S0-BDM-943

Suspect

The chances of discovering the frenzied killer of Muriel Brown were remote by any standards. The twenty-seven year old had been raped and murdered in her own car. Fifteen years ago.

Detective Superintendent Mark Pemberton's ambition was to solve the case before he retired; it was the only undetected murder on the books. But his determination suffered a setback when his special team of three detectives was replaced by one sick senior officer, Inspector Vic Hadley.

According to specialists, Hadley, on sick leave due to stress, needed some undemanding work to aid rehabilitation. The Muriel Brown case seemed ideal. But Hadley had shot and killed a man during an armed raid; there were allegations that Hadley had murdered him and that there had been a cover-up. Even the robbers claimed the dead man had not been with them but Hadley maintained he shot an armed robber to save a detective's life. The accusations and doubts had driven Hadley to his sick-bed.

As Hadley began his new duties, Pemberton needed to satisfy himself of Hadley's innocence. While investigating Hadley's past, further deaths occurred and new evidence emerged about Hadley's actions at the shooting, forcing Pemberton to re-evaluate his personal and professional attitude to colleagues and to his law enforcement rôle. Pemberton is forced into an armed and dramatic conclusion.

Nicholas Rhea, creator of the books from which the highly popular ITV series 'Heartbeat' is derived, has produced a drama of high tension in this riveting story of a professional under unbearable pressure.

Books by Peter N. Walker

CRIME FICTION

The 'Carnaby' series (1967–84)
Carnaby and the hijackers
Carnaby and the gaolbreakers
Carnaby and the assassins
Carnaby and the conspirators
Carnaby and the saboteurs
Carnaby and the eliminators
Carnaby and the demonstrators
Carnaby and the infiltrators
Carnaby and the kidnappers
Carnaby and the counterfeiters
Carnaby and the campaigners
Fatal accident (1970)
Panda One on duty (1971)
Special duty (1971)
Identification Parade (1972)
Panda One investigates (1973)
Major incident (1974)
The Dovingsby death (1975)
Missing from home (1977)
The MacIntyre plot (1977)
Witchcraft for Panda One (1978)
Target criminal (1978)
The Carlton plot (1980)
Siege for Panda One (1981)
Teenage cop (1982)
Robber in a mole trap (1985)
False alibi (1991)
Grave secrets (1992)

Written as Christopher Coram
A call to danger (1968)
A call to die (1969)
Death in Ptarmigan Forest (1970)
Death on the motorway (1973)
Murder by the lake (1975)
Murder beneath the trees (1979)
Prisoner on the dam (1982)
Prisoner on the run (1985)

Written as Tom Ferris
Espionage for a lady (1969)

Written as Andrew Arncliffe
Murder after the holidays (1985)

NON-FICTION

The courts of law (1971)
Punishment (1972)
Murders and mysteries from the North York Moors (1988)
Murders and mysteries from the Yorkshire Dales (1991)
Folk tales from the North York Moors (1990)
Folk stories from the Yorkshire Dales (1991)
Portrait of the North York Moors (1985) *as Nicholas Rhea*
Heartbeat of Yorkshire (1993) *as Nicholas Rhea*
Folk tales from York and the Wolds (1992)
Folk stories from the Lake District (1993)
The Story of the Police Mutual Assurance Society (1993)
Yorkshire days (1995)

THE 'CONSTABLE' SERIES

Written as Nicholas Rhea
Constable on the hill (1979)
Constable on the prowl (1980)
Constable around the village (1981)
Constable across the moors (1982)
Constable in the dale (1983)
Constable by the sea (1985)
Constable along the lane (1986)
Constable through the meadow (1988)
Constable at the double (1988)
Constable in disguise (1989)
Constable through the heather (1990)
Constable beside the stream (1991)
Constable around the green (1993)
Constable beneath the trees (1994)
Constable in the shrubbery (1995)
Heartbeat Omnibus I (1992)
Heartbeat Omnibus II (1993)
Heartbeat – Constable among the heather (1992)
Heartbeat – Constable across the moor (1993)
Heartbeat – Constable on call (1993)
Family ties (1994)
Heartbeat – Constable along the lane (1995)

EMMERDALE TITLES

Written as James Ferguson
A friend in need (1987)
Divided loyalties (1988)
Wives and lovers (1989)
Book of country lore (1988)
Official companion (1988)
Emmerdale's Yorkshire (1990)

SUSPECT

Nicholas Rhea

Nicholas Rhea

Constable · London

First published in Great Britain 1995
by Constable & Company Ltd
3 The Lanchesters, 162 Fulham Palace Road
London W6 9ER

ISBN 0 09 474580 3
Reprinted 1995
Set in Palatino 10pt by
Pure Tech India Ltd, Pondicherry
Printed and bound in Great Britain
by Hartnolls Ltd, Bodmin

A CIP catalogue record for this book
is available from the British Library

1

'You're happier these days, Mark, and it shows.' The Chief Constable's smile was warm and friendly. 'You're more at ease, more relaxed.'

Detective Superintendent Mark Pemberton, seated on a chair before his boss's desk, sipped a black coffee. 'Yes, I am, sir, thank you.'

'You've got over your wife's death?'

'Not entirely, but I've come to terms with it. And I'm taking more time off, making friends outside the job too. It's not easy, mixing a social life with police work, but I'm managing.'

'So what are you doing in your spare time?' Charles Moore was showing a genuine interest in Mark's welfare.

'I've joined a rambling club, we explore the dales and moors. I'm discovering parts of Yorkshire I never knew existed.'

'I'm glad you're making the effort. I must admit I prefer the new, relaxed and not-so-gloomy Mark Pemberton. There was anger in you. You'd become very introverted, you know, and you were working far too hard.'

'I had to keep busy, sir, there was nothing to keep me at home. I used work to get rid of my anger, get me over my loss, I suppose.'

'I understand.' Moore's tone was sympathetic. 'But it's down to business now. I'm faced with the ever-present need to spend less money while making better use of existing manpower and resources and at the same time I have to detect more and more crime.'

'Hoary old regulars!' grinned Mark Pemberton. 'So long as I've been in the job, we've been told to spend less, get more officers on the streets and detect more crime, but I'd say we're detecting a greater number of crimes than we did say, fifty years ago . . .' He realized Moore was regarding him calmly and began to appreciate why the Chief had called him in. 'If it's cuts we're talking about, I suppose it'll affect the Muriel Brown enquiry?'

Mark could envisage that investigation being wound up. It wouldn't be a great surprise. Being allowed three detective constables to work full-time on that old enquiry was something of a luxury – Pemberton's long-term worry was that a lack of funds and a shortage of staff could result in that murder remaining forever unsolved. That thought was highly frustrating – that a lack of money could enable a killer to evade justice seemed very wrong indeed. The Chief now addressed Pemberton's concerns.

'Don't forget that Muriel Brown was murdered a long time ago, Mark, before I became Chief Constable of this force. The chances of discovering her killer are remote by any standards.'

'But not impossible.' Mark wasn't going to let this crime be forgotten.

'To be honest,' Moore spoke softly and smoothly, 'I can't see that we need to fret unduly about an undetected murder which is some fifteen years old. Besides, even if we do crack it, it'll be just one more crime detected. A single clear-up. That won't make a very large contribution to our "Detected Crime" figures – give me a batch of a hundred detected burglaries any day. They're much more impressive on paper!'

'You can't compare burglary with murder, sir!' Pemberton had to defend his desire to keep this old enquiry active. 'Some yobbo admitting a string of break-ins is no comparison with a murderer caught by good police work. Paper-pushing policemen and Home Office clerks will be our downfall! Statistics of that kind make nonsense of our work! I regard it as my duty to do all in my power to identify the murderer. The fact that the crime's an old one doesn't matter – in fact, this one ensures that my officers remain up to date with HOLMES and current investigative techniques. It allows them an opportunity to work with computers and it's taught them how to abstract important data from statement forms, even very old ones. It's highlighted mistakes made by their predecessors, mistakes that will benefit future enquiries. All that is most important – we all learn from mistakes. Muriel Brown has been a first-class means of providing extra training for young detectives, far better than any exercise we could devise. It's real too, which means there's the job satisfaction aspect. We might get a result – we might identify the killer. That's important even if it is only one detected crime.'

'I appreciate what you say, Mark, and I admire your spirited defence. You'll be pleased that Muriel Brown is not going to be totally abandoned. I'm replacing your three plain-clothes officers which means the murder enquiry can continue. Inspector Hadley will join your staff, he will replace those detectives.'

'Vic Hadley? George Washington incarnate?'

'George Washington?' grinned the Chief. 'Who calls him that?'

'Most of the force, sir,' smiled Mark Pemberton. 'It's because he says he cannot tell a lie.'

'That's a lie in itself.' The Chief was bemused by this. 'I don't believe anyone goes through life without telling some sort of a lie. I must admit I've never come across that nickname for Hadley. Anyway, Inspector Hadley, George Washington or whatever you call him, is going to join your department.'

'I thought he was on sick leave, sir, something to do with stress?'

'He is, Mark, but he's on the mend, he needs to be usefully employed.'

'But he's a uniform inspector, sir, they're detective constables.'

Pemberton's instinctive response was adverse. Why choose Hadley? Of all the officers in the force, Hadley was the last person Pemberton would have selected for any task in the CID.

'I know what you're thinking, Mark. But his advisers – doctor, psychologist, therapist and counsellor – are all agreed that some undemanding work, free from operational pressures and stress, will help towards his rehabilitation and restore his confidence. That's why I want him to work in your department.'

'Undemanding work, sir? In a CID office?'

'If you gave him the Muriel Brown case, more as occupational therapy than anything else, he'd feel useful. He needs to believe he's still a skilled operational policeman who can be trusted with important work. I don't have to remind you, Mark, that it's best he keeps out of the public eye, at least for the time being; you'll need to keep him away from the attentions of ex-Councillor Newton and his family too. That man's never off our backs – I still get letters from him, demanding justice or wanting to reopen the enquiry. He's still as bitter as hell about his brother's death. That aside, I'm sure you can usefully employ Inspector Hadley.'

And as he issued that challenge, the Chief flashed one of hi
handsome smiles.

'There's always work in a CID office, I'll grant you that,
Mark Pemberton responded without enthusiasm and place
his empty cup and saucer on the Chief's desk. This morning'
meeting was almost over and his gut feeling was that Hadle
would be a burden rather than an asset. The Chief had mad
it impossible to refuse – but to take away three good, kee
young detectives and replace them with a sick senior office
who would work shorter hours and require very careful hand
ling didn't seem a good bargain for Pemberton and the Crim
inal Investigation Department – or for the Muriel Brow
enquiry.

Pemberton's ambition was to solve that case before he retire
it was the only undetected murder on the force books. Some fi
teen years ago, Muriel Brown, then a twenty-seven-year-old se
retary, had been raped and murdered in her own car, her deat
resulting from a bout of frenzied stabbing.

The car, with her body inside, had been abandoned on th
moors but her killer had never been traced. That crime had o
curred prior to DNA testing, HOLMES and the other moder
support services and computers which had become such a
integral part of murder investigations. Old techniques had bee
used and Pemberton felt that if all the relevant data could be fe
into a computerised data-processing system, the enquiry coul
be revitalised. The case of Muriel Brown might yet benefit fro
modern technology. In any case, undetected murder files we
never officially closed. Nonetheless, Pemberton felt that th
chore of logging all that old data into a computer was not reall
demanding enough for a high-ranking officer, even one wh
was recuperating after a long illness.

But orders were orders and you couldn't deflect the Chief Co
stable once he had made up his mind – and it was clear that h
decision had been made. Whatever Pemberton might think
say, Inspector Victor Hadley, the former officer in charge of th
force firearms unit, would join Pemberton's team.

'He will start on Monday morning.' Charles Moore flashed o
of his dazzling smiles. 'And I shall require weekly reports on h
progress.'

*

Hadley's illness was officially described as 'stress-related'. The file of the incident which had brought it about was kept under confidential cover at force headquarters. The documents were therefore beyond the immediate reach of Pemberton while he was operating from Rainesbury police station, but even without access to that file he could recall the event.

It was the sort of incident that no one in the force could forget. There had been a tremendous outcry throughout the country and the facts were etched in the minds of every local police officer. The drama had made unwelcome national headlines and had led to questions in Parliament about the actions and supervision of armed police officers.

Known as the 'Millgate supermarket incident', it had achieved notoriety because a so-called innocent bystander had been shot dead by Inspector Victor Hadley. His action had created turmoil in the press, it had generated fear among the public and it had resulted in accusations that the police had committed murder, the accusers being members of the dead man's family led by his militant older brother. Even now, some two years later, the drama was by no means forgotten.

As he returned to his office, Pemberton recalled the tragedy. An informer had tipped off the CID that there would be an armed raid on a security van as it delivered a large and special consignment of cash to Millgate supermarket in Fawneswick. An armed response unit, led by Inspector Hadley, had concealed themselves nearby to await and ambush the raiders. CID officers had also been hidden while other detectives had waited inside the supermarket and within other nearby buildings. The security van with three guards on board had arrived at 8.25 a.m., five minutes earlier than anticipated.

Three raiders had been waiting. They had gone about their intended objective, two of them being armed with sawn-off shotguns. The third raider, the getaway driver, was not armed.

As the police had emerged from hiding to make their arrests, one of the raiders had fired shots but none of the officers had been hit. The shots had gone over their heads. Realising they were surrounded by armed police, the raiders had quickly surrendered and all were immediately arrested. The raid had failed; the tip-of had been a good one. Those aspects of the incident had not pro duced any problems.

During the early, very tense moments of the intended robbery however, as the raid was in progress, a fourth man had unexpec tedly appeared on the scene. Inspector Hadley claimed he wa armed and said he had been aiming his sawn-off shotgun at detective – Hadley had reacted instinctively and had shot th man dead. The deceased's name was Joseph 'Joss' Newton and h was twenty-nine years old.

After news of the killing had been made public, there had de veloped a massive protest at Inspector Hadley's action. The cam paign was led by Newton's older brother, Brian, who was a forme trade unionist, an ex-town councillor and now a shift worker in food-canning factory. His fierce antagonism was directed agains the police and was based on the claim that Joss Newton had ha nothing to do with the raid. It was claimed he was merely an inno cent bystander. Later, the arrested raiders said that Newton wa not involved and had never been associated with them. Accordin to them, he was not, and never had been, a member of their tean Of greater importance was the claim by ex-Councillor Newton tha his brother had not been carrying a shotgun and that he had nc been armed in any way. His persistent theme was that the polic had murdered an innocent man, the father of two little childre who happened to be in the wrong place at the wrong time.

Newton had openly said that his brother had been shot in col blood, the deliberate victim of the police. He had accused the police c murdering Joss and had repeated those allegations in a long-runnin campaign, aided by some of the tabloid press. He said he would neve rest until Joss's killer, i.e. Inspector Victor Hadley, had been dealt wit for the crime and until his brother's name had been cleared.

Brian Newton's campaign was supported by the fact that Jos had no previous convictions and that Joss's wife, Lara, claime he had gone to the supermarket as soon as the doors were ope that morning, at 8.30 a.m., to get some cereals for their tw young children's breakfasts. He was an innocent member of th public, a dad shopping for his family, she said. Brian Newto and his supporters claimed that Joss had simply walked into th ambush and had been shot dead by trigger-happy police.

Inspector Hadley had claimed otherwise; he'd insisted that Newton had been carrying a sawn-off shotgun which had been pointing towards a detective. A highly trained and reliable police officer, he had killed Newton to save that detective's life. It had been a split-second decision by a highly trained policeman who was also an expert marksman.

Two sawn-off shotguns, both double-barrelled, and four spent cartridge shells had been recovered at the scene; one of the cartridges had come from Hadley's police-issue shotgun. Four shots had been heard, although some witnesses, including police officers, said there had been only three. Some suggested that the sound of a fourth shot was an echo produced by the high-walled surrounding buildings but they had all been so close together that no one was quite certain.

Inspector Hadley claimed that one loaded shotgun belonged to Newton, but it was later claimed by one of the arrested men, Roger Pollard, that he, not Newton, had been carrying that particular weapon. Newton's brother, Brian, had established that claim during a prison visit to Pollard. Later, Pollard's fellow raiders, called Sykes and Gill, had confirmed that Pollard, not Newton, had had possession of that gun. During that same visit, Pollard had admitted that at the moment he'd realized he was surrounded by armed police, he had broken the gun to render it harmless and had thrown it to the ground in front of him as a gesture of surrender. It had come to rest some five yards from him and had contained two unused twelve-bore cartridges. When that gun had been recovered by the police, it had contained two such cartridges, thus verifying that statement.

Pollard had added that, in being caught red-handed, he had never contemplated a denial of his involvement in the raid, nor had he intended to dispute his ownership of the shotgun. The question of ownership of that gun had not been raised at the time because Pollard had simply admitted his guilt. The prosecution of him and his colleagues was quite distinct from the official investigation into Newton's death. Similarly, at the time, none of the others had been questioned specifically about ownership of the guns although Sykes had been charged with additional offences under the Firearms Act because he had discharged his weapon. That shotgun, with empty barrels, had been

recovered from Robert James Sykes. It was that gun which ha
been discharged over the heads of the police by its carrier – ther
was no argument about that and its barrels had been empty.

Sykes had admitted firing the gun, albeit not at the police – h
said he'd deliberately discharged it over their heads as a fin
gesture of defiance. He'd insisted he'd only fired two shots an
was unable to provide any information about the suppose
fourth shot. The driver of the getaway car, Shaun Gill, had n
been carrying a gun.

Later, a ballistics examination confirmed that no shot had bee
fired on that occasion from the loaded twelve-bore gun althoug
it was never disputed that it had been carried during the rai
But even now, two years after the event, the identity of the ca
rier of that shotgun still remained in contention. Some said it ha
been Newton, others were sure it had been Pollard.

An examination of the weapon for fingerprints had been incon
clusive. There had been prints on various parts of the gun, bu
they were too indistinct for positive identification. Thus it coul
not be scientifically established who had handled that weapo
even though Pollard, questioned later during a searching poli
enquiry into the incident, persisted in his claim that it was hin
He was emphatic that he had thrown it aside while it was sti
loaded, albeit broken to avoid accidental discharge.

Some time after the raid, the inability to account for all fou
spent cartridge shells also caused a little concern, particularly
there had never been a satisfactory explanation for the myste
ous fourth shot, also from a twelve-bore weapon. The cartrid
shell from Hadley's own gun and the two from Sykes's twelv
bore could be accounted for. Thus three were beyond di
pute. It was the fourth empty cartridge shell which created th
puzzle.

None of the recovered weapons had fired it and it was ther
fore assumed it had nothing to do with the raid. Empty cartrid
shells were not unusual in Fawneswick – they were sometim
discarded by young farmers when buying fresh supplies. They
pocket them during a shoot rather than litter the moors, then fo
get their presence in their shooting jacket pockets until the
came into town. Then they'd find them and throw them aw
like litter. Sometimes they were found in the gutters but main

in waste bins outside sports shops. Children picked them up as play-things and then threw them away when their use was over. Slightly smaller than a tube of Smarties, they were, of course, quite harmless.

Thus the presence of an unidentified cartridge shell near the supermarket was not particularly remarkable and the gun which might have fired it was never traced. Nonetheless, the fact that the cartridge shell had been recovered from the scene of a crime, plus the unresolved puzzle over the fourth shot, did render it of some importance and it had been recorded in the file of the incident.

Throughout the inevitable enquiries which ensued, Inspector Hadley had been adamant that the villains' account was not true. He did suggest their story had been concocted in prison as a means of discrediting the police, especially as Brian Newton had been the one to break the story of Pollard's claims. Those villains had had plenty of time to concoct such a yarn, Hadley had suggested. Throughout the resultant aftermath, Hadley had insisted that Newton had been carrying a sawn-off gun when he had entered the forecourt of the supermarket.

He never wavered in his claim; he had never wavered in his story that Joss Newton had aimed it at a detective and that he, Hadley, had had to shoot Newton to save the life of that detective. The detective in question – Detective Sergeant Philip Swanson – had been concentrating his attention upon events at or near the security vehicle and, in a written statement, said he had not noticed Newton's approach. Under oath, he had therefore been unable to confirm Inspector Hadley's interpretation of events.

The problem was that no one else had noticed Newton's arrival. All the police officers engaged at the scene, and the three security guards from the Cerberus security vehicle, were all quizzed in depth but in the midst of the ongoing drama, none had noticed Newton's arrival from the opposite side of the forecourt. Everyone was concentrating upon their own aspect of the drama around the security vehicle, with Sykes's gun being on open display and Pollard being momentarily out of sight at the rear of the vehicle. Faced with some confusion and a lack of coherence, Hadley's version had been accepted by the coroner at the inquest on Joss Newton; it had also been accepted by the official enquiry into the shooting of Joss Newton. There appeared to be some nagging official doubts as to the veracity of the claims made by Newton and Pollard, particularly as they had not emerged until a private conversation had been made during a prison visit.

Nonetheless, vociferous members of the family of the dead Newton, led by Brian, remained convinced there had been a cover-up.

Fuelled by his intense activity to throw blame on the police and aided by lurid newspaper reports in the tabloid press, there had persisted a widespread belief that Hadley had killed an innocent bystander, that the British police had murdered the unarmed father of two infants and that there had been a cover-up.

Ex-Councillor Newton's fervent and ceaseless attempts to prove that his younger brother was not part of that armed raid resulted in further demands for the truth from a motley assortment of anti-authority and anti-police factions. They included left-wing protesters and others with political rather than humanitarian motives. Several hard-hitting television programmes and newspaper features had ensued, all critical of the police action and all publishing their own, often biased, version of the drama. The fact that no additional enquiries were instituted was, in their minds, further evidence of a cover-up.

When someone is shot dead by the police in the course of their duty, the name of the officer who fires the fatal shot is not released until the inquest. Some interpret this well-established procedure as a cover-up of the truth. It is, on the other hand, a procedural method of establishing the truth by forensic and scientific means so that the public can be properly informed at the inquest and at subsequent hearings. It takes time and effort to establish such a truth – there have been instances of police marksmen themselves believing they have shot someone when in fact the victim had shot himself. Thus what is sometimes regarded as the truth at the time may be later countered by scientific evidence. Newspaper stories published before the inquest can therefore be misleading.

Prior to the inquest on Newton, therefore, Hadley's role as the man who had actually pulled the trigger had never emerged.

Nonetheless, as the officer in charge of the firearms unit, he'd had to carry the weight of those public accusations and the responsibility for the incident. The allegations of the murder of an innocent man by the police had affected him deeply, particularly when the Chief Constable had announced that a formal investigation into the killing would be implemented, with Hadley being suspended from duty pending its outcome.

In claiming he had been taught as a child never to tell a lie, Hadley said he had already openly and truthfully given his version of events and could do no more, but he continued to be vilified by the public and the press for months after the shooting. Meanwhile, Pollard, Sykes and Gill had been dealt with at the Crown Court where all pleaded guilty to attempted armed robbery and each received three years' imprisonment.

Following the inquest and trial, an official investigation into the shooting of Newton had been conducted by Detective Chief Superintendent Chambers of Staplefordshire Constabulary and failed to establish that Newton had been one of the raiders. He found no evidence to link Newton with the raid or with the other participants. From that aspect, it began to look as if Hadley had shot an innocent man – but one important factor went in Hadley's favour. He said that when his shot had hit Newton, Newton's sawn-off gun had been dashed from his grasp and had fallen to the ground. He could not be sure whether the falling gun had discharged a shot – the sound of his own gun had drowned all other contemporaneous noises.

The enquiry did support Hadley's version, i.e. that Newton had been carrying a gun, that no shots had been fired from it, and that it had been been dashed to the ground by the force of Hadley's shots and later recovered complete with two cartridges up the spout. That finding implied that Pollard's story had been concocted in prison, a suggestion that was never forgiven by Brian Newton. The very detailed report by Chambers had been submitted to the Crown Prosecution Service who had ruled there was insufficient evidence to prosecute Hadley for murder or manslaughter. The official verdict was that Newton had been shot by Hadley in the course of his duty and that it had been justifiable homicide.

It was during the inquest that Hadley's personal role in the killing was made public, even though he was showing signs of great

distress and mental suffering following his instinctive actions
He persisted in his claim that he was telling the truth, even
though few seemed inclined to believe him. After his name had
been publicized, he had been subjected to hate mail, faeces from
dogs and humans being pushed through his letter box, graffiti
on his house doors and walls, damage to his car, obscene and
threatening correspondence and antagonism in the street.

It was thought that Newton's family were responsible, either
directly or by organizing others to carry out some of the acts of
vengeance. Brian Newton, through his union links, had managed to recruit the help of several anti-police factions who had
been delighted to capitalize on Hadley's vulnerability. Hadley's
wife had suffered too, being subjected to harassment in the
supermarkets and in the street.

As a consequence, they had moved home from Fawneswick
to Rainesford at police authority expense, and that had given
them some welcome anonymity and a respite from attention.
In spite of that, on each anniversary of Joss's death, hate mail
was pushed through their letter box. And whenever the
police, anywhere in Britain, were compelled to use firearms
ex-Councillor Brian Newton managed to resurrect newspaper
stories of Hadley's shooting of young Joss. Inspector Hadley
would never be allowed to forget his actions that day and the
resultant stress caused him to be declared unfit for duty. He
had been on sick leave for the past eighteen months. Following his ordeal by press, public and innuendo, the Police Feder-
ation's welfare advisers had arranged the necessary
counselling and therapeutic treatment, but Hadley's life and
career had been ruined. He had grown a heavy beard and
moustache which had changed his appearance, and his hair
was now thick, grey and untidy, not thick, brown and well
cared for as it had once been. Lately, there had been a big improvement in his outlook and demeanour and, in spite of
everything, Hadley remained determined that he would not
let the protestors and critics hound him from the police service. Now that he was recovering, he had made a resolute effort to establish the truth, one of his persistent pleas being that
no one believed his story. He felt that that no one trusted him
and that upset him greatly.

Indeed, during the following months and throughout his on-going treatment, he had maintained his innocence, repeatedly vowing to discover the truth about Newton's presence and actions that day. Inspector Hadley maintained he had done his duty – no one could ask more of a policeman.

Now, as Mark Pemberton recalled the trauma of that time and the debilitating effect of the case upon all police officers, he wondered how his officers would react to Vic Hadley. Pemberton hoped he would not use the opportunity to give everyone an ear-bashing over his alleged innocence and mistreatment. In preparing for Hadley's arrival, though, Pemberton realised he must know more about the Millgate supermarket incident, so upon his return to the office, he rang force headquarters.

'Pemberton here,' he announced himself to Detective Chief Superintendent Ray Castle and after some preliminary chat, asked, 'Can I have sight of the Millgate supermarket file?'

'Can I ask why?' asked the head of the force CID.

Pemberton explained his reasons and Castle listened intently.

'I can't say I envy you, Mark, having to work alongside George Washington. But yes, of course you can see the file – but keep it out of the sight of everyone else, especially Hadley himself. It remains a very sensitive document. From my own experience, all I can say is that it's a miracle he wasn't charged with murder. There were a lot of loose ends in that enquiry – I wasn't happy with it. Anyway, Mark, it's all over now, so I'll send the file through the internal mail. Look after it.'

And so, with some trepidation, Detective Superintendent Mark Pemberton prepared to receive a new member of staff.

2

It was ten minutes to nine on Monday morning and Detective Superintendent Mark Pemberton was in his office. He would have arrived earlier had that lorry not shed its load of timber at White Horse roundabout – that delay, followed by a diversion around the housing estates, had cost him at least forty-five minutes. In that time, his in-tray had been filled with mail from both internal and external sources. It was astonishing how much correspondence a weekend could generate – but crime wasn't a nine-to-five Monday-to-Friday job, however, and much of the paperwork had arisen from the weekend activities of the local villains. He was wondering whether to tackle the pile or ring for a coffee when there was a knock on his door. And he hadn't even read his first piece of paper.

'Come in,' he shouted, thinking it was his secretary, Barbara. Maybe she'd brought a coffee? If so, it was a good start to the week. But instead of her cheery tones, he was surprised to hear a soft Scots voice bid him, 'Morning, sir.'

Turning in his chair, he saw Inspector Hadley standing in the doorway. He was a tall, broad and very powerfully built man in a loose-fitting sweater which comprised various shades of dull brown. His outfit was enhanced with heavy brown corduroy trousers with no creases and a pair of unkempt white trainers upon his large feet. He looked like a heap of dead bracken from a Highland glen.

His thick greying brown hair appeared to have been dressed by a force nine gale while his face of forty summers and more was adorned with a thick grey-brown beard and moustache.

A pair of dark brown eyes peered at Pemberton through the mass of hair. The fellow looked as if he'd just arrived from a session of gardening in an October gale and his untidy appearance was in direct contrast to Pemberton's elegance. Pemberton, considered the smartest man in the force, was always immaculate in his dark suits, white shirts with crisp clean cuffs and polished shoes. With no sign of greying in spite of having turned forty, Pemberton never had a blond hair out of place and in-force folklore said he could walk across a ploughed field and emerge at the other end without dirtying his shoes. One outcome of his appearance was that the officers in his department also took care over their mode of dress – they were all smart, clean and tidy. Except for the new arrival.

'Morning, Vic.' Pemberton rose and shook the other's hand, deciding not to comment on his casual method of dress. He realized he must treat this man with gentleness and tact; he needed compassion and care, not criticism. 'Come in, shut the door and sit down.'

Hadley padded into the office and settled on the chair that Pemberton indicated. Pemberton returned to his own chair behind the desk and asked, 'Coffee?'

'Thanks, sir. White, no sugar.'

The beautiful Scots burr was a joy to Pemberton. He loved the Highlands, the heather, the lochs and the nectar-like malt whiskies from the glens. He pressed the intercom and said, 'Coffee, please, Barbara, for two. One black, one white, no sugar in either.'

The coffee arranged, Mark found he had difficulty asking a sensible question.

'How's it going, Vic?' he began.

Pemberton was fully aware that a careless word might trigger some unwelcome response or reaction. Stress, and the individual's reaction to it, was a terrible thing. One wrong word or one word out of place could compound the problem.

'Can't grumble,' said Hadley.

'Who suggested you return to work, Vic?'

'Me. It was my idea. I was bored, sir. I wanted something useful to do, you know, so the medics said I might benefit from some unstressful police work. And the Chief agreed.'

'Right, well, that pleases me. I can use your talents. You know the Muriel Brown case?'

'Aye, I remember it.'

'We're busy programming it into HOLMES. A chore really, very undemanding, almost to the point of being boring if I'm honest with you, but it's potentially very valuable. We think the killer's still out there, Vic, waiting to be nicked, and we want to feel his collar while he's young enough to do a stretch for the crime. To help us, I want all the data from the Muriel Brown file to be programmed into the computer. Once it's there, we'll let the computer do its work. I hope it'll lead us to the villain. That's my aim – to nail Muriel Brown's killer.'

'Aye, right, thanks. I can do that. I'd love to nail him too. I hate to think that any criminal can escape without punishment.'

'I'm sure many would echo your thoughts. Now, once you get into our routine, you might find yourself helping with other enquiries, a sort of overseeing office manager. With regard to your hours, Vic, I'm not going to demand that you work a full eight-hour day. You decide when you want to work and for how long. Take every weekend off, come and go as you want, but keep in touch with me. Let me know what you're doing. If you don't wish to come in, just ring and say so. Ask if you want any help and don't be frightened to come to me at any time about anything that might be bothering you. Right?'

A faint smile showed beneath the heavy beard and Hadley nodded. 'Aye, thanks, sir. You know, I was in CID for a while, sir, early in my service. A DC for two years. At Fawneswick, it was. I expect things have changed a wee bit since then, CID procedures and so on.'

'Quite a lot hasn't changed, Vic, and I'm sure the knowledge you gained will be useful. Now, we've set up the Muriel Brown enquiry in a separate office, so you'll be working alone. If you'd rather work with people around you, you can move the stuff out and relocate yourself in the general office. I'm sure we could find a corner somewhere. Work as you feel best, Vic. There's no pressure to get results, it's a job you can do exactly how you please. You can take as long as you want – I'll not be putting pressure on you and there's no deadline for what you'll be doing. All I ask from you is a competent job of work.'

'Thanks, I understand. It'll be nice doing something useful again.'

After a gentle knock on the door, it opened to admit Barbara who was carrying a tray bearing two mugs of coffee and a jug of milk.

'Vic, this is Barbara Meadows, secretary of the department. The place couldn't function without her. Barbara, this is Inspector Hadley, Vic Hadley. He's joining the department on attachment – he'll be processing the Muriel Brown data.'

She smiled at him and he shook her hand. Barbara knew about Hadley; Pemberton had informed his staff that he would be joining them but few had met him personally. Barbara was a stranger to him but she would be the one person who would have most contact with the newcomer. She was a tall, slender woman in her early thirties with long eyelashes, grey eyes, a neat figure and shoulder-length dark brown hair. Unmarried, she had been with the CID, as a secretary, for some six years and was totally familiar with the demands of the department. Pemberton had often wondered why she had never married although she did have a succession of male friends, escorts who wined and dined her. But true, everlasting romance had not come her way. It was a pity – she was a lovely woman both in appearance and in personality.

'If you need any help, just shout.' She flashed one of her lovely smiles at him. 'My office is just round the corner, on the left.'

'Aye, I will, thanks,' he said.

Over coffee and between telephone calls which he ignored, Mark explained the general running of the CID office with Hadley proffering little more than one-word answers or comments, but the fellow seemed keen enough to begin.

Then followed a tour of the large CID office with introductions to the key figures like Detective Inspector Paul Larkin, Detective Sergeants Keith Duffield and Stuart Egerton, along with the other detectives, male and female. They were on duty this morning; others would be coming on duty later in the day for the back shift. Some of them nodded a greeting, one or two shook his hand, but Pemberton wondered how many associated the dour, untidy inspector with the dramatic shooting of a member of the public in Fawneswick some two years ago.

Eventually, Mark showed him to the office currently being used for the Muriel Brown enquiry. Somewhat on the small side, it contained two desks each with a chair at either side so that four people could operate here even if it was a bit cramped when everyone was working. There were also four filing cabinets and the other requisites of an active murder investigation plus the keyboards, monitors and accoutrements of a terminal of HOLMES set upon its own custom-built stand. Pemberton then called in Detective Constable Duncan Young to explain to Hadley the mechanics of operating the computer components, the system of extracting facts from the mass of papers which comprised the Muriel Brown case file and the method of entering them into HOLMES.

'I'll leave you two to get acquainted.' Pemberton turned to leave. 'Don't let him baffle you with science, Vic – ask him to speak in normal language, not computer jargon! Call me if you need anything or have words with one of the others. We're all here to help each other, that's how my department works. No man is an island, as somebody famous once said.'

'John Donne, sir, the poet. He wrote that,' and there was a flash of a smile from Hadley.

'You learn something every day,' grinned Pemberton. 'It's the sort of thing Shakespeare might have written.'

And so for the first time in months, Inspector Victor Hadley was back at work as a policeman.

Almost three weeks after Inspector Hadley started work with Rainesbury CID, news of a murder was received via the fax. As the machine began to spew forth its lengthy roll of paper, Detective Constable Lorraine Cashmore chanced to be passing. She halted to read the message and noticed it had originated in Langbarugh County, the murder having occurred this Saturday lunchtime.

She waited for the fax to complete its four pages, tore off the message, scanned it and took it to Barbara's office where she placed it in the in-tray. Barbara would set it upon its route through the system and it would reach Pemberton in due course; there seemed to be no local urgency with that murder because the crime had been committed beyond the force boundaries.

Langbarugh CID were dealing with it and no specific enquiries had been requested from Pemberton's team at Rainesbury. The fax was for general information, being circulated to all northern police forces, and after Pemberton had read it, copies would be circulated around the department with one being pinned to the notice-board. Pemberton's detectives would bear it in mind during their routine enquiries, particularly as Langbarugh's boundaries adjoined their own.

It was around that time that Charles Moore, the Chief Constable, telephoned Pemberton from his office at Great Halverton police headquarters.

'Mark.' His voice was strong and clear on the telephone. 'This is just a personal check call about Inspector Hadley. I'm getting your weekly reports and it seems he is coping very well.'

Pemberton confirmed that the inspector was indeed doing well. He told the Chief that Hadley appeared to be enjoying his work and had developed a determination to find the killer of

Muriel Brown. Although he worked only half-days, sometimes in the mornings and sometimes in the afternoons, he did undertake a concentrated four hours' work, broken only by a coffee or tea break. He didn't work weekends, however, unlike other members of the CID who operated a rota system of duties. Happily, the staff had accepted him and he appeared to be popular with them during work hours but didn't mix with them during his off-duty time.

'He goes fishing when he's off duty, sir,' Pemberton told the Chief. 'He has a motor bike and off he goes, armed with rods, nets and gaffs, dressed up like an aged biker. But it gets him into the fresh air and he can be alone if he wishes. I must say that his confidence does seem to be returning. He's rather quiet, though, he doesn't mix with my officers either on duty or off, preferring to work alone and not to socialize. My lads often go out for a drink before going home after duty, but Hadley never joins them, even when he works during the afternoon.'

'That might be his natural Scots thrift!' chuckled the Chief.

'Maybe, sir, but I think he's rather shy. He doesn't say much, but there again, he never has; he's always been taciturn and so I don't read too much into his silences and lack of conversation. He's never been one for small talk.'

'And his mental condition? Any improvement there?'

'It doesn't appear to be a problem, sir. He's never given me cause for concern, he behaves quite normally, quite rationally. I've not noticed any uncharacteristic behaviour. He is continuing to visit his therapist and his counsellor, I make sure he never misses those sessions, and not once has he referred to the Millgate supermarket incident. I must admit that surprises me. I thought he might want to discuss it.'

Pemberton wondered why the Chief was ringing for this information when it was all contained in his weekly reports, but Moore's next comment provided an answer.

'It's time for my report on his progress to the Police Committee. As you know, there comes a time when a sick officer's future needs to be looked at, a decision reached as to whether we retain him or retire him on ill-health pension. Because of his long absence, Hadley's now in that category, Mark. I'm sending a detailed questionnaire for you to complete, but what's your own view on his long-term potential?'

'I think he'll make a full recovery, sir. He's a stolid individual, very strong both mentally and physically, I'd say. Very honest and open, too honest at times, and I do know he loves police work. He's useful to my department – I've spoken to DC Young, our computer wizard, and he tells me Hadley's making a really sound job of entering the data; he has a ready grasp of the basics of the computer and his years of police experience have told him what to look for in reports and statements. He's very useful and there'll always be work to do, although I must remind myself that he is functioning at a level well below the rank he carries.'

'I can hardly demote him, Mark, just to program the facts of an old case into a computer. Anyway, let me have your views and recommendations in writing.'

'Understood, sir,' and Pemberton replaced the telephone just as Barbara entered with the in-tray. As she placed it on his desk, he asked, 'Anything of immediate interest, Barbara?'

'Some letters for signature before the post goes,' she smiled. 'A list of last night's crimes at divisional level – a lot of burglaries and a spate of breakings into cars with cash being taken. Druggies needing money for their regular fixes, no doubt. Normal stuff really. The only additional thing worthy of mention is a murder in Langbarugh sir, this afternoon. A shooting. A gangland assassination by the sound of it. Robbery wasn't the motive. The cash in the victim's till wasn't touched. The dead man is Harry Pearle, a second-hand car dealer from Tulleypool – he was shot in his office by a crash-helmeted gunman who got away on a motor bike bearing a false registration plate.'

'That's one for Barry to sort out,' smiled Pemberton without any real sympathy for his friend and colleague, Detective Superintendent Barry Brennon of the neighbouring force. 'It'll prevent his weekend becoming a bore! There's no request for our involvement is there? No specific enquiries to be made in our division?'

'No,' she confirmed. 'It's purely for information. I've made copies for the usual distribution.'

'Good, but get Paul Larkin to check it through – ask him to see if there are any links with our area. I know Barry will call me if he wants enquiries made in our patch.'

As Barbara went about her work, Pemberton settled down to study the fax in more detail. He knew that he had previously come across the name of the victim, Harry Pearle. But where? And in what context? It was some years ago, he was sure. Determined to find an answer, he left his office to examine the Criminal Intelligence File. This had not yet been computerized – another task for Hadley perhaps? It was simply a strip index system of the names of suspects, convicted criminals and people with shady backgrounds and criminal associates. Adjoining each name there was a file reference.

It was the work of a moment to locate the name of Harold Edwin Pearle.

3

According to this piece of intelligence, Harold Edwin Pearle, born in 1957 at Turnerville on the north-east coast of Yorkshire, had been arrested in August 1982 following a chase on foot through the streets of Fawneswick. He was suspected of breaking into an off-licence in the early hours of the morning by smashing a small rear window, climbing through and taking money from a cashbox. The sum taken, all in used notes, was reputedly £850, although the file noted that the off-licence proprietor might have over-stated the sum allegedly stolen. A check on the stock showed the sum was probably closer to £300 but the proprietor insisted that his figure of £850 was correct – he insisted he had counted the cash that evening before locking up and it was destined to be paid into his bank the following morning. It had been stolen before that transaction had taken place.

When Pearle was caught, after a chase of some three-quarters of an hour by several officers through a network of streets, he was not in possession of any money other than a few coins totalling £3.75. He claimed he was innocent; he said he had not broken into the premises. He had gone up the alley for a pee and had run away when a policeman had suddenly appeared and shouted at him. He'd fled because he thought he might be in trouble for 'committing a nuisance in a public place' as the local newspaper politely put it. Male holiday-makers were regularly fined for that breach of the by-laws, having been taken short upon leaving the pubs and clubs. Pearle, who had been alone, readily admitted to being in the passage which led to the rear of Alliker's off-licence but insisted that he had not burgled the premises.

He also said he had not seen anyone else loitering in the area at the time – his presence in the passage had totalled some thirty seconds in all, just enough to achieve his urgent purpose. Reading the file, Pemberton saw that a uniformed constable had sighted him whereupon Pearle had fled; sensing that something illegal had occurred, the constable had radioed Fawneswick Control whereupon a patrolling police car, literally one street away at that very moment, had joined the chase. Furnished with a description of the suspect, the car's crew joined the fun. As the Control staff leapt into action with a flurry of radio messages, other officers had converged upon the scene and soon three more foot patrol policemen and three night-duty detectives had joined the chase. All this had happened within five minutes of the first constable's alarm call. This posse had scoured the streets and from time to time they had caught sight of the running man, but capture was difficult because of his use of the narrow alleys and passages which formed a maze between the streets of the older part of the seaside town. These often divided into two or three, thus making pursuit very difficult, and it was evident that their quarry was very familiar with this veritable labyrinth of alleys and passages. After a chase lasting some forty-five minutes, Pearle was caught, arrested and taken to the police station to be searched. In the meantime, the break-in at the off-licence had been confirmed. When searched, Pearle had had no cash upon him, the later theory being that he had taken the opportunity to hide it during the chase. Without the real evidence of a large sum of cash upon him, it would be difficult, if not impossible, to secure a conviction.

A search of the route believed to have been taken by Pearle during his dash for freedom had failed to locate any hidden cash – but no one really knew the precise route he had taken. All the evening's sightings had been but fleeting glimpses. In his statement, the constable who had surprised Pearle said he'd wanted to know why the fellow had fled and so, once the chase had attracted other officers, he had checked the rear of the shops along the passage and had discovered the broken window. That had taken only a second or two. Both the front and rear doors of Alliker's were locked, however, the thief having apparently made his exit by dropping the Yale latch of the rear door upon departure. The proprietor had been roused from his bed, standard procedure in such cases. He lived away from the premises but within twenty minutes had attended the scene of the crime to confirm that the premises had been unlawfully entered via a rear window and that £850 in cash had been stolen. An examination of the scene by SOCO had not produced any fingerprints nor any other evidence which would link Pearle with the crime. His persistent denials, a lack of independent witnesses and a dearth of evidence at the scene had persuaded the duty inspector that Pearle could not be charged with that crime. Quite simply, he could not be linked to the burglary and he had been released without charge.

A note attached to the file, dated 1982, said that Pearle was believed to be an active and very clever criminal in Fawneswick, specializing in break-in offences at commercial properties such as bookmakers' premises, off-licences, public houses and shops of all kinds – all businesses that dealt in cash.

He had been a target criminal for a year (1981) and although several premises had been attacked during that time, all using his MO, Pearle had not once admitted guilt nor had sufficient evidence ever been found for a prosecution. In spite of his known activities, Pearle had never been prosecuted.

The break-in at Alliker's had all the hallmarks of his work. There was a further note which suggested the proprietor might have staged the raid himself, but that was not proved either. It was known that the proprietor was deeply in debt, a good reason for staging a robbery and claiming an inflated amount from his insurance. These were recorded observations made by the police at the time.

Pemberton had remembered the name because one facet of Pearle's character was that he always operated alone. A friendly man with a ready smile and considerable charm, he enjoyed an active social life around the pubs and clubs, but so far as his criminal activities were concerned, no one, not even his closest friend or his current lover, knew the precise details of his criminal work. He kept his activities strictly to himself, never boasting of his successes or announcing his plans in advance. In other words, Pearle was a highly professional and highly successful criminal. Nonetheless, he did associate with known criminals and a list of those was included in the file. Pemberton felt sure that a copy of this information would be beneficial to the Langbarugh enquiry.

Sitting quietly in his office that afternoon, Pemberton studied this file with deepening interest. He was about to pick up the telephone to call Barry Brennon in Langbarugh, when he noticed the name of the arresting officer.

On Pearle's Refused Charge Sheet was the name and signature of Detective Constable Victor Hadley. As it was a Saturday, Hadley was not working and so Mark was unable to discuss this with him, but he made a note in his diary to have a chat with him on Monday morning. It would be interesting to obtain Hadley's recollection of that incident and his impressions of the guilt or otherwise of the running Pearle. Meanwhile, Mark rang Barry Brennon at the Langbarugh police headquarters.

'Hi, Barry, Mark Pemberton here.' They chatted informally for a while about their days together at the training school and at the police college, and then Pemberton told his pal of his own Criminal Intelligence Department's records about Pearle. He outlined the contents in brief, referring to the abortive arrest, and asked if the information was of any value to Brennon's murder enquiry teams.

'Brilliant!' enthused Brennon in his rich Irish brogue. 'Great stuff. We've had our eye on Pearle for a long time, but he's never let us catch him. He was always one jump ahead; there was never any evidence to link him with any job we suspected him of. On paper, he was a fine upstanding fellow and an ideal citizen even if we thought he was a dubious dealer in second-hand cars. We knew he was a crook.'

'But somebody got to him!' commented Mark Pemberton. 'He wasn't as clever as he thought, eh?'

'The killer never took a penny,' Brennon went on. 'That's what's so bloody puzzling. There's no sign of a theft, no indication of fraud or dodgy dealing in cars, the bloody killer just walked in with a sawn-off shotgun and bang – Harry was dead. No reason, no words, no chance of a plea, no bargaining, nothing. It smacks of a criminal execution to me, Mark, an assassination, and if it is, it's something new to this area. Anyway, let me have a copy of that file, there might be some interesting names in it, names we can check out.'

'I'll send it off in a few minutes by car – I'll get our Control to arrange a rendezvous point with one of our patrol cars and one of yours.'

Mark asked Barbara to make two photocopies of the complete file on Pearle, then send one to Langbarugh and return the original to its place for future reference. He would work from a copy.

On Monday, Pemberton called Hadley into his office for a coffee, and referred to the murder of Harold Edwin Pearle. Hadley nodded; he had read the circular on the notice-board and told Pemberton the killing had featured in the morning papers and on local radio.

'You knew him?' Pemberton asked.

'Not really.' Hadley shook his head. 'I arrested him once, you know, years ago, after a chase through Fawneswick. I nicked him for doing Alliker's off-licence, but the charge wouldn't stick. Lack of evidence.'

'We have the file,' Pemberton told him, indicating the papers on his desk. 'I've dug it out for Langbarugh. I see you were the arresting officer.'

'A fluke really, sir, it could have been any one of us. I can't remember how many of us were chasing Pearle that night, but I happened to be the one who got my hand on his collar. We cornered him eventually, like a wee rat.'

'A good arrest?'

'Aye. Guilty as hell, he was, but we could'nae prove it.'

'The money was never found, was it? He didn't have it with him.'

'He'd ditched it somewhere. He was too crafty to be caught in possession of stolen cash. He'd managed to hide it somewhere. It was never found. We kept him under surveillance for a week or two after that job, just in case he went to retrieve the loot or went on a spending spree, but he never did. He knew we were on to him, sir, he's as slippery as an eel. *Was* as slippery as an eel. He won't offend any more, will he? He's got his just deserts, sir, he lived on crime and now he's died by it. It's one less villain for us to worry about. Serve him right. I have no sympathy for him or his like, no sympathy at all.'

'We don't know he was still an active criminal, Vic. He might have reformed.'

'And pigs might fly, sir! His sort never change. I saw that circular and I thought, good riddance.'

'Our file's been copied for Langbarugh,' Pemberton told him. 'I wanted you to know. They might want words with you – they're interested in his cronies and contacts.'

'I'll be here,' said Inspector Hadley.

'So, how's the Muriel Brown programming coming along, Vic?'

'Fine, no problems. They were a wee bit casual in those days, if you don't mind me saying so. I get the feeling that lots of evidence was overlooked, the scene wasn't properly examined, and the way some of those statements were taken leaves a lot to be desired. Some of the things said by witnesses were never checked out, theories and clues not followed up. Sloppy bloody police work, if you ask me.'

'So we might have to reinterview some of them?'

'That might be an option, sir, even after all this time – that's if they can remember anything after such a long gap or if they're still alive. But yes, Mr Pemberton, the work's going well and I'm enjoying it. It is doing me good, by the way, being useful again, doing something positive. Not too demanding and there is an end product – to catch the killer. You know, sir, I'd really like to get my hands on the bastard who killed Muriel Brown.'

'Perhaps you will, Vic, perhaps you will!'

'That's what I'm aiming for, sir. Feeling another collar – and having enough evidence to get him put away for a long, long time.'

While Hadley was in his office, Mark Pemberton rang the Langbarugh incident room and spoke to Detective Inspector Ron Whiteley. He explained that the arresting officer named in the file recently delivered to the Langbarugh incident room was now working in the CID office at Rainesbury and was available for interview. Whiteley thanked him – the Alliker file had arrived and a team had been allocated that old crime as an action; they would undoubtedly be in touch with Hadley, and the other officers and witnesses named in the report.

Whiteley added that there had been no significant developments with that murder hunt, other than confirmation that the registration plate on the offender's getaway motor cycle was false. The actual number was allocated to a Rolls-Royce.

Thanking Hadley, Pemberton dismissed him, then the untidy inspector returned to his work on the Muriel Brown enquiry.

Mark's next task, before the day's business intruded, was to visit the Scenes of Crime Department to discuss the condition of some fingerprints found at the scene of several local burglaries. He wanted a word with Detective Sergeant Derek Thornton so rang him to ensure he was in his office and set off for a chat. When he arrived, he found Detective Inspector Philip Swanson, visiting from Fawneswick.

'Morning, Phil,' greeted Pemberton as he entered the busy office. 'So what brings you over to Rainesbury?'

'Car crime,' said the dark-haired detective. 'BMWs and Rovers. The MO used for nicking them on our patch is just like yours. The crimes are linked, I feel, so I'm here to examine the pics of some of your local cases.'

'Let me know what transpires. It seems we have professionals at work?'

'Taking cars to order, I reckon, sir,' said Swanson. 'Chummy from the Continent rings up, orders a new black BMW and it's nicked, number plates changed and on board the ferry before the real owner realizes its gone. Your lads have got some gen on the likely villains.'

'They're good lads, ours,' beamed Pemberton with pride, now heading for the sergeant's office.

Before he reached it, however, Swanson said, 'Sir, a minute if you've time. A walk around the car-park?'

'Sure,' Pemberton agreed.

He was never totally happy in Swanson's company – the man never seemed sincere. He never looked you in the eye, and yet he had an amazing rapport with women. It was said he could charm the pants off any woman and yet he treated them like dirt

– he used them, and discarded them. In Pemberton's view, Swanson was not a very nice person. But he was a competent detective and a walk and a chat away from flapping ears suggested something confidential and something important. In the brisk coolness of that early autumn morning, with the trees shedding their leaves and the grass around the car-park looking jaded and pale, the two detectives walked away from the vehicles. In those first moments, they chatted about the weather, the state of English football and the effects of the Sheehy Report upon the police service.

'So,' said Pemberton when they were striding across the tarmac away from the vehicles, 'what can I do for you, Phil?'

'It's Vic Hadley, sir. They tell me he's back at work, in your department?'

'Yes, he is. He's not full-time, it's supposed to be therapeutic work.'

'I was there, sir, at the Millgate supermarket job. He shot that man deliberately, you know that?'

'I don't know anything, Phil, other than what's contained in the official reports. There was no evidence to suggest what you imply. So what was your role?'

'I was a DS at the time, sir, teamed up with DC Watson. Dave Watson. We'd got this tip-off, from a reliable source, I might add, that the raid on the security van delivering cash to Millgate would go ahead. We'd had some preliminary gen, but this was the confirmation we needed. The operation was set up, using plain-clothes and uniform officers, both inside and outside the supermarket. We had armed officers with us too. I was one of those detailed to be outside. Me and Dave were in a disguised van parked on the street outside. Both of us were unarmed. A bread van, it was, looking empty. We were hidden in the back, in radio contact, and we could see into the parking area in front of the supermarket. I told all this to the enquiry, sir, and at the inquest, but nobody believed me. I know Hadley shot Newton, sir.'

'He admits he shot Newton, Phil. He's never denied that.'

'I know, but he did it in cold blood, sir, that's the point I'm making. That man should have been done for murder – he executed Newton. It was a cold-blooded assassination. I'm sorry to plague you with this after all this time and after all the enquiries into the shooting, but I was there, only feet away from him. He never gave Newton a chance to surrender, he never gave the warning —'

'We know. He was disciplined for that,' interrupted Pemberton.

'I know, sir, but Newton was not armed. If he'd been pointing a gun at me, I'd have known about it. I'm not blind, I am alert in circumstances of that kind. I know there's nothing I can do now, I can bang my head against a brick wall until I drop from exhaustion or brain damage, but I thought you ought to know what sort of man you've got in your department. He can't tolerate a criminal getting away with a crime, sir. He's paranoid about lawbreakers. If he lived in the Wild West, he'd be stringing up suspects from trees, lynching them without a trial, innocent or not.'

'That's a bit strong, Phil!'

'Maybe, sir, but that man is a killer and I don't care who hears me say so.'

'That's a serious allegation to make against a senior colleague, Phil.'

'So what can be done, sir? I mean, I know he's been off duty sick for months, the pressure they said it was, the stress of killing an innocent man, a bystander, a young chap with a family. Even if Newton was part of the gang, there was no need to kill him, sir. We'd got the whole lot contained. But Newton wasn't on that job, Mr Pemberton. There was nothing to link him with that raid, sir, nothing at all. Not a shred of evidence. He was a passer-by, a chap popping into the shop to get something for his kids' breakfast. He just turned up at the wrong time. So now that Hadley's returned to duty, sir, what's he going to do next, eh?'

'He has been sick, a stress-related illness they say, and experts with far more knowledge and experience than you and me have said he's fit for therapeutic work. I've got him programming an old crime into HOLMES. The Muriel Brown case.'

'Well, if he finds out who killed Muriel Brown, he's good enough to go out and knock him off, sir, that's if the courts won't prosecute.'

'I'll pretend I never heard that comment, Phil.' Pemberton was shocked by the vehemence of the detective inspector's remark.

'Somebody has to say it, sir. You'll never get me to work alongside him, that's for sure.'

Pemberton halted and regarded his colleague.

'Phil,' he said, 'I respect your opinions, you're a detective with a vast amount of experience, but you know, and I know, that we can't resurrect that old case. There's been a court case, an inquest and an official enquiry with emphasis on Newton's death and Hadley's role in it. He's been exonerated, Phil. It's all over.'

'But you've not looked into the case, sir? In depth? Not even out of interest?'

'I looked at the file when I knew that Hadley was going to join me. I wanted to refresh my memories of the Millgate raid, and I'll be straight with you. I have no desire to challenge the outcome of the official investigations.'

'Can I ask you to get the file out, go through it and ask people who were there, like me, what they thought of it all? Then make your judgement.'

Pemberton, aware of the depth of Swanson's concern, said, 'All right, Phil. I'll have a closer look at the case. But I'll do it out of interest only, I'm not going to reopen it, you know that's impossible.'

'That's all I ask, sir. I'd appreciate another chat when you've made your assessment.'

And so Swanson and Pemberton parted and entered the building, Swanson going to the studio section to examine the photographs which were awaiting him, while Pemberton went to Sergeant Thornton's door, knocked and was admitted. But Pemberton was wondering why Swanson continued to air his views on the Millgate supermarket case.

When Pemberton returned home that evening, Lorraine had prepared a meal. Detective Constable Lorraine Cashmore now lived with Pemberton, an arrangement not entirely acceptable to the hierarchy of the force due partially to the wide difference in their ranks. A detective constable sleeping with her boss was not considered conducive to good personnel management, but as both Pemberton and Lorraine were able to separate their work relationship from their domestic set-up, the arrangement was tolerated, albeit never with open or official approval.

When Pemberton walked in, he could smell the herbs, celery and mushrooms of her beef crumble, rich with Worcester sauce and flavouring, and covered with a baked topping of oats, wholemeal flour, butter and grated Cheddar cheese all flavoured with mixed herbs. They kissed, then he went to the bedroom to change into something casual while she poured a malt whisky for him and a dry Martini and tonic for herself. Meanwhile, Mark opened a bottle of Bordeaux in readiness for the meal. Over their aperitifs, they chatted about the day's events, Lorraine highlighting her own investigation into a paedophile ring while Pemberton gave her an appraisal of his own supervisory role that day. It was a chance to unwind, to discuss the minutiae of the office within the privacy of their home, and, for Pemberton, to chat about work in an informal atmosphere. In the confines of the office, they adopted a formal approach to one another, with Lorraine even calling him 'sir' as the others did – but not at home. Here, they were lovers.

'Lorraine,' he said, draining his whisky, 'what's the general feeling about Hadley?'

She smiled. 'Some feel sorry for him,' she said. 'They know he went through a rough time, but he doesn't say much, does he? Some of the lads have invited him out for a drink, but he won't go along with them.'

'And the others?' he smiled. 'Those who are not sorry for him? How do they feel?'

'There's a bit of unease in the office, Mark.' She had to be honest with him.

'Unease? What sort of unease?'

'There's a feeling that Hadley shot Newton on purpose – an excuse to be rid of a villain, as one detective said. Inspector Swanson resurrected the arguments when he called in. And Hadley is well known for his tough attitude towards wrongdoers, Mark; he never gives an inch. If a teenage joyrider gets killed in a stolen car, Hadley reckons it saves the courts a job and reduces the cost to the taxpayer. Why do you ask?'

'It's something that Swanson said to me today.' He explained about his chat with the detective inspector. 'He could be stirring things up for obscure personal reasons, but I do get the impres sion there's a lot of submerged feeling, antagonism really, tc wards Hadley – which could explain why he doesn't want t socialize with his colleagues.'

'He has been very sick,' she said. 'If I'd been through what he' been through, I don't think I'd want to socialize after work.'

'What's the feeling about his response in the Millgate super market shooting?'

'Mixed,' she said. 'Some say he should not have fired his gu even if Swanson was threatened, others say he did a service t the force, saving Swanson's life. It seems odd that Swanson is s much against Vic Hadley, Mark, it doesn't add up, but I don know the ins and outs of it all, I've not read the file.'

'I must confess I don't like Swanson,' admitted Mark, drainin his glass. 'I think he's very devious, I wouldn't trust him wit my granny or with my wallet. Even so, I think much of the fee ing against Hadley is based on gossip and innuendo, and o how the papers interpreted events in the heat of the moment. think I'd better refresh my memory of that day. I'd be intereste to see precisely what Swanson said at the time.'

'I hope you're not going to get involved in something th doesn't concern you, Mark Pemberton!' She rose from her chai 'That incident is over, Mark. Finished. Concluded. Come alon it's time to eat; time to forget you're a detective.'

And obediently, he followed her into the dining-room.

4

The Millgate supermarket file was very comprehensive. It con prised the original statements, crime reports and SOCO accoun of the investigation of the scene, plus the deliberations of the i quest, the trial and the subsequent enquiry by Staplefordshi Constabulary. It was a mammoth document and, in the securi of his own home, Pemberton allowed Lorraine to examine it her leisure. Had she been in the office, her rank of detective co stable would have meant she was not allowed access to the mo confidential of these pages, but as the lover and companion of Detective Superintendent Mark Pemberton, she was granted this privilege. And she would not abuse it.

Mark allowed her several evenings during the week to read it because he valued her opinion; from time to time in some complex cases, her feminine intuition had highlighted factors which he might have missed and he hoped that her perspicacity would reveal more than the official scrutiny had uncovered.

'So what do you think?' Mark asked when she had completed her task.

'I'm not quite sure,' Lorraine admitted. 'Even now, no one's sure whether Inspector Hadley murdered Newton or not. Hadley is the only one to state that Newton was carrying a gun. No one else saw Newton arrive on the scene; no one can say whether he was armed or not, not even Swanson. Hadley shot him, yes, we know that. He did so to save Swanson's life. The official enquiries accepted Hadley's version of events. Hadley has never denied killing Newton but killing is not necessarily murder. And no one has proved that Hadley acted outside the law.'

'Some would say he did.'

'I agree, Mark, plenty have suggested he did, but there's never been any proof.'

'Do *you* accept Hadley's version of events?'

'I don't accept anything, Mark. I'm just thinking aloud, trying to sort out the vital elements.'

'Look at it from another angle,' Pemberton suggested. 'Does it matter whether or not Newton was part of the raiding gang? Does it matter whether or not he was a crook?'

'Are you saying it's acceptable to kill a crook who's in the act of committing a crime?'

'No, I'm not saying that. What I'd like to establish is whether Hadley killed an innocent man. What I want to know is whether Newton was involved in the raid on that security van, and whether he was armed at the time.'

'The official enquiry —' she began.

'I'm not concerned with what the official enquiry concluded, Lorraine. I want to know for myself. I want to know because there seem to be some grave doubts about the whole affair. There's a deep feeling, even among our own officers, that

Hadley did kill an innocent man and somehow managed to cover up his crime. When that belief persists among our own people, Lorraine, we can't ignore it. *I* can't ignore it.'

'Newton was known to the police, Mark – that could be a factor.'

'He was never convicted,' he reminded her. 'He had no criminal record, but the file does record that he came to the notice of the local CID from time to time. He had no job, yet he had a comfortable life-style. He was getting an income from somewhere, the theory being that he lived off the proceeds of crime. But nothing was ever proved, no identifiable proceeds of crime were ever found in his possession or at his home.'

'That's rather odd,' she mused. 'In some ways, it's rather like that man Pearle. He was never convicted and now he's dead. But we know he was murdered.'

'A vigilante revenge, eh?' He smiled.

'It's the sort of thing vigilantes might do if they got out of hand,' Lorraine said. 'An eye for an eye, a tooth for a tooth . . .'

'Hand for hand, foot for foot, burning for burning, wound for wound, stripe for stripe,' Mark completed the biblical quote. 'So should we investigate the background of Joseph Newton, otherwise known as Joss, the so-called innocent father of two?'

'You can't, Mark! That would have been done at the time. It's all over, enquiries into Newton's death have been completed, there's nothing you can do, nothing you should do. You know that.'

'Lorraine, I want to get to the bottom of this – I need to know the truth about Hadley's action that day. I would hate to have a cold-blooded murderer working in my office!' and Mark Pemberton shuddered at the thought. 'You know, looking back at Millgate, I do wonder about Hadley's mental state that day. We know he's been ill since that time, but maybe he was ill both before and during the incident. Has that been considered? I'm asking whether he was in total control of his actions that day, as indeed a firearms trained police officer should be. Was he controlled enough to kill if necessary, yet brave enough not to pull the trigger when there was doubt?'

'If he was sick at the time, it might explain some of the confusion and doubt,' she said.

'He could have been ill without anyone knowing,' Mark mused. 'He might not even have realized himself. I must admit he could have shot Newton in cold blood. And that thought worries me. It worries me a lot. For that reason, and because the chap is working in my department, I might just do a little investigating of my own, in my own time, just to satisfy my curiosity.'

'You'd be stirring up a lot of mud, Mark, especially if you start asking questions all over again,' she cautioned him. 'There'd be real trouble if the press, or Newton's family, got wind of your activities, more so if they knew Hadley was back at work in the CID! It's over, Mark, it's finished, you'd better forget it.'

But she knew Mark Pemberton would not rest until he had thoroughly investigated the events which occurred outside Millgate supermarket two years ago.

In spite of Lorraine's reservations, Pemberton decided that a visit to the forecourt of the supermarket was a good start. In the investigation of any crime, a visit to the scene was vital.

He decided to undertake the trip next Saturday because some groceries were required. He and Lorraine were off duty that weekend, so they could combine their domestic routine with a spot of quiet and unofficial police work in Fawneswick.

As Mark said, 'You can shop and I can snoop. We can shop and snoop at Millgate. How's that for a slogan?'

'Terrible!' She cringed.

On the Saturday morning, they arrived at the supermarket just as the doors were opening at 8.30 a.m. The raid had occurred around that time, albeit in midweek, and on this occasion Mark and Lorraine managed to park their white Vauxhall Astra in the street outside. That street was called Millgate, a steep, cobbled road. There was a two-hour limit at this point, adequate for their purpose, and Mark was pleased that he had been able to park in the precise place occupied two years ago by Detective Sergeant Swanson and Detective Constable Watson. From the same spot, they had kept observations on the premises and Mark realized they had had a clear view of the forecourt.

In large bold letters across the entrance, and in line with the pavement which ended at each end of the supermarket forecourt, was the legend 'No Parking' and Pemberton's front wheels were al most touching the demarcation line of that restricted area. Th tiny forecourt was not the main car-park, however. A far large public car-park lay behind the supermarket and it led into th rear entrance of the shopping complex. Most of the shopper used that park, rather than the one now being scrutinized b Mark and Lorraine.

When full, the entire forecourt could accommodate only eigh cars, four at each side. Four spaces were for disabled driver with a two-hour limit, the other four being for shoppers with one-hour limit. Each of these parking areas was at an outer edg of the forecourt – as you looked at it from Millgate towards th supermarket, the disabled park was on the right with the othe four spaces on the left. Parking was not allowed upon the oblon area between the two series of parking spaces, this being use for delivery vehicles and, of course, to allow the incoming an outgoing cars to manoeuvre.

The front wall of the supermarket, which overlooked the fore court, comprised two storeys, the upper one being used for sto age and offices and the lower one being the shop floor. Th upper storey had several small windows high in the brick wa while two large doors provided the supermarket entrances one, the goods entrance, opened almost on to the disabled park ing spaces, and adjoining this was a small door for use by th staff. The goods delivery entrance was a large metal slidin door, most unattractive and in need of a coat of paint. It wa identified by a sign on the wall, announcing, 'Goods Entranc No Smoking. No Parking. Authorized Personnel Only.' For th customers, there was a revolving door of sturdy glass and th was situated close to the four public parking spaces. The lengt of wall in between the entrances was of ornamental brick an bore the logo of the supermarket, a millwheel superimpose upon a five-bar gate. A gaudy clock adorned the high centre the wall, also with the logo upon its face. The entire forecou was cobbled in keeping with both the neighbouring street an the town's ancient image. The only other furniture was a met litter bin standing against the wall behind the invalid parkin places, and a bench alongside. It would accommodate three perhaps four persons.

Prior to their visit, both Mark and Lorraine had examined photographs and plans of this forecourt, and they now sought to familiarize themselves by matching the actuality with the official photographs and plans. In silence, each examined the layout of the entrance, the disposition of the disabled and general parking lots and the relative position of the adjoining houses, shops and offices. They also measured the distances to where each of the discarded cartridge shells had been found and where the loaded shotgun had been located.

Some of the windows of the adjoining premises overlooked the parking area, Pemberton knew, and some of those premises had been utilized by the police as they had established their ambush on the day. Although Pemberton's memory was clear and his powers of recollection very good, he had brought a selection of the documents with him, plus some notes of his own. He carried these in his pocket, not wishing to leave sensitive material in his car. One factor was that the abortive and tragic raid had occurred two years ago which meant that the forecourt might have been altered in some material way. Each bore that possibility in mind.

From the anonymity of the car, Mark pointed immediately to his right. 'Four disabled parking spaces,' he said partly to himself and partly to Lorraine. 'At the time of the raid, there was a van parked there. It used the space closest to the goods entrance. It was a small van, a Ford Escort according to one witness, and in the rear, seen through a window at the back, was a wheelchair. It had been stolen and bore false number plates. It was used by two of the raiders, Pollard and Sykes, to hide in as they awaited the arrival of the Cerberus security vehicle. It was to be left behind when they made their escape in the waiting getaway car.'

'Did anyone see it arrive, Mark?' Lorraine asked. 'Just to our right there are two shops – a shoe shop and a wool shop immediately across the pavement from us. Maybe the staff noticed something?'

'No, they were questioned about that. No one saw it arrive, which implies it came very early, before the shop workers reported in, before the supermarket staff arrived,' he reminded her. 'There's a house next to the shoe shop and its windows overlook the goods entrance and the far end of the disabled car-park.

No one in the house or shops noticed the arrival of that van, even though the shop windows overlook the parking spaces. The shop assistants in both places were too busy preparing for their day to worry about things happening on the supermarket forecourt. Similarly, the lady in the cottage, who lives alone and is a pensioner, did see the van in position about 8.15 a.m., but didn't notice its actual arrival. She suspected nothing sinister because disabled people often arrive early so that they can tour the supermarket without the hassle of crowded aisles and overloaded trolleys. No one in any of the premises overlooking the forecourt witnessed the actual raid.'

Lorraine was studying the other side of the parking area. 'Four spaces there,' she commented. 'Were any of them used as the raid was under way?'

'No,' he said. 'The getaway car was parked on the street, Millgate that is, facing the same direction that we are now, with a man at the wheel, engine running. That was Gill, unarmed. He parked at the far side of that "No Parking" area, engine running and ready for off. All four parking spaces were empty. The getaway car was stolen and it bore false plates. Gill was arrested at the same time as the others and the car was impounded before it could be driven away.'

'And overlooking that side of the parking area is a solicitors' office and a restaurant.' Lorraine was peering at the respective premises.

'Yes, the solicitors' office has two floors. One of its upper windows overlooks the whole area. There was a police marksman in that window, which was open. It is normally open to allow a circulation of fresh air when the office is being used. That marksman had a first-rate view of all the front doors of the supermarket and of the rear of the security van as it reversed into position ready to deliver the cash. The other place is a restaurant which is on the first floor – access is by a flight of steps which led from this street, they ascend with the car-park spaces on your right. As you climb, there is a window which overlooks the parking spaces, and there is a further window on the landing, looking in the same direction. Inspector Hadley was on that staircase because it commands a broad view of the forecourt, with ready access through the door which is on the corner formed by the forecourt and the pavement. The downstairs accommodation of the restaurant is used as a holiday cottage; it's fully equipped but it was empty at the time. The police did not see fit to make use of it – they had enough vantage points.'

'And I can see an alley in the far corner, Mark. Where's it lead?'

'The wall of the supermarket extends along that alley, Lorraine, and you can see that it reaches along the hidden side of the solicitors' office. Further along there is a flight of steps which turns a corner, and the alley then leads to a narrow street. Cholmley Street, it's called. The alley's called Acorn Alley.'

'And that's where Newton appeared from, if I remember correctly?'

'Yes, according to Hadley. Now, the reports from waiting police officers state that the two raiders, Pollard and Sykes, emerged from their van which was parked on the disabled area. They made their move as the security guards were emerging from their vehicle, having reversed it into position near the tradesmen's entrance. The raiders' first job was to deal with the guards as they prepared to deliver the cash. As they were carrying out this raid, armed with guns, the waiting policemen went into action. It was at that precise moment that Newton came out of that alley. It was unexpected, a total surprise. Hadley, who had, at that instant, also just emerged from his hiding place, was the only person to see him. In statements taken from the police and the Cerberus guards, none of them noticed Newton's arrival – their minds were on other more urgent things! Not even the raiders saw him turn up. But Hadley did. Hadley saw him and reacted, all within a split second because he swore Newton was bearing a gun which was pointing at a detective. Hadley's official firearm was at the ready for instant use in case he had to assist in the arrest of the perpetrators and halt the raid. According to Hadley, DS Swanson was crossing the forecourt over to Hadley's right to assist with the arrest of the raiders, which meant that Newton's gun was pointing at him. Swanson, according to both Hadley and Swanson himself, was totally unaware of the danger and Hadley, acting with the speed of light to prevent his death, thought he had no alternative but to shoot Newton. Other shots were discharged – we know they came from Sykes. In the chaos that followed, no one seems quite sure what happened in the next few seconds, or how many shots were actually fired or in what sequence the shots were fired, but the raiders were disarmed and arrested. Some moments, minutes even, passed before Newton's body was approached by armed police but no weapon was found on the body or lying nearby. However, there was a shotgun lying some five yards away; it was loaded but broken. One theory is that Hadley's shots propelled it from Newton's grasp when it fell to the ground and broke open without discharging any shots. Another gun, empty, was recovered from Sykes. Out of all this, Lorraine, a gun seems to be missing. So what in the name of God happened to it? Swanson maintains that Pollard was armed and that the fallen, broken gun belonged to him. Pollard also said that, albeit some time later when interviewed by Newton's brother. Sadly, no one else can confirm that. Other officers were concentrating on Sykes and Gill; the security van's guards were out of the sight of Hadley, the security vehicle stood between them. Pollard was at the rear of the van beyond the vision of all the officers at the critical moment; he was there to prevent the guards escaping via that route. Out of all those people, only Hadley saw Newton come on to the forecourt which means that no one except Hadley can say whether or not he was armed. There are holes in this, Lorraine, and we are left with a mighty mystery.'

'The gun?'

'Yes, the loaded gun. Is there any way of finding out who had it in his hands at the time of the raid?'

'There were other policemen hidden around the forecourt, in the buildings?' Lorraine said. 'Surely one of those saw Newton's arrival? Surely someone noticed Pollard with a gun?'

'No.' He was emphatic. 'That's the problem. The raid was under way, they all had their orders and were concentrating on other things, a very tense time for all. It's interesting to speculate that if Newton had turned tail and run, no one would have noticed him, but he didn't. He came forward and died as a consequence.'

'If Hadley is telling the truth,' observed Lorraine, 'he reacted with remarkable speed and confidence and undoubtedly saved the life of one of his officers.'

'Perhaps. Or he shot Newton in cold blood and managed to cover up his crime,' said Pemberton. 'Whatever he did that day, Lorraine, I must know the answer. That's why we are here.'

5

'Look,' said Lorraine eventually, 'you mooch about while I do the shopping. You might even get around to asking if any of the locals saw anything on the day. They'll still remember it.'

'If they did see anything, the police should have interviewed them at the time. But yes, I would like to savour the atmosphere.'

He drove on to the forecourt, none of the four spaces having yet been taken, and reversed into the marked area nearest the entrance. This was outside the solicitors' office, he noted.

'I'll meet you back here in half an hour?' Lorraine suggested.

'Fine,' he agreed.

His main point of interest was the route by which Newton had gained access to the forecourt. Hadley had been quite clear in his statement that Newton had emerged from the narrow confines of Acorn Alley at the point where it led on to the forecourt; that was at the north-west corner. The alley was almost concealed; a stranger might be unaware of it and people might think it was the entrance to private premises rather than a public thoroughfare. As the tall, elegant and slender figure of Lorraine, armed with her shopping bags, made for the revolving entrance, Mark locked his car to inspect Acorn Alley.

It emerged only some ten or twelve feet to the nearside of his car and, even in the morning light, was dark and rather sombre.

High walls shielded the footpath on both sides, one being that of the solicitors' office, devoid of windows, the other being the wall of the supermarket, also without windows. The alley ran at ground level for the width of the solicitors' office, then turned at right angles up a flight of stone steps. The wall on the right was another one which belonged to the supermarket while the one on his left appeared to be that of a private terrace house which fronted Cholmley Street. At the end of the house wall, the alley turned sharp left and led between two terrace houses, neither with ground-floor windows overlooking the alley. Each had two bedroom windows which overlooked the alley, Pemberton noted. Acorn Alley was only some four feet wide at its maximum breadth and it emerged on to Cholmley Street. To the right and left was a row of terrace houses, the alley splitting the terrace at this point, and Cholmley Street featured a one-way traffic system from Millgate. He noticed that car parking was permitted upon one side of Cholmley Street for thirty minutes within every hour.

Behind the supermarket, there was a large public car-park with a compulsory payment system allowing one hour, two hours or a maximum of three hours for varying payments. As he stood at the Cholmley Street exit of Acorn Alley, the large car-park lay to his right with the entrance about one hundred yards along the street. On the wall of one of the houses which overlooked Acorn Alley was a large metal arrow pointing towards the supermarket and bearing the words 'Millgate Supermarket'.

If Hadley's version was accurate, Newton could have been waiting in the darkness of Acorn Alley as he prepared to raid the security van. It provided a very useful place of concealment. It was sparingly used when the supermarket was open; those who parked at the rear would use well-signed rear entrances while those using the smaller front door would park on the forecourt.

Pemberton decided to walk along Cholmley Street towards the car-park but after some forty yards he was hailed by an old man who was clipping a privet bush in his tiny garden. The neat terrace house with its brown painted door and window frames overlooked Cholmley Street; there was one large window on the ground floor and in front of the house was a tiny garden comprising a neat lawn and borders, with a pair of privet shrubs in each corner. A low wall with a brown wooden gate in the middle led on to the street.

'You're Joe Pemberton's lad, aren't you?' he greeted Mark with a toothy smile. 'I remember you when you started grammar school. Jim Green, caretaker that was, that's me. Me and your dad played cricket together, he was capped to bits when you joined the force.'

Mark smiled at the old character; stoutly built and grizzled with a few days' growth of beard, he would be in his late seventies and limped around his garden as he pruned the bush with his shears. Braces over a white striped shirt, a flat cap and heavy black boots formed his gardening outfit. He took the opportunity to rest awhile now that he had someone to talk to, and it was clear he had a remarkable memory.

'I remember you now, Jim – it's a few years since I was at school, mind!' Mark recalled Green cutting the grass on the cricket fields and hockey pitches. 'You've retired, eh?'

Jim came to the wall and sat upon it. 'My old legs get tired these days, I can't spend all day standing like I used to. Anyroad, I've packed it all in, got my pension book now. This is all I've got, a few square feet of garden instead of acres of sports fields to look after, but it's enough at my age. I'm seventy-eight now, getting on a bit. Anyroad, enough about me. You're still a policeman, are you?'

'I am,' smiled Mark. 'And heading rapidly towards my own pension.'

'So where are you stationed now?'

'Rainesbury. They moved me around a lot when I was a young policeman, but I'm settled now.'

'Got on, have you?'

Mark smiled. Parents were always proud of children who 'got on' in the world, and old Jim was the same. He loved the reflected glory of those children he remembered from 'his' school and had a remarkable memory for those who had made a success of life. 'I'm a detective now, Jim. Detective Superintendent in charge of Rainesbury Division.'

'One of the bosses, eh? By gum, you *have* got on! Your dad would have been so proud. So you've come to see where it all happened, have you?'

'Where all what happened, Jim?'

'That shooting job round the corner, on the supermarket front. Joss Newton.'

'A nasty business,' Mark said. 'I wasn't on the case, though. It wasn't on my patch.'

'He got what he deserved, that young bugger,' Jim said. 'He'd nick anything, lived off crime, he did. Your lot could never catch him, he was too cute for that, so we were all chuffed to bits when he got his come-uppance. Rough justice, but it stopped him.'

'Did you see the raid, Jim?' Mark asked.

The old fellow shook his head. 'No, it's not often I go into that place, I prefer old Mabel's shop along the street, you get personal service there. She knows how I like my smoked bacon and what sort of bread I want.'

'So what kind of things was Joss Newton up to?'

'Nicking cash, a sneak thief. Leave your back door open and he'd be inside like a flash. He'd take cash, Mark, nowt else but cash. He'd never break in – too cute for that. My mate had a fish shop on the seafront years ago and Joss went in to buy some kippers. After he'd gone, there was nearly eighty-five quid missing from the till. There was no way he could prove Joss had taken it, but he had. He'd done it while Fishy Fishwick's back was turned for nobbut a couple of seconds.'

'Did Fishy tell the police?'

'No. No point, was there? What could they do? Joss'd never admit he'd taken the money. That's the sort of trick he did, Mark, and most of the local tradespeople knew him for that, that's why they kept an eye on him whenever he came into their shops or houses. He'd go round the houses sometimes, when the menfolk were out at work, charming the women into thinking he was doing some kind of social survey, and then nick cash from their mantelshelves and tea caddies while they made him a coffee. The odd quid here and there, it all mounts up. He knew where to find it, they all hid it in the same place. He'd take cash left out for the milkman or the insurance. He didn't stick to Fawneswick mind, he went off to other spots too in his car, like a salesman going off on his rounds. He got into loads of women's houses and their knickers too by using the survey trick. They said he even had special forms printed on headed paper to make it look real, went off with a briefcase and clipboard, he did. I've no idea what his wife thought he was doing for a living, but he had a good life, Mark, and a nice house, wife and kids. Mind you, Mark, that wife of his wasn't much better. Go with any bloke, she would, especially them in uniform! They said a few of your chaps were getting more than a cup of coffee from her while he was out stealing. He was from a decent family, though – his dad did well in business in town, a general store, he had. Then his dad left him that house up on Kirkdale Avenue, a smart part of town, and without a mortgage to worry about or rent to pay – that's how he got such a nice spot to live.'

'Did the police know all this?' Mark asked.

'Oh, aye, they knew all about it but never did owt. What could they do, Mark? I know gossip's not good enough for you blokes to take action and most of the folks he took money from never complained. I mean, some of those women would never dare admit what he'd done in their houses while their husbands were out. I'm not daft, I know the police hands are tied when it comes to putting blokes like Joss away, but he made a bloody good living off crime, tax free an' all, while poor sods like you and me had to pay our taxes on less money than he was making.'

'So you reckon he was involved in that supermarket raid?'

'Sure as dogs is dogs,' he grinned. 'A man with a growing family needs more money, a bit of security, so he was hoping to get into the big time, wanting to do bigger jobs for huge sums . . . but he was beaten, eh, by the police. That time, they were one just ahead of him, waiting for him. If you can't lock 'em up, shoot 'em, eh? It's one way of cleaning the town up.'

'Is this all gossip, Jim, or is there some foundation for what you're telling me?'

'Oh, it's right enough,' Jim said. 'I go down to the club every Monday, Wednesday and Saturday night, and it was all the talk down there. Folks knew him, you see, they'd had dealings with him, they'd lost money to the little bastard. I'll tell you summat, Mark, they all cheered that night when they heard he'd got his come-uppance. Best thing to happen in this town for years. Some said it should have happened to that brother of his, an' all.'

'Why his brother?'

'Big Brother Brian, we call him. Union man he was. They said he was as bad as young Joss. Nobody would give him work in this town, Mark, he was allus causing trouble, stirring up strikes if he worked in a factory, or demanding too high wages. Anyway, he got sacked that many times they said he was into crime to make ends meet. There was talk of him working with Joss on some of the big jobs.'

'What's he doing now?' asked Pemberton.

'He's got a job in the factory, canning. But I bet he's soon out on his neck. He never holds a job down too long, trouble-maker through and through he is.'

'Was he ever caught? Brian, I mean,' Mark asked.

'Nay, he was too clever, just like his little brother. Good at planning ahead, they were. A right pair of villains if you ask me.'

'There's no proof of all this, is there, Jim?'

'Nay, lad, but we all knew. Folks aren't daft, you know.'

Pemberton returned to the supermarket incident. 'Jim, do you know if anyone saw the shooting? Nobody seems to have witnessed the actual shooting of Joss Newton.'

'If anybody who knew him had seen it, they'd not say so, would they?' smiled the old man. 'They'd say good riddance to bad rubbish, they'd not want to get involved, would they? They'd be only too glad he was stopped. Did you know that one old lady lost all her life savings to that bastard? Three thousand pounds she'd got saved up after a lifetime's hard work – he smarmed his way into the house reckoning he was from the council checking on her water supply, and nicked a shoe box from under her bed. We all knew it was him. The police were called but they couldn't prove anything. She couldn't even describe the bloke who'd been in the house, except he was well dressed, young with dark hair. It was him all right, we all knew that. She was a bit fuddled, poor old dear, she died six months later when they sent her a big gas bill. She couldn't pay, the shock was enough to finish her, Mark.'

As Mark Pemberton listened to a continuing catalogue of accusations against the late Joss Newton and his brother, along with more tales of his erring wife, he knew he could never be sure how much was gossip and how much was an exaggerated version of the truth. Certainly, he recalled, there had been no comparable account of Newton's supposed criminal activities in the file but he knew, as a policeman, that unless a complaint of theft was received, no police action could be taken. If the victims hadn't reported the thefts, they could not be investigated, neither would they be entered in the official statistics. On the other hand, Pemberton was sufficiently experienced to realize that local gossip could contain a great deal of truth, but he had to accept that unsupported accusations and mere gossip could never feature in a formal investigation. The formal judgements on the death of Joss Newton would be based on what had occurred that day, irrespective of his rumoured past or his mysteriously lucrative mode of life. And it was a fact that he had no criminal record – and that served only to enhance his status as Mr Innocent Passer-by.

Mark remained for ten minutes or so to reminisce with Jim Green, then bade him farewell before inspecting the car-park behind the supermarket. This told him little. He counted eight cars in the park and saw that the rear entrance was open with rows of trolley awaiting inside. It was just nine o'clock now, and the day's business was getting under way. He stood near the ticket machine for a few minutes, trying to determine whether or not this entrance to the supermarket was in any way relevant, and decided that it wasn't. He was on the point of using this entrance to the supermarket to find Lorraine, but decided to return via Acorn Alley.

He would follow the route used by Joss Newton to see what view the deceased might have enjoyed in the final seconds of his life. Old Jim had gone into his house by the time Mark returned, and so he walked along the pavement beside Cholmley Street, against the direction of the traffic. He turned into Acorn Alley, seeing the supermarket sign and noting that no windows overlooked him. It was so easy to traverse this alley unseen. Ideal for a loitering armed robber? Or one rushing to cope with his intended target which had surprised him by arriving five minutes early?

Mark turned right, walked down the steps, turned left and finally moved along the flat stretch which opened on to the forecourt. From the first few yards leading from the foot of the steps, most of the area of the forecourt was not visible – he could see the revolving doors to his left, but little else. As he stepped nearer to the exit of Acorn Alley, the forecourt opened up before him. A bread van was parked there now, its rear doors open as members of staff and the delivery man unloaded tray after tray and hurried them inside. He guessed it was parked in a very similar position to the security van – it was the logical place for any delivery van to park.

The bread van blocked his view of two of the disabled parking spaces, those being the two nearest the goods entrance, and he realized that Newton, if he was involved in the raid, would not know whether his partners in their stolen van had arrived. It would have been concealed by the parked security van – unless, of course, he had made an earlier recce? Pemberton realized that as Newton had walked the final yards along Acorn Alley, it was quite possible he would not have known whether or not the raid was actually in progress.

The guards and his fellow raiders would have been concealed from his view by the Cerberus vehicle and no police would have been visible. If he was totally innocent, as had been vociferously suggested, there was every chance he would have had no idea that an armed raid was in progress, and so he would have continued his journey.

To Mark's right, as he entered the forecourt, were the four public parking spaces and these were now occupied, the nearest being his own car. On the day of the raid, the police reports said none of those were in use; thus Hadley, upon emerging from the entrance to the restaurant further to Mark's right, would have had an uninterrupted view of Newton the moment he emerged from Acorn Alley. The distance was about fifteen yards, a very short distance for a trained firearms officer to see and be seen.

In spite of Pemberton's attempt to gain an impression of the scenario which had prevailed that day, he knew it would be impossible to reproduce events with total accuracy. He had to tune his mind to think in seconds and even parts of seconds – he had to know precisely what was happening around the Cerberus vehicle as Newton entered from stage left and as Hadley made his appearance. The pair of them must have made their appearances almost simultaneously. Pollard must have been behind the van at that very moment. The time between Newton appearing from the alley and meeting his death would be a split second.

Hadley's subsequent actions would be instinctive – he would freeze for a few vital seconds.

A videotape of the raid would have been ideal, with the action reduced to its slowest pace so that the precise relationships and positions of the key players could be determined. What was needed was a choreographed re-enactment, not pieces of paper with theoretical movements upon them. Standing at this place, Pemberton felt that Pollard had thrown his gun into the arena at that same instant, with Pollard concentrating his attention upon Swanson and not noticing Newton's arrival.

Having examined the scene of Newton's death, Pemberton realized that the truth of Hadley's actions might never be determined. Hadley and only Hadley had the answer – and he had given his version of events, not once but several times, and he had suffered as a consequence. And he'd always insisted that he spoke the truth, a habit imposed upon him since childhood.

Lorraine was not waiting at the car, so Mark went into the store and found her. It was small by some supermarket standards and lacked a cafeteria. He decided he would like a coffee when the shopping expedition was over – and what better place than the very café that had concealed Hadley as he had awaited the arrival of the Cerberus van? Their shopping complete, Mark placed the goods in the car and told Lorraine there was just time for a quick coffee before their parking time expired. They walked across to the restaurant which overlooked the forecourt from the west. Climbing the stairs, Mark stopped to examine the view from the window which was midway up the flight; this was the window used by Hadley as he awaited the would-be raiders. He saw that the bread van had now departed.

'It provides a good view,' he explained to Lorraine as they peered across the forecourt. 'Hadley would have been able to see the parked van over there, in the disabled space, and then watch the arrival of the Cerberus van as it reversed into position. Earlier, there was a bread van parked over there,' and he pointed. 'It obscured my view of the disabled parking area. That means the Cerberus vehicle, which would be slightly larger than a bread van, would have obscured Hadley's view of what was happening on its far side, and at the rear. Hadley and Newton would have had an open view of the driver's side only. The raiders would have had to wait for at least two of the Cerberus men to leave the vehicle before they made their move and in turn, the police would have had to wait for a signal to begin their counter-action. It all takes time, precious seconds I know, but time nonetheless. Now, according to the file, there was a firearms officer in the ground floor of the house which overlooks that parking space – a sergeant – and he was in radio contact with Hadley. Once he gave the order to move, Hadley would have emerged from here and run on to the forecourt. That would take, what? Two or three seconds. No more, less even.'

'But from here, Mark, you can't see that alley, can you?'

'No, and that's important. It means there could be no sighting of Newton by Hadley until both had emerged on to the forecourt. Hadley was very surprised to see Newton suddenly appear; he'd been no part of the scenario, no part of the build-up. Because he was carrying a gun, he was shot dead. It would take a mere split second, Lorraine, it could only have been an instinctive reaction from Hadley.'

'Where exactly was Swanson when Newton was allegedly aiming at him?'

'It's difficult to be precise. We know he was walking across the forecourt, probably diagonally and heading towards the centre of it, and also towards the offside of the Cerberus vehicle. He was unarmed, by the way. Another factor in Hadley's mind, perhaps? Imagine this, Lorraine,' continued Pemberton. 'Just suppose that Newton was carrying a shotgun, suppose that he did enter the arena just as the raid was getting under way. If he was carrying a gun, he'd need it in a position so it could be seen and used instantly; it would be pointing towards that detective. It couldn't really be pointing anywhere else, could it? Even if it was aimed at the rear of the van, Hadley would think it was pointing at the detective who was walking into its line of fire. Perhaps it might not have been deliberately aimed at Swanson, but if the detective was walking towards the rear of the security van, via the side nearest to Newton, then he would automatically enter the line of Newton's fire. Hadley, from his excellent viewing position, would assume that Newton was aiming at the detective when in fact he might not have been.'

'Was Newton carrying something else that might have been mistaken for a gun?' asked Lorraine.

'That was considered in depth at the time. He wasn't carrying anything else, he had nothing with him that might have been mistaken for a weapon. He wasn't carrying a toy gun or a replica. Besides, that isn't the sort of error that a trained firearms of ficer would make. If the truth-telling Hadley says Newton was carrying a shotgun when he materialized upon the scene, then I should – and I emphasize should – have no cause to disbelieve him. But enough – come along, if we don't get our coffee, we'll be heading for a parking ticket. These seaside traffic wardens are pretty keen! They operate with split-second timing too!'

They continued to the restaurant on the first floor, selected a window overlooking the forecourt and ordered two coffees. As they enjoyed the drink, Mark told Lorraine about his chat with Jim Green and of his perambulations, offering to show Lorraine the length of Acorn Alley before they departed. Due to a shortage of time, they had to hurry their coffees but there was just sufficient time to show Lorraine along Acorn Alley. She undertook the short trip with Mark, peered along Cholmley Street in both directions and then they hurried back to the car just as a traffic warden appeared. They drove off with grins on their faces.

'Mark, you know Fawneswick fairly well, don't you?'

'Yes, I would say so.'

'So where is Kirkdale Avenue?'

'In the suburbs, not far inland from the cliff-top.'

'Some distance from the supermarket?'

'A mile or so, yes. Why do you ask?' He was puzzled by this sudden question.

'You told me that the old man, Jim whatever-his-name-is, said Newton had been left a house by his father, in Kirkdale Avenue.'

'You've a good memory!' he smiled. 'But yes, that was Newton's address.'

'So if he came to Millgate to get his children something for breakfast, as the file suggests, he would come by car?'

'Yes, we know he did. His car was found after his death. It was in Cholmley Street, right outside the far end of Acorn Alley in fact.'

'So why didn't he drive into the supermarket forecourt, Mark? The spaces were empty, there's an hour's free parking.'

'I don't know why. I would have done as you say . . .'

'And so would I,' she said.

'Is it important?' he asked her.

'I think so, Mark. I think he parked away from the forecourt because he knew what was happening there. If he'd been innocent and in a genuine rush to buy his kids something for breakfast, he would surely have parked as close as possible to one of the entrances. I'd say he didn't want his own car to be associated in any way with the raid. I think he had a shotgun in his car; I think he parked at the end of Acorn Alley knowing he could walk on to the forecourt unobserved while carrying a gun; I think he knew he could be in the thick of the action within seconds, and all without his approach being observed. And I think the early arrival of the security van caught him by surprise.'

'Taking that argument a stage further,' Mark pursed his lips, 'if he was interested only in cereals, why bother to come all this way? Surely there are corner shops closer to his home? I know for a fact there are shops on The Crescent close to where he lived.'

'Exactly, Mark, so for all those reasons, I think Newton *was* part of the raid.'

'It still doesn't explain why the other raiders denied he was operating with them and it doesn't explain the mystery of whether or not he was carrying a gun,' said Pemberton. 'But would you raid a heavily guarded security van without a gun?'

'No, of course not. So we think Newton was involved in some way?' Lorraine put to him. 'If we can be certain of that, it must help us to understand Hadley's actions.'

'And it means we must read that file all over again!' he sighed.

'Then let's waste no more time,' she urged him.

6

A downpour that same Saturday afternoon presented an ideal opportunity for Mark and Lorraine to reappraise the Millgate supermarket file. They examined it line by line, word by word, but found nothing to supplement their existing knowledge and nothing to explain the puzzle about the loaded gun. They pondered the fact that Pollard's claim had been made in prison, undoubtedly with some prompting from Brian Newton. They discussed and read until their heads ached.

'Mark,' Lorraine called from the kitchen where she was making a cup of tea, 'have the raiders been reinterviewed about any of this?'

'Not to my knowledge, there's never been any need. Besides, we don't want them to think we are reopening the case.'

'They are out of prison, aren't they?'

'Yes, there's a note in the file. They all got full remission.'

'So what did the Cerberus guards say about it?'

She came through to the lounge and placed a tray of tea things on the floor, squatting before it. He joined her.

'Not a lot,' he recalled. 'Two of them saw two armed men, both with sawn-off shotguns. The description of one fitted Sykes, but the other could have been either Pollard or Newton, they looked very similar. They were even dressed alike – jeans and a dark blue sweatshirt.'

'But they never saw Newton as he entered the fray?'

'No, that was checked. We're sure it was Pollard they saw.'

'Armed?' she asked. 'Was Pollard armed?'

'Yes, if their testimony is reliable.'

'Knowing who is telling the truth is the problem. I suppose we have reason to think that Pollard was telling the truth?' she persisted.

'Yes, I'm aware of that, he does have some support. If he was truthful, then Hadley is lying. It means Newton didn't have a gun. And that is a most worrying thought.'

'Mark,' Lorraine was pouring the tea, 'quite honestly, I can't see what's going to be gained by all this research. We're not getting anywhere, we're going round in circles. I don't think you can improve on the outcome of the various investigations. Everything that can be said, has been said. There will never be a clear answer to the questions that bother you. I think we might be wasting our time.'

'Not if it means Newton could have been murdered by the police, Lorraine.'

'Mark . . .' There was a long silence. 'Who tipped the police off about that raid?'

'It was never stated in any of the files; the informer's name and means of contact would remain secret. I don't know who it was nor do I know which police officer was originally given the tip-off. They're not obliged to let anyone know – it's almost a legal privilege, keeping one's narks to oneself. Why do you ask?'

'I wondered if it might have been Newton.' She frowned. 'Joss Newton, I mean. If it was him, he might have been hoping for some reward money. Some organizations do offer substantial rewards for information leading to the arrest of thieves. If he was the informer, it might explain why he arrived late on the scene. He would have had to turn up at the raid to convince the others he was not the informer, but by being late, he might avoid being arrested.'

'I'd guess that someone within the supermarket's organization had tipped off the raiders. The security van undertook a regular delivery to the premises, albeit at different times, and this was just one of several drops. It wouldn't be hard to work out when it was due to arrive at 8.30 a.m. on a particular day of the week. In this case, it had extra cash on board to cater for a bank holiday in the height of the season – extra staff wages, part-timers' remuneration and so on. Plus cash for the servicing of tills and those who wish to cash cheques, which is a facility they offer. But if those raiders suspected Newton was an informer, Lorraine, they wouldn't have protected his reputation the way they did, surely?'

'Wouldn't they?' She smiled. 'I think they might. Just think of the police embarrassment at killing an informer, and then being accused of killing an innocent bystander, a member of the public . . . a wonderful result for the villains, a spot of good criminal PR, an own goal for the police.'

'I think that logic is rather too advanced for villains like Pollard, Sykes and Gill. Besides, after what Jim Green said, I doubt if Newton would become an informer; the share-out from the raid would be substantial enough for him without risking his reputation because he grassed, and, if he was the criminal Green says he was, then he would want to commit further crimes of this kind, with the same team if this one had succeeded.'

'Maybe he planned it then?'

'It's possible. He might have been the brains behind the raid, but I'm sure he was not the informer, Lorraine.'

'So was there a fifth man?' She looked into his eyes across the top of her mug.

'A fifth one?'

'Yes, the real informer. We suspect there were four raiders. Three were caught and one was shot dead. If none of these was the informer, who tipped off the police? Someone knew all about it. There was enough detail for the police to be waiting at the right place at the right time.'

'It was certainly spot on,' Mark admitted.

'Most informers go along to the job as a means of concealing their activities, so I am asking the question, Mark – was there another person at that raid? A fifth one?'

'There's never been any suggestion of that.' He frowned.

'Well, there wouldn't be, would there? But suppose he, or she, had been with Newton, waiting in that alley? Suppose he, or she, began to move forward, with Newton going first, he being the one who was armed. The moment Newton popped out of the alley, he was shot by the waiting police – by Hadley, that is. His gun was sent flying from his hands . . . it discharged a shot, a harmless one which could account for the fourth sound of a gunshot. But where did it come to earth? In the alley perhaps, or very close to it? I wonder if the fifth person, the informer, had not emerged from Acorn Alley, but as Newton fell, fatally wounded, the informer recovered that gun and made good his or her escape, never to be seen again. With the protection from the walls of the alley, it could be possible, especially in the midst of all the confusion we know existed. If the gun did discharge a shot, it would account for the fourth empty cartridge shell too.'

'That would depend upon Newton's gun dropping very close to the exit of that alley, wouldn't it?' He nodded. 'Even inside it? And it could explain how Hadley saw Newton with a gun and how that gun has never been satisfactorily explained.' Mark saw the possibilities in Lorraine's argument. 'I wonder if that possibility was ever examined?'

'More scrutiny of the files?'

'More scrutiny of the files,' he sighed.

The papers failed to reveal even a consideration of the presence of a fifth person. Furthermore, there was no suggestion, by any investigator, that Newton's firearm had been spirited away during that split second when everyone's attention had been diverted or concentrated upon specific people or places. Pemberton knew that the participating officers would never accept that a gun could be removed from the scene of a crime virtually under the noses of armed officers. To admit that likelihood would be tantamount to admitting failure. Indeed, Pemberton himself would have said it was impossible but, having traversed Acorn Alley and having seen Newton's likely means of arrival married with Hadley's place of concealment, then he conceded that this just might have occurred.

It was possible – just – but extremely unlikely. Yet if Lorraine's suggestion had any merit, then who was the fifth person? If the gun had been removed, then it must have been done by a fifth villain – and that suggested yet another robber!

So who was the fifth raider? Was it the informer? Whoever it was, he or she had escaped without trace.

The introduction of this possibility swung Pemberton's support back towards Hadley; in another change of mind, Pemberton accepted that Hadley could have saved the life of a colleague while preventing a serious robbery and injury to the guards of the Cerberus security vehicle. If so, he deserved a medal, not continuing criticism. His response had been of the very highest order.

'It's time to knock off,' said Lorraine as the clock struck five thirty. 'Time to clear those papers from the table, time for a drink before we prepare the evening meal – and time to forget all about police work, wrongdoers, firearms and informers!'

'Spoken like a true lady!' he enthused, rising to take her in his arms.

It was three o'clock in the morning, it was Sunday and the telephone was ringing. Pemberton stirred in his sleep, reached out and seized the noisy instrument, if only to silence it. With Lorraine stirring at his side, he put the handset to his ear and whispered, 'Pemberton.'

'Inspector Morton, sir, Control Room. Sorry to disturb you.'

'It must be important, Stan.' Pemberton knew that such a call would never be lightly made. 'Trouble, is it?'

'A shooting, sir. Murder by the look of it.'

'Oh, bloody hell! All right, where do you want me?'
'You'll need a map, sir.'
'Hang on then, I'll have to get a pencil and paper, and a light . . .'
'I'm awake.' Lorraine's voice was at his side. 'I'll put the light on.'
Sitting up in bed, naked and feeling the coolness of the night air on his skin, Detective Superintendent Pemberton was already wide awake and in control of his actions. He had a pencil and notebook in his hands, props he always kept beside the bed, as he said, 'Right, Stan. Fire away.'
Inspector Morton, in charge of the night shift in the Control Room, explained that the body of a man had been found in a small tent in an isolated part of Kesterdale. The tent was beside an unnamed tributary to Kester Beck and he provided the map reference. A uniformed constable was with the body and would remain there until the arrival of a senior officer from the CID – i.e. Pemberton. A doctor had been called. The man had been shot through the chest and the wound was consistent with having been made by a shotgun.
'Right enough, I'm on my way. Are we sure it's not a suicide?'
'The constable reports no firearm at the scene, sir.'
'Fair enough. Who found the body at this time of night, and in such a remote spot?'
'It was a farmer and his wife coming home from a party at a friend's house. They came through the gate which leads up to their farm; that's on a hill above where the body was found. The house is about a mile from the gate. As the farmer opened the gate – his wife was driving because he'd had a few drinks – he heard a shot. He thought it was poachers then heard a motor-bike engine strike up. Then, as he was driving along the track towards his house, a motor bike hurtled past him, towards the gate, towards the road. He was worried about hearing the shot because he knew there was a camper on his land. He parked his car, took out a torch and very soon found the deceased.'
'Any identity yet, Stan?'
'No, sir, we've not touched anything pending your arrival.'
'Right, I'll be there within the hour,' Mark said. 'Raise DI Larkin and DS Thornton of SOCO will you? Tell them to rendezvous with me at the scene. And radio the scene to keep the

doctor there till I arrive, and tell the constable not to let anyone else upon the scene, certainly not into the tent. I'll make my assessment at the scene and will call you from there, probably to make a full call-out and to set up an incident room. And have all motor cycles seen on the roads tonight stopped and checked, detain any suspicious riders – and tell your patrols that any motor cyclist they stop could be armed and could be dangerous.'

'Very good, sir,' said Inspector Morton who had, in fact, already circulated details of the motor cyclist to all night patrols both within the county and across the boundaries.

'I'm coming with you,' said Lorraine as Mark left the bed to dress and shave.

'There's no need, not yet, not until you get the call to set up the incident room.'

'That call will come as sure as eggs are eggs.' She was already standing beside the bed completely naked as she sought her dressing-gown. 'So I might as well come now.'

'I'll have a cup of tea before we go,' he said. 'And a plate of corn flakes, and some toast. It's no good starting a murder investigation on an empty stomach!'

'You get shaved, leave the domestic arrangements to me.' She clutched a dark green silk dressing-gown around her slender form.

Twenty-five minutes later, they were heading for the remote Kesterdale deep in its moorland setting. Pemberton, in his new-found hobby of walking the moors and dales, had explored this beautiful region and was moderately familiar with the area. A further twenty-five minutes later he was easing to a halt at a gate beside the narrow lane; the gate was controlled by a uniformed constable with a small police car whose blue flashing light allowed no doubt they were approaching the scene of the crime. He recognized the detective and his companion, and ushered them through the gate.

'Is there somewhere the incoming cars can park?' Pemberton asked.

'On the left, sir, about fifty yards along that track, a nice level patch of solid ground.'

'OK, I'll set the example. Tell them all to park there. Now, where's the body?'

'Go upstream, sir, use the right-hand side of the beck and it's about a hundred yards, just behind that clump of rocks. In a small green tent. Well out of sight.'

'Anybody there?'

'PC Atkinson, sir.'

'Doctor?'

'Not yet, but I understand he has been called, sir.'

'Good, send him to me the moment he arrives. Other CID members will be coming too, send them to me. Now this is important, I want as few people as possible using the footpath beside the beck, I want it preserved and examined for motorcycle tyre marks.'

'Very good, sir.'

Parking his white Astra on the spacious patch of grass, Mark with Lorraine at his side made his way to the scene of the murder. Armed with powerful torches, they walked away from the footpath – even in the light of the torches, they could see the tyre marks of a motor cycle and it was vital they be preserved for the Scenes of Crime team to examine. Moving quickly through the heather beside the beck, Pemberton came upon the tent; a uniformed constable stood outside, torch waving in the darkness.

'Pemberton, and DC Cashmore,' Mark introduced himself. 'Anyone been inside the tent?'

'I'm PC Atkinson, sir, the local constable. I looked inside, sir, and saw the extent of the injuries. There was no firearm anywhere near the body and I knew no man could survive that . . .'

'And the chap who found the body? Did he go into the tent?'

'Yes, like me, sir, he looked inside, then ran up to his house to call us. He's a farmer, sir, Baxton. Henry Baxton, I know him well.'

'OK. Now I want the footpath alongside the beck preserving for SOCO. That's vital. DC Cashmore will show you some motor-cycle tyre marks. Your friend Baxton saw a motor bike leaving the scene . . . so off you go, PC Atkinson, and prevent any flat-footed officers ruining the scene! That's the most important task anyone could be asked to do right now . . . make the incoming cavalry walk about five yards away from that track. If they question it, say it's upon my orders. OK?'

'Yes, sir.'

'And I'll look after the body and the tent until SOCO and the rest of them turn up.'

As Lorraine and the constable retraced their steps to undertake their task, Pemberton, hampered by the darkness to some degree, stood and examined the exterior of the tent. It was a small ridge tent, suitable for one or possibly two persons, and it was a light green colour. Guy ropes and tent poles supported it, a rather old-fashioned method in these days of light plastic inflatable structures, but there was nothing outside that he could see. No motor cycle, no car, no pedal cycle, no boots, nothing.

Realizing that the entrance would contain evidence of the culprit, either in the form of footprints or some other thing he might have left at the scene, Pemberton approached the tent from the rear and opened the rear flap.

He shone his torch inside. It illuminated the body of a man in late middle age, perhaps in his sixties or seventies, with grey hair. He was half out of his sleeping bag and his chest had been blasted open with a shotgun – the wound bore all the hallmarks of that weapon; no one could have survived that injury. It had blasted through his clothes to produce a ghastly mixture of blood and fibre. He was dressed in what appeared to be a sweatshirt, but his legs and lower parts were hidden by the sleeping bag. As the constable had said, there was no sign of the gun. Pemberton could see his hands too; they were free from the confines of the sleeping bag and neither contained a weapon of any kind.

Somewhere, Mark knew, there would be the cartridge shell – that would have to be found, by fingertip search if necessary. It would probably be outside the tent, close to the entrance but among the undergrowth.

This was murder, of that there was no doubt. He closed the flap and walked back to where PC Atkinson and Lorraine were waiting.

'Can I use your radio?' he asked Atkinson. 'Mine's in the car.'

Using the constable's personal set, he called the Control Room and confirmed that the incident beside the Kesterdale beck was a murder; he ordered a full call-out and the setting up of an incident room.

'Right,' Pemberton continued. 'There's nothing further I can do until our wizards arrive. So, PC Atkinson, you know the farmer, Baxton. What can you tell me about him – and his family?'

Baxton, as finder of the murder victim, was immediately under suspicion and would have to be eliminated through interrogation. Before interviewing him, Pemberton wanted some background details and who better than the village constable upon whose patch the farmer lived? PC Atkinson said that Baxton was in his late forties, married to Jenny, and had taken over Kester Heights Farm upon the death of his father ten years ago. The Baxtons had two grown-up children, a son and a daughter both away at university, and PC Atkinson said that the family was well respected in the locality, with no known enemies.

It was true, said Atkinson, that there would be shotguns on the farm and so they would have to be examined – the Baxtons would begin to feel they were under suspicion as their life was examined, their guns were tested and their movements checked in detail. PC Atkinson added that the Baxtons did permit campers to pitch tents on their land; the rough land bordering the stream had no agricultural use, other than being grazed from time to time by moorland sheep, and a public footpath did run through that portion of the farm's extensive land. There was room for half a dozen small tents but it was not a formal camping site and certainly not one which would be utilized by caravans or mobile homes.

It was while he chatted to PC Atkinson that other members of Pemberton's team began to arrive.

Official vehicles and private cars were now flowing through the gate and parking on the selected site. The darkness of the night was lifting too, and for Mark Pemberton a new enquiry was beginning.

Having preserved the scene, the next task was to identify the body.

7

Identification of the elderly man in the green tent did not appear to present any major difficulties. When the preliminary examination of body and scene was complete, and when experts such as the forensic pathologist, forensic scientists, scene of crime officers, photographer and others had completed their meticulous work in and around the tent, the body was removed to the mortuary in Rainesbury.

There it was undressed with immense care, but only after the fully clothed body had been placed on a plastic sheet so that the smallest matter such as fibres, hairs, pieces of vegetation or grains of dust and dirt would be collected for later laboratory analysis. As each article of clothing was removed, it was catalogued by the coroner's officer and searched for belongings, particularly objects which would provide a name for this man. His sweatshirt and vest had been shredded by lead shot fired from close range and burn marks were evident upon the fabric, all likely to provide useful scientific evidence.

Although he had removed his cagoule, he had slept in most of his hiking gear and in the rear pocket of his green corduroy trousers was a small black fold-over wallet containing his credit cards, library card and other papers in the name of Frank Scott. The address was given as Spring Cottage, Cressford. The wallet contained more than £80 comprising one £20 note, two £10 notes and the rest in fivers.

The moment the wallet was found, the coroner's officer, PC Mick Partridge, rang Pemberton from the mortuary to inform him that identification seemed a simple matter.

Pemberton said he would immediately despatch a team of two detectives to Cressford to inform any relatives of the victim's untimely death. One of his relations would have to visit the mortuary to examine the remains and make a formal identification of the body – after all, the dead man might not be Frank Scott. He might be a thief and the wallet in his pocket might belong to one of his victims.

As the steady process of formal identification got under way, the remains were subjected to a further detailed examination by the pathologist. He began by dictating into an intercom system. His secretary was not in the operating theatre of the mortuary but was snug in her office, her only link with the smelly disinfected place being that intercom. The pathologist, Dr Stephen Philips, began by describing the body: male, five feet six inches tall, approximately sixty-five years of age, bald head with thin grey hair around the neck and temples, grey eyes, round face

with a bulbous nose, a small grey moustache clipped and neat,
clean-shaven otherwise. No spectacles were upon the head, although a pair of horn-rimmed ones were found in a leather case
among his clothing. There were no marks of violence or bruising
to the face or head. The body, when stripped, was found to
be clean and well nourished with no tattoos or other marks o
identification and no operation scars. The only mark of violence o
the torso was the massive open wound in the chest area. The hand
were rough, suggesting manual work or even long hours of domes
tic gardening, and the fingernails were damaged, probably from
the same reason, although the feet and toenails were clean an
well manicured. From an external visual examination, it seeme
that death was from a shotgun blast at close range.

The pellets had entered the chest cavity. And as the intern
examination began, so two detectives were already heading f
Spring Cottage in Cressford. It was eight thirty in the mornin
and the worst part of their duties was to break the awful news
Scott's relatives.

While these procedures were under way, Detective Superinten
ent Mark Pemberton returned to his office in Rainesbury to br
his officers. They were already establishing the incident room
Rainesbury divisional police headquarters. Although it w
some distance from the scene, that police station offered all
necessary accommodation and systems of communication.
had most facilities *in situ*, meaning the incident room could
operational within a very short time. HOLMES was being set
for this new enquiry and very soon, the investigation of
Green Tent murder would be under way.

Pemberton explained that he would hold the first conferenc
detectives at 10 a.m., exhorting as many as possible to attend
was during this activity that Inspector Hadley entered the ro

'Ah, Vic!' Pemberton had noticed his arrival. 'Problems
you! There's been a murder. We're installing HOLMES in the
cident room which means that we've got to put Muriel Brown
a back burner for a while.'

'I heard it on the news at eight this morning,' Hadley said. '
a domestic, is it?'

'No, it looks like being a runner,' and Pemberton provided the inspector with a brief outline of events. 'So how do you feel about helping us? You're quite a wizard with HOLMES now.'

'Well, I have learned a good deal.'

'I know you'll cope, you know what to look for, you could oversee the statement readers and make sure they program all the right data into the computer.'

'Sounds fine to me,' said Hadley, nodding his head. 'I'll enjoy that.'

'Like the Muriel Brown murder, work the hours you want, Vic,' said Pemberton. 'Any help will be gratefully accepted.'

And so Inspector Vic Hadley became a member of the Green Tent murder team. As Pemberton went into his office to ring headquarters and brief the Chief Constable about the crime, Hadley made his way downstairs to the large muster room which housed most of the detectives in its new role of incident room. Already, a blackboard had been erected at one end and it bore the name Frank Scott and his address, giving his age as between sixty-five and seventy, together with a brief physical description and details of his clothing.

His clothes had already been photographed and they were on display so that the teams of detectives would be aware of his appearance as they went about their enquiries. Also on show were the contents of his pockets, including the wallet, his credit cards, the £80 in cash and a further £6.50 in coins found in his trouser pocket, along with a comb, handkerchief, house keys and spare boot laces. There were coloured photographs of the green tent, both interior and exterior, shots of the campsite and its surrounds, shots of the motor-cycle tyre marks in the soft earth and an awful series of pictures showing the terrible wound to Scott's chest both in his undressed state on the slab and in the tent. A map of the area was spread across a large blackboard with the tent's location pin-pointed by a red ribbon. This showed the murder scene in relation to the surrounding countryside and gave some idea of its remoteness. The nearest village of any consequence was four miles away, this remote moorland area being dotted with lonely farms and isolated cottages.

By the time of the planned conference, ten o'clock, when many organizations were just beginning their day's activities, the Green Tent murder teams had completed several hours of very

important work. They were assembled in the incident room to present their first findings to their incoming colleagues, veterans of earlier murder investigations who were recruited from around the force area. Barbara had organized coffee for the forty or so detectives and also present were the administration support teams with their word processors and photocopiers, specially installed telephone lines and fax machines. Everyone was keen to begin – all nursed an ambition to arrest a murderer.

Pemberton stood on a chair to address them.

'Morning, all,' he said, giving his name for the benefit of those who had never met him in the flesh. 'Just before four o'clock this morning, I visited the scene of this murder, along with other officers. The scene is beside the beck on land belonging to Mr and Mrs Baxton, Henry and Jenny they're called, at Kester Heights Farm, Kesterdale which is some ten miles from here. We have a video of the approach and of the scene itself with the body in position; this will be available to everyone at the end of this conference. The Baxton family, whom we do not seriously regard as suspects, do allow campers to pitch their tents on a patch of land bordered by a small beck which flows through some scrubland on their property. The land has trees upon it, young oaks in fact, but it is not cultivated. The deceased had sought their permission to pitch his tent, which was granted. In the early hours of this morning, Sunday, the Baxtons were returning home from a late-night social outing. Mrs Baxton was driving, Henry had had a drink or two but was by no means drunk. As Henry opened the gate which leads on to his property, the idea being to allow his wife to drive through, he heard a gunshot. It was dark, and he had no real idea where the noise came from. His immediate thought was that it was poachers, this being a common occurrence, especially around the outskirts of his large acreage. This campsite is on the extremities. Henry decided to investigate. But moments later, as the Baxtons were preparing to park the car, they were startled by a motor cycle which was being ridden very quickly towards them – it passed them and made for the gate. Baxton knew there was a camper on the site and for a brief moment wondered if the camper was leaving, or had had a visitor. But the shot bothered him. Putting two and two together, and bearing in mind the demeanour of the departing bike, Henry became alarmed. In the meantime, the biker had reached the gate; he'd had time to dismount and open the gate, an easy task because it is fitted with a hunting sneck, and rode off into the darkness before Henry had time to turn his car around and go in pursuit. Henry went to the tent where he found the remains of our victim. From home, he rang his local constable, PC Atkinson, who was the first officer on the scene and who acted very well indeed; he realized it was murder and rang Control who immediately put out an All Stations to trace and detain the the motor cyclist. He has not been found, nor has his motor cycle and neither has the murder weapon. We need to find them all. It might be that the motor cyclist is not the killer – he might have stumbled across the body and fled. We do know that a motor cycle visited the tent because there are fresh tyre marks in the soft earth. They lead from the track to the tent and back again, and further marks reveal the machine was placed on its rest near the tent, on a piece of firmer ground. The biker might be a thief who raids the tents of campers – he did not burgle the farmhouse, though, nor is any other property missing from the outbuildings. The motor cyclist therefore has a lot of questions to answer. Whoever he is, he must be found, if only for elimination purposes.

'Now to the deceased. His name is Frank Scott, he is sixty-nine years old, slightly older than we first thought, and he is a widower. He is a retired master plumber from West Yorkshire who settled in Spring Cottage, Cressford where he lived alone. He has no relations in the village but does have a son in the Lake District – he has been informed of his father's death. He is on his way to Rainesbury at this moment to make a formal identification and to take possession of his father's belongings. Scott has no criminal record. However, a team is examining his background and contacts to see what motive there might be for this killing. He was in business, in a fairly successful way, and might have made enemies; he might have been involved in some dodgy deals in the past, and that is something we shall be investigating. According to the owner of the shop next door to his cottage, he often went out walking and rambling. He was very fit for his age but a theory is that he carried a lot of cash and so he might have been a target for a thief, a robbery which went drastically wrong. If theft was the motive, the thief did not succeed because Scott had more than £80 cash in his possession when the body was found, neither his wallet nor credit cards being taken. I feel we can rule out robbery as the motive. He has no car; we do not know how he arrived at the remote camping site but the theory is that he either walked the whole way or caught a local bus for part of the distance. Local buses will be checked to see if he used them, and so will taxis.

'As I mentioned earlier, in spite of early and speedy publicity through inter-force links, the motor cyclist has not been traced. The Baxtons cannot give us a description of the machine, except that it looked dark-coloured and sounded like a recent model, not a scrambles or track machine, but a conventional road motor cycle of modern design. It had low-slung handlebars and seemed to be in newish condition. Henry Baxton did think there were lighter coloured flashings upon the fairings – they reflected in his headlights. Baxton could not provide us with a registration number. A description of the rider is equally vague – he was clad in dark leathers with a dark helmet, the visor was down and there is no further description. It was impossible even to estimate his age. Judging from the nature of the wound, the murder weapon was a shotgun. This view is supported by the pathologist; the wounds are not consistent with bullet wounds, thus ruling out a revolver, pistol or rifle. The murder weapon has not been found. A fingertip search is being conducted in and around the campsite in the hope of retrieving the cartridge or cartridges used and all roadside verges on both sides of the farm exit will be searched. The backs of all hedges, walls and ditches will be examined in great detail by the task force – if the cartridge was kept and thrown away during the escape run, it will be found. The beck is very shallow and the waters are clear – divers are not needed but the beck will be searched as well.

'The best evidence from the scene comes in the tyre marks. There are front and rear wheel markings of the tyres in the soft earth. Plaster casts have been made and photographs taken. I'm assured by SOCO that if we can find the tyre in question, we can make a comparison with our casts and so obtain evidence which should be good enough for court purposes. We are also endeavouring to find the manufacturer of such tyres to determine which motor cycles are fitted with them, and therefore which dealers sell those bikes. I have two teams visiting all local motorcycle dealers, tyre specialists and garages.

'Now, there is another very important angle. There was a recent murder in Langbarugh when a businessman was shot dead by a gunman who used a sawn-off shotgun. The killer arrived and made his escape on a motor cycle so there are interesting similarities between the two murders. One difference is that although our victim is a retired businessman, the victim in Langbarugh was younger and was known to have been a crook, even though he has never been prosecuted. We have no such knowledge of Scott.

'I have not yet spoken to the Langbarugh incident room about these similarities, but that is my first task when the conference is over. Obviously, I will let you know the outcome. I refer to it now because I want you to bear the Langbarugh murder in mind when you are conducting your enquiries. I do not know of any other murders in this region which have borne these similarities.'

When Pemberton had finished his speech, he asked if any of the teams had anything further to offer. The team which had initially questioned the Baxtons added that when the Baxtons had given Scott permission to camp on their land, they had not known his name. They sought no fee from such campers. Scott had been alone, on foot, when he had arrived at the farm. That was around 4 p.m. yesterday afternoon, and the old fellow had been carrying a backpack bearing a tent with a rolled-up sleeping bag and warm clothing. His appearance and demeanour were those of an experienced camper and hiker, and he had expressed a desire to stay for two nights. He'd not said whether anyone would be joining him but had commented that he was studying the wildlife which depended upon the oak tree, or which lived in woodlands comprising mainly oak trees.

There being no further comments at this point, Pemberton told his detectives to get themselves a coffee and then set about their task of finding Frank Scott's killer. Half an hour later, they had all gone about their urgent task, leaving the office staff to their work. Among the incoming calls was one from Inspector Les Dodd, the force press officer.

'Anything further, sir?' he asked. 'I'm getting calls from the local radio stations, they want to be up to date for their bulletins.'

'We haven't had the positive identification yet, Les,' said Pemberton. 'So we can't release any name. Just say he is an elderly gentleman camper and that robbery does not appear to be the motive. Ask for witnesses who might have seen him in or near Kesterdale yesterday before 4 p.m. A man aged sixty-five to seventy, medium height, balding with light grey hair, clean-shaven, wearing bottle green corduroys, hiking boots and an orange cagoule. We'd like to know if anyone noticed him and whether he was alone at the time. If he was with someone, we need a description of that person.'

'Fine, sir, that'll keep them happy for now,' and so Pemberton's request for witnesses would now hit the evening news bulletins and tomorrow's editions of the daily papers, evening papers and local TV. Sunday was never the best day for securing widespread media coverage.

Pemberton's next job was a discussion with Barry Brennon in Langbarugh and so, using the private telephone network, he rang his opposite number. Mark's purpose at this early stage was simply to alert Brennon to the similarities between the killings; if further similarities emerged, then the question of closer liaison between the forces would have to be considered. As the two senior detectives chattered, it seemed doubtful if there was any positive link between the murders. The second might be a copycat of the first, done by a totally different individual, but each felt it wise to maintain contact.

It was the team whose action was to delve into the life and background of Frank Scott who established a possible link between the two murders. Before the arrival of Scott's son from Keswick, Detective Sergeant Ernie Boothman and Detective Constable Gordon Warren took a door key found among the deceased's clothing and went to examine his house. It was a pretty cottage built of limestone and it had a smart red pantile roof, a green painted wooden conservatory at the front, and a tiny stream trickling through the garden. The stream emerged from a spring high in the hills and ran down the sloping garden where it had been harnessed, through Scott's knowledge of water and its behaviour, to drive a small watermill and to supply a pond containing goldfish.

After passing through his garden, the water vanished into a drain which led beneath the shop and disappeared somewhere under the village.

The purpose of this visit was to establish that Scott did live at the house. This was evident when the key fitted the front door, which swung open to reveal a neat and tidy cottage with old-fashioned furnishings, clip rugs on the floor and an array of family photographs upon the mantelpiece and bookshelves. Some pictures showed the man whose body now lay on a slab in Rainesbury mortuary – the detectives were fairly clear that the identity was genuine and the son's visit would confirm that.

There were no flowers in the house, an indication of no female presence. But their next task was to try and establish a motive. Threatening letters perhaps, a diary – anything which would provide a clue as to why someone would shoot an old man in a tent in the middle of the night. Had he gone camping to get away from some kind of threat, perhaps?

A preliminary search of the downstairs bathroom, the living-room and its cupboards and the conservatory proved fruitless – nothing of any evidential value was retrieved. Upstairs there were two bedrooms, a small guest room and the old man's main room, with the bed neatly made and the room tidy and free from dust. Photographs of his wedding day and his family stood on the dressing-table; the drawers contained personal belongings, clothing and souvenirs from his business along with some copies of old advertisements and press coverage. He was clearly proud of his business achievements. And then they found a locked cupboard. It was built into the wall of the room to the left of the fireplace, an old wooden cupboard of the kind found in most cottages which had been built in the last century.

'The key'll be in the chest of drawers,' said Boothman, knowing that most people used similar places in which to hide their secret things, a fact known to burglars and police officers alike. They found a key and it fitted the cupboard. Every shelf was stuffed full of brown envelopes and booklets and when Warren removed one and opened it, he was horrified.

He opened more and realized he had discovered a treasure trove of child pornography.

8

The discovery of the paedophilic literature, followed by the outcome of some speedy and productive enquiries in Cressford village, led Lorraine to express an opinion that the Green Tent murder had been committed by the same person who had executed Pearle. She sought Pemberton to explain her views.

'Tell me why you think that.' Pemberton was standing next to the computer as Hadley was entering data from statements already filed. She approached him with a smile.

'Scott was a paedophile, sir.' She made sure she referred to Pemberton in the formal manner. 'He specialized in little girls – eight- to ten-year-olds. We know that from the stuff he kept at his house and from enquiries in the village. After Boothman and Warren found that literature, they asked around and discovered the locals all called him Sexy Scotty, Dirty Old Frank, Mucky Ducky and other filthier names. He's been at it ever since he settled in Cressford, inviting little girls into the house and interfering with them, or getting them to interfere with him. The locals always warned their little lasses never to go into his house but inevitably some ignored these warnings. He had quite an unsavoury reputation in the village.'

'He was never prosecuted?' Pemberton asked.

'No. It's the old, old story, Sir.' She winced. 'His word against that of a little girl who doesn't know the nastiness of what she's being asked to do. Because a man who says he loves her and who is kind in other ways asks her to do terrible things, she thinks it's all right, she doesn't know it's naughty. She keeps it from mum and dad because he says it's their special secret. When these sadist characters are with a little victim, they always say it's nice, they say it's their special secret and that she must tell nobody. We came across some cases where Scott had struck little girls to ensure their co-operation – they're adults now and are prepared to talk. According to the postman, a couple did try and prosecute him eight or nine years ago – he'd been performing fellatio with their eight-year-old – but the police just couldn't get the evidence. The CID prepared a file but the case never got to court – and Scott kept on persuading little girls to go to his cottage.'

'Is there anything in our intelligence files on him?'

'No, the older files of inactive suspects are destroyed every ten years, sir, so according to us, he's clean. I wish the parents of paedophiles' victims would make official complaints then we could compile a dossier – in fact, I'm sure some don't think the activities are against the law. They just think it's mucky behaviour by sad and lonely old codgers, but this man was a cunning bastard, sir, pardon the French! And he had no criminal record either. And that's why I believe there's a link with the murder – I think both were shot because they were criminals who were never caught. Never brought before a court, never presented to the public as the rogues they were. Now, they'll offend no more. It's a form of rough justice.'

'If that's true,' butted in Hadley, 'whoever killed that mucky old sod deserves a medal!'

'A serial vigilante? Is that what you're suggesting, Lorraine?' Mark smiled.

'It might well be, sir, there's two deaths so far. More to come? It wouldn't surprise me.'

'It sounds to me as if he's doing society a favour,' grunted Hadley.

'All right,' said Pemberton. 'Let's suppose the same killer did both jobs. Who would know all about Pearle's activities and also about Scott's? The two victims are so different and lived a long way from each other. I accept that neither had been to court and they were of totally different backgrounds. That one person should know about both men's activities seems rather unlikely.'

'That's what we have to find out.' She smiled at him. 'That's our job – but if it is the same person, then he —'

'Or she,' beamed Pemberton.

'All right, he or she must have some inside knowledge, sir. Some knowledge of police intelligence files, or those of some other agency.'

'If there is a mole, sir, he's putting his knowledge to good use.' Hadley came in again. 'I'm all for getting rid of scum like that, preying on innocent kids.'

'We're not concerned with the ethics of these crimes, Vic,' snapped Pemberton. 'Most decent people would say good riddance to bad rubbish, but as policemen, as law enforcement officers, we can't think like that. We have a job to do and that is to enforce the law. It's illegal to murder people, no matter what they've done and how evil they are, and these people, for all their faults, have been murdered. That is wrong, Vic, it's against our laws, and so it's our duty to track the killers down and present them to the courts.'

'I know all that, sir,' retorted Hadley. 'I'm very aware of my official role and duties, but I still think those killers have done a good job, a service to the public. They've done something that neither the police nor the courts can do, they've eliminated some pretty rotten people, sir, and I reckon that society will thank them for it. If I was a parent of a little girl in that village, I'd be as chuffed as hell that the old sod's been got rid of. Full marks to the killer, I say.'

'If Lorraine's hypothesis is correct, it does look like the work of a lone vigilante,' Pemberton said. 'Someone who's seeking vengeance, someone who has a detailed knowledge of the victims, knowledge that might have been obtained from confidential sources. A former police officer? A police employee of some kind? One whose work crosses force boundaries? A social worker? All right, Lorraine, I'll have further words with my oppo in Langbarugh. We might find more links now.'

'HOLMES will do the work, sir,' said Hadley. 'Just establish a data base between us and Langbarugh and it'll identify all the similarities.'

'Give the computer a go, Vic, but remember there's no substitute for officers on the ground, police officers with local knowledge,' Pemberton said. 'Pearle was shot in the early afternoon of a Saturday in broad daylight in a town environment with people around him; Scott was alone in the middle of nowhere at the dead of night or, to be precise, in the early hours of a Sunday morning. The scenes are forty miles apart in separate police areas and the victims have nothing in common. For those reasons, the murders are quite different.'

'Think of the similarities, sir,' Lorraine insisted. 'A shotgun was used, perhaps the same one for both deaths; in both cases, a motor cycle was used to arrive and escape on, perhaps the same one for both deaths . . . and both victims were unconvicted criminals, although of widely differing styles. One dirty old man, one crooked dealer.'

'Unless Pearle was also interfering with children?' The thought occurred to Pemberton. 'I wonder if that's a possibility?'

Neither of the others had considered that likelihood and it was Hadley who said, 'It's worth a word with your mate in Langbarugh, sir.'

'My very next job,' said Mark Pemberton.

The enquiries by the murder teams that morning did produce a little more information. There was one witness who had heard a motor cycle travelling along Kesterdale after midnight. She was an elderly lady who had been unable to sleep due to indigestion and as she had pottered down to the kitchen of her roadside cottage for a Rennie, she had heard the distinctive sound of a motor cycle heading up the dale. But she had not looked out and could provide no further details, except that it did not seem to be moving very rapidly. She was not sure of the time either, but was convinced the motor cycle was heading up the dale, towards Kester Heights Farm entrance. Although there was a frustrating lack of detail in that piece of information, it could be reasonably assumed that it was the same rider who had later been seen by the Baxtons. Traffic of any kind was rare in that dale, especially in the early hours of the morning.

No other cars or motor vehicles had driven along the remote road, and the old lady had not heard that motor bike, or any other, make a return journey. It was not known by which route the killer had made his escape because the road followed a circular route around the dale head and emerged at a point some two miles from its place of entry. Enquiries at farms and cottages along that circuitous route had failed to elicit any supportive information. No one else had heard the motor bike, and no one had noticed the lone hiker earlier making his way towards Kester Heights Farm.

The fingertip search of the area around the tent did locate a single cartridge shell; its appearance was clean, suggesting it had not lain there for very long, and it was of the kind normally used in a shotgun. Manufactured by Burrard and comprising a red plastic barrel with a brass ignition cap, it bore the imprint of the firing pin in the centre of its cap. If the murder weapon was ever found, comparisons could be made and the marks of the firing pin, almost as individual as a human's fingerprints, might prove that the killer's shotgun had discharged this cartridge. Similarly, the mark left by the ejector bar might also determine from which weapon the cartridge had been ejected. If the cartridge fired in the Langbarugh killing had been recovered, then ballistics examination of the marks might determine whether or not the same weapon had been used for both murders. Thus the finding of this piece of evidence, the only cartridge shell on this patch of ground, was considered to be of prime importance.

It would be some hours before the examination of the scene of the crime could be considered final – although it had been examined once in great detail, the detectives could have overlooked something. The murderer might have left other evidence of his or her presence – footprints somewhere among the vegetation maybe, deposits of other kinds, fibres from clothing or human hairs left on the tent doorway while entering or leaving . . . and had the motor cyclist's helmet been removed during the crime, for example? If so, where had it been deposited? Hairs inside it might have been transferred to its resting place – and human hairs, however small, could be matched to their owner. It was a long, tedious but very necessary examination of the scene. Looking for a single human hair in a wooded area was like trying to find the tiniest of needles in the largest of haystacks.

Away from the scene, teams of detectives, with two officers to each team, went around asking their questions in the neighbourhood of the scene and further afield; they produced shoals of long handwritten statements which were typed, photocopied and read by the statement readers in the incident room. Their job was to identify references which would be of further use – names of people, descriptions of motor vehicles, noises heard, the timing of important occurrences and a whole host of other data would be noted, checked, compared and logged into HOLMES, the Home Office Large Major Enquiry System, which was specifically designed to cope with murder investigations, particularly those which spanned the boundaries of police forces.

From a very slow but meticulous beginning, therefore, the Green Tent murder began to generate its own impetus and excitement, accompanied by a steady and encouraging accumulation of evidence.

But while all this was happening, Mark Pemberton rang Barry Brennon in Langbarugh. He explained Lorraine's theory and asked, 'Was Pearle a sexual deviant, Barry? Interfering with kids, for example?'

'No, he was normal in that sense. He loved fully-grown women – he never married but he got his oats without too much effort!'

'Thanks, another link gone! Now, did you find a spent cartridge case at your scene?'

'We did,' said Brennon. 'Burrard, red casing.'

'Same here,' countered Pemberton. 'We need to liaise with the ballistics people at Nottingham. Has your sample gone down there?'

'Yes, we sent it immediately.'

'Right, I'll have words and get ours despatched by courier right away, Barry. It looks to me as if we might have a serial killer in our midst.'

'The Helmeted Avenger, eh?' chuckled Brennon. 'So if that's the case, we need to establish contact, Mark. A liaison officer. Any ideas at your end?'

'I've a bright young detective on my teams. She's called Lorraine Cashmore,' Mark suggested. 'She's proved herself in the past.'

'If you're happy with her, then I'll not object. What will you do? Send her over to our incident room to examine our records?'

'Yes, every day after our morning conference, then she'll be as up to date as possible before she visits you. Thanks, Barry, I think we're going to need this kind of co-operation.'

And so the personal connection as well as the computer link was established, even though the press had not yet conjectured on links between the crimes. That would surely come later and it would be welcomed by the investigating officers, especially when the initial impetus had lessened and when some angle for a rejuvenating news story was required. The detectives themselves would release news of their suspicions when they were ready.

Throughout the remainder of that Sunday and the following days, the enquiries continued without any spectacular developments. Nonetheless, useful evidence was accumulating, thanks to careful ballistics examinations. It was confirmed that the two cartridge shells had come from the same shotgun, a twelve-bore. Thus the same gun had been used in both murders and that fact alone indicated, but did not prove, that the same person had pulled the trigger on both occasions. And so the two murders could now be officially linked.

Further investigation into Scott's life before coming to live at Cressford established that he had been involved in child pornography while running his plumbing business – there had been several complaints to the West Yorkshire police, none of which could be substantiated through lack of evidence. His name was in their older records, records which had escaped destruction due to an old superintendent who believed that crime records and intelligence notes should be kept for ever. Those old files had been sent along to the Rainesbury incident room. So far as Pearle was concerned, however, it was confirmed that there was no record of him being involved in pornography of any kind, certainly not with children. Although many of his alleged deals were illegal and dishonest, he had never touched pornography, masochism or even the so-called video nasties.

Thus that link between the two killings could not be established. It seemed that the killer was not specifically against child molesters. It remained possible, however, that Lorraine was correct in believing that there was a further link in that both victims were alleged criminals, albeit unconvicted. It began to look as if the killer was violently antagonistic towards all unconvincted criminals.

In addition to the positive evidence of the cartridge case, another development involved the motor-cycle tyre marks. None had been left on the tarmac and concrete outside Harry Pearle's premises, but from the casts of the very distinctive tracks made near the Kesterdale green tent, experts were able to say that the heavy-tread tyres were of Italian manufacture, made by Masseria for use in country areas rather than towns, but fitted as standard equipment to certain new machines. A list of the motor cycles which used these tyres included Yamaha, Kawasaki,

BMW, Honda, Suzuki, Triumph and even Piaggio scooters and mopeds. They were not fitted to all models, however, and thus the gap could be narrowed by careful enquiries. Dealers in such machines, throughout the entire north-east of England, were being visited with a view to tracking down any machines recently sold which were bearing such tyres. Tyre outlets were also being checked for sales or fitting of such tyres in recent weeks. The detail on the tracks left at the Green Tent scene was of such good quality that the tyres were clearly in excellent and probably new condition. This made the work of the detectives that much easier.

So far as the mode of travel for Scott was concerned, none of the local bus companies could recall him using their services on the Saturday before his death; two buses per day left Cressford in the direction of Kesterdale, and only two buses passed along Kesterdale on Saturdays, one at 9.15 a.m. and the other at 3.45 p.m. These were sometimes used by people shopping in the nearby market towns, but none of the drivers or conductors could recall picking up or dropping the old man with the back pack. Photographs of him, and of his clothing, failed to elicit any response. This lack of sightings along the road did suggest he might have obtained a lift, perhaps as a hitch-hiker, but no one had come forward to say so, although another possibility was that he had walked across country. There was a network of paths upon those moors, and it was quite feasible that he might have walked from Cressford to Kesterdale rarely touching a metalled road. Widespread publicity in the huge conurbations to the north, west and south of Kesterdale, such as Newcastle, Middlesbrough, Leeds, Hull and York, had failed to produce any motorist or lorry driver who had given him a lift, this dale being upon the tourist trail where drivers meandered, pottered and gawped their way along the valley. Similarly, no hikers or ramblers reported seeing him upon the cross country routes.

As the enquiry entered its fifth day on Thursday, the impetus began to falter because there had been no new leads in either the Langbarugh or the Green Tent enquiries. The respective incident rooms were busy, nonetheless, their work revolving around the never-ending chores of endless interviews, checking of facts, taking of statements and assessment of material.

So much of the material entering the files was of a negative nature – statements from people saying they had seen nothing, heard nothing and knew nothing – but even this had value because it could eliminate a lot of unnecessary enquiries. One nagging gap was the failure to find the murder weapon. Witnesses to the Langbarugh killing had said it was a sawn-off shotgun, probably double-barrelled, but no one had seen the weapon which had been used in the green tent. The small spread of shot in Scott's corpse, however, did suggest a sawn-off weapon had been used at fairly close range; such a gun could have been concealed either upon the motor cyclist in his leathers, or perhaps in the panniers of his machine.

The fact that the weapon had not been found, and that the same gun had been used to commit two murders, did suggest the killer might be retaining it for further killings. That alone suggested a confidence in his ability to avoid detection and capture and it also indicated that a very dangerous, determined and clever criminal was at large.

That theory was proved the following Monday.

At eight o'clock in the evening, a young man was shot dead outside the King's Head public house in Turnerville. The killer used a sawn-off shotgun and escaped on a black motor cycle.

9

If the investigations into the Green Tent murder and that of Harry Pearle had been out of the headline news due to a persistent lack of newsworthy excitement, the murder at Turnerville, and its possible links with the previous two, brought a swift response from the press. Officers in the control rooms in both forces were bombarded during the remainder of that late evening and throughout the night with questions from journalists, all of whom were asking, 'Are the three murders connected?' In the case of the first two, no journalist had considered a possible link, probably because not every detail of the killings had been released to the media. The use of the sawn-off shotgun and the departure of the killer by motor cycle at the Turnerville killing had changed all that – the coincidences were too strong to be ignored by the press.

The problem was that confirmation of a link was something the Control Room staff could not provide – that answer could only come from detectives on each of the cases because the Control Rooms were not in possession of all the facts. The investigation of murder was not their duty.

An added problem was that the Turnerville murder had occurred within the boundaries of Langbarugh, the second on their patch, but Pemberton's own divisional boundaries came within a mile of that town – and criminals know no boundaries. These close links, plus the growing concern about the motor-cycling killer, had resulted in a speedy decision for both forces to pool their resources.

Lorraine Cashmore was their liaison officer but the respective press officers would produce a joint statement for issue to the media at the main news conference the following morning. Meanwhile, a holding statement said that the possibility of the crimes being linked was being investigated and that the respective forces would co-operate. A representative selection of detectives from each force, led by Detective Superintendent Mark Pemberton of Rainesbury and Detective Superintendent Barry Brennon from Langbarugh, had been summoned to a conference at 9 a.m., an hour before the joint news conference was due to be held. The conference was at Rainesbury police station because there was sufficient accommodation and car-parking for the visitors – and Rainesbury was less than one hour's drive from Langbarugh. Brennon was first to speak.

The packed room awaited him, as in his distinctive Irish accent, he began.

'Ladies and gentlemen, it is apparent that we have a serial killer at large in the region.' He went on to outline the similarities between Pearle's murder and that of Frank Scott, before continuing:

'Last night, at eight o'clock, Wayne William Hardisty, aged twenty-one, was shot dead outside the King's Head Hotel in Railway Street, Turnerville. He was standing outside the main entrance of the inn, alone but within sight of other witnesses, when a motor cyclist approached. The motor cycle halted outside the main door, not mounting the footpath but remaining on the road, whereupon the rider pulled a sawn-off shotgun from his leathers, shot Hardisty once in the chest at close range and drove off. Hardisty died almost immediately. Witnesses took the number of the departing bike and it was the same as that which had been used in the Pearle killing – a false registration number. Preliminary examination of the cartridge shell recovered at the scene suggests it came from the same gun which killed both Harry Pearle and Frank Scott. Ballistic examination will be made jointly with the cartridge shells found at the scenes of the other murders.

'Now, we know that Hardisty was a drugs dealer. He had several convictions but in spite of that, continued to sell drugs in Turnerville. A quantity of adulterated heroin was found upon the body, in small packs ready for sale. We believe he was awaiting a customer because he often waited outside the pub to complete his sales, this being his regular pitch and his way of not implicating the pub landlord. In fact, the landlord had, in no uncertain terms, told him not to sell drugs on the premises. You will have noticed a slight difference between this death and the earlier ones – the victims of the previous killings had no convictions even though their activities were known or suspected. Hardisty did have convictions. It is possible, ladies and gentlemen, that the killer is wiping out criminals who persist in following a life of crime – remember that Pearle was known to us as a confidence trickster and thief who had never been convicted and Scott was a known paedophile who had avoided conviction. Hardisty was a known drugs dealer who continued to ply his trade in spite of convictions and in spite of continuing surveillance by our drugs officers. There are those amongst us, and within the public sphere, who would rejoice at such killings, but we must not be seen to do so. We have a job to do. We must find that motor cycle and the killer and bring him to justice before he kills anyone else.

'I fear we have a desperately urgent task ahead of us and I need, we all need, the co-operation of everyone, police, press and public alike, if we are to prevent further bloodshed. That motor cycle has to be found and the killings halted. A news conference will follow this meeting, with both forces represented, and we shall be seeking the co-operation of the media in tracing our suspect. Somebody somewhere must have seen that motor cycle, somebody somewhere must have made that false number plate or sold the machine or fitted it with tyres . . . Our job is to find those people.'

He went on to describe to the detectives the result of the post-mortem on Hardisty – death had been caused by gunshot wounds to the chest – and how Hardisty's friends and contacts were now being interviewed, not the easiest of tasks due to their involvement with drugs. Few would willingly talk to the police.

Had Hardisty's death not been associated with the previous two killings, his murder would have been regarded as part of a drugs war or a narcotics-related dispute of some kind. That aspect had not been dismissed entirely, however, and it remained a consideration, but it was the opinion of those who had undertaken the investigations to date that the death had to be viewed within the context of the other murders.

In his beautiful accent, Brennon delivered a professional address, following which he highlighted aspects of the Pearle murder with due emphasis upon the similarities with the present case. Detective Superintendent Pemberton then followed and he outlined the known facts of the Green Tent murder, emulating his friend's example of highlighting the similarities and known links between all the cases.

In this way, the teams of investigating detectives, from both forces, were provided with as much background information and relevant detail as was possible. From this day forward, every statement, every fact and every suspicion from each incident room would be offered to the other for joint information and comparison.

As the teams of detectives returned to their normal duties, all flushed with a new determination to find the killer, Pemberton and Brennon settled down with their respective press officers to discuss their presentation at the news conference, now only minutes away. They decided to concentrate on the hunt for the motor cycle and its rider, rather than the life-style of the three victims. They would refer to the bike's false number plates without revealing precisely what number it carried – the killer might not be aware of their knowledge of this. The public would be asked to report all sightings of a dark-coloured modern motor cycle carrying a man in black leathers. Many would have to be eliminated – it was worth the effort if it found the murderer. The latest sighting, outside the King's Head, suggested the machine was black with silver markings and that it was of modern design. The manufacturer was unknown. The description was very similar to the bike seen leaving the scene of the Green Tent murder.

Witnesses outside both the King's Head and Harry Pearle's premises said the rider was a large man, about six feet tall, broad in build with a powerful appearance. Several said he did not look like a youthful man, there was an air of maturity about him and his conduct. He strode with confidence, he did not run, he was not particularly agile in his movements and he was not furtive in what he did.

The only time he raised the visor of his helmet was when he lifted the gun to his shoulder to take aim. In those seconds, he flipped up the visor, aimed, fired and shook his head to drop the visor back into position. No one had seen his face, consequently no one could state whether or not he was clean-shaven or wore spectacles or had any other facial characteristics. Witnesses to the Pearle murder and to that at the King's Head affirmed that the killer had never spoken a word. He had simply pointed his gun and fired; in both cases, the victims had pleaded for mercy, a brief but screamed request which had been callously ignored. Each had known that death was but seconds away – perhaps neither knew why.

In all cases, the names of the victims could and would be publicized, albeit without any mention of their criminal activities. Pemberton and Brennon each agreed that if the criminal nature of the victims was made known, the public might not respond with such fervour. Some might relish the death of a child molester or a drugs dealer. To harness the sympathy of the public, therefore, the killings must seem to be the deaths of ordinary people going about their daily routine, deaths of innocent victims, deaths without a motive.

The police knew, of course, that details of each man's criminal activities, even without the supporting convictions, could be published after death: it is not possible to libel a dead person and so, if necessary, those allegations could eventually be made public. It was decided that the most sympathetic response would come from Frank Scott's lonely death in his little green tent and so details of that would precede the Langbarugh killings.

It was hoped that a sympathetic public would respond to police requests for information. And so, as the day's publicity and co-operative methods were determined, Brennon and Pemberton felt they had engineered a positive start to their joint operation.

'Ready?' asked Pemberton.

'Sure, lead the way,' grinned Brennon as they left for their news conference.

When the Langbarugh contingent left, Pemberton spent the remainder of that morning checking the Actions Register to ensure that every task had either been fulfilled or was still ongoing. Every question raised at the CID conferences had to be answered, every detail confirmed, every statement scrutinized for lies and factual errors, every alibi checked and double-checked. In reading the Actions Register, he was able to refresh his own memory of events since the Green Tent murder was discovered: firearms dealers were being quizzed about shotguns and sales of cartridges, motor-cycle dealers were being quizzed about bikes and tyres, house-to-house enquiries were continuing in an effort to trace the movements of Scott and his killer, the Baxtons had been questioned almost without mercy until they could be absolved from any links with the death of the man near their stream. The parents of the little girls who were known to have associated with the old man were quizzed too, every dad being interviewed about his whereabouts, every dad being asked whether he had access to, or possessed, a dark-coloured motor cycle . . . The tentacles were spreading, information was flowing into the files and into the computer.

But no new positive leads had emerged.

Pemberton returned to his office; he'd packed himself a salad sandwich, a tub of fruit-flavoured yoghurt and an apple for lunch, and Barbara would produce a cup of coffee when he was ready. It was 12.30 p.m. now and he felt he could give himself half an hour's break for refreshments. He asked Barbara if she would make his drink and she agreed. He said he was going to do some intensive reading at his desk and did not want to be disturbed. She said she would put the 'Do Not Disturb' sign on his door when she brought his coffee and he decided he would, in fact, do some intensive reading while having his lunch. He would study the statements from all the fathers of the little girls who had been visiting Scott during the past three years – all were kept in one large file. Revenge of this savagery might well appeal to some angry dad. Young people conned by Pearle, sexually assaulted by Scott or made into druggies by Hardisty were likely to have very angry fathers who might want to mete out their own brand of justice.

When Barbara brought his coffee, Pemberton said, 'Can you fetch the father's file, please? I'm going to do some suspect hunting!'

As she turned away to fetch it, Vic Hadley appeared at Pemberton's office door.

'I'm away now, sir,' he said. 'I've a wee headache, all that concentration.'

'Fine, thanks for your help this morning, Vic,' Pemberton smiled. 'How's it going, dealing with this murder? A bit more hectic than Muriel Brown, I guess?'

There was a half-smile on the heavy bearded face. 'He's certainly causing a bit of a wee flap, is our motor-cycling murderer. You know, sir, I'm really pleased to be involved in the hunt for him.'

'We'll find him,' said Pemberton with as much confidence as he could muster. 'So we'll see you tomorrow, Vic?'

'Aye, I'll be in at 8.30 a.m., for the morning at least.'

'So what are you doing this afternoon? Anything exciting?'

'A wee spot of fishing, sir. An hour or two on the river bank does me the world of good.'

'Right. Well, see you tomorrow.'

And Vic Hadley walked from his office. Pemberton watched him leave with a heavy, even ponderous walk. A man who had suffered, a man now recuperating well and recovering fast. Then Barbara entered with the file of fathers' statements, and placed it on his desk beside his mug of coffee. She smiled and left, closing the door as she went. Standing over his desk, Mark Pemberton, lonely without Lorraine but for the moment content with his own company, opened his sandwich box and removed one of its offerings. He walked across to his window and looked out; he was on the first floor of the police station and commanded a fine view of the car-park and various exits and entrances. And as he stood there, he heard a motor-cycle engine burst into life. Hadley, he thought. He'd heard the inspector had a motor bike. He waited and saw the black-leathered figure of Inspector Hadley ride from the police station upon a black and very modern machine.

Silver markings along the fairing flashed in the sunlight.

'Oh my God . . .' muttered Pemberton to himself as he sat down at his desk, shocked and disbelieving. He sat there for a long time, his coffee growing cold and his mind reeling from the terrible suspicion that had been thrust upon him. As the sound of Hadley's motor cycle faded, Pemberton found himself thinking about the Millgate supermarket shooting. His own brief and rather superficial study of the case file had practically convinced him of Hadley's innocence; he had managed to persuade himself that Hadley could have shot Newton in order to save the life of a policeman. But had he? Could Hadley in truth have shot Newton in cold blood, knowing of his criminal activities?

All the doubts which had nagged at Pemberton now resurfaced and he began to compare the Millgate shooting with the latest three murders. Certainly, there were similarities: sawn-off shotguns had been used during the Millgate raid and there was an unresolved query concerning them. There had been no motor cycle there, however, but Hadley now owned a motor cycle. So had he also access to a sawn-off shotgun? Did he own one, illegal though it was? Most police firearms officers used firearms as a hobby too, either with target shooting, clay pigeon events or grouse and wildfowl shooting. As he sat in his office, Mark realized he knew so little about the man who had recently joined his team. He said he went fishing in his leisure moments, but was that true? Where was he when the last three murders had been committed? Fishing? Or riding that black motor bike with a sawn-off shotgun hidden in his leathers? A shiver rippled down his spine, the thought made him cold.

Pemberton, seasoned detective that he was, had a horror of having to investigate one of his colleagues, and yet this now seemed inevitable. Quite suddenly Vic Hadley was in the frame – in that instant, Inspector Hadley had become a suspect for three murders. Mark drew a deep breath and decided he must first inform the Chief Constable. The decision about any subsequent action in such circumstances was not for Pemberton alone, it was for higher authority. If Hadley was even remotely suspected, then his superiors, and Pemberton's superiors, must be informed. Mark knew that even police telephone lines are notoriously insecure and so it meant a personal trip to police headquarters, a time-consuming but vital journey. The Chief must be told face to face, and it must be done immediately.

He rang his own secretary.

'Barbara,' he said, his voice sounding croaked with the emotion of his discovery, 'ring the Chief's secretary, will you? See if he's likely to be in his office this afternoon. I want an urgent meeting with him. Emphasize that it is very important and highly confidential.'

She made the call immediately and came back to say, 'Mr Moore is in his car, sir, in fact he's in town *en route* for lunch with the Town Clerk. He says he will call in. He'll be twenty minutes or so, his secretary says. He will come and see you, he has a few minutes in hand.'

And so it was that Mark Pemberton took the Chief Constable for a brief walk in Rainesbury Central Park and made known his deep suspicions about Vic Hadley.

Charles Moore listened carefully as Mark explained his suspicions and the reason for them as they strode along the wooded footpath. Pemberton, smart and alert, took care to guide his Chief away from people who might eavesdrop on their conversation.

When he had finished his explanation, Moore said, 'This is supposition, Mark, is it not? You have no evidence to support your belief?'

'No, not yet. The suspicion has just dawned on me, I've not investigated it yet. I felt you had to know though, before I started to make deeper enquiries and before word gets around.'

'I appreciate that, and I respect you for reacting so speedily to your own suspicions. However, you will appreciate that I cannot suspend Hadley from duty, not without some substantial evidence.' Moore was emphatic. 'I cannot take that kind of action merely based on your suspicions, Mark, much as I respect your professionalism. But I do agree there is cause for deep concern. You need to carry out a very discreet and careful investigation, a secret enquiry, Mark. And if Hadley is the murderer, we must make sure he commits no more, mustn't we?'

'Yes, sir.'

'All right, pick your team, large or small as you think necessary. Use subterfuge if you have to. I don't envy you this one, Mark. But thanks for alerting me. You know, I liked Hadley, I really thought he was on the road to recovery.'

'Perhaps he is, sir, perhaps I am wrong,' said Pemberton.

'I hope so,' said the Chief Constable.

10

Before deciding whom to appoint as his team in the forthcoming examination of Hadley's life-style, past, present and future, Mark Pemberton wanted to check the duty sheets. These would enable him to determine Hadley's whereabouts at the material times; they might even show he could not have committed the murders. He rather hoped that was the case. He should have done so before alarming the Chief Constable, but in his excitement he'd overlooked that simple routine.

Back in his office, he asked Barbara to fetch them. Examination of the duty sheets was not out of the ordinary: the hours worked by the detectives were all logged so that any overtime payments could be arranged, and regular checks were made by senior officers.

'Are you all right, sir?' she asked as he placed the file on his desk.

'All right? Yes, I'm fine.' He grinned at her. 'Why? Do I look ill or something?'

'No, it's just that you rushed out and didn't finish your lunch or drink your coffee – and you never said where you'd gone!'

'Sorry, something important cropped up. All will be revealed in due course,' he added in an attempt to prevent any further speculation on her part. 'Anyway, thanks for these papers. And how about a replacement coffee?'

'Settle down to drink it this time!' she exhorted with good humour.

And so he did.

Alone again, he noted that Hadley had meticulously logged his hours of work, both on the Muriel Brown case and on the current enquiries, and his entries had been countersigned by Detective Inspector Larkin. Thus they could be accepted as accurate. It was the work of a moment to trace the dates of the three murders – one on a Saturday, one on a Sunday and one on a Monday, all with a week in between. And on each occasion, with a sinking heart, Pemberton discovered that Hadley had not been working in the CID office. At the time of Pearle's death, he'd been off duty, probably fishing. He was off duty when Hardisty had been killed in mid-evening, probably fishing again, while Scott's death, in the early hours of the morning, was not so positive a bet. Certainly, Hadley had not been at work at that time of the morning, but Pemberton did know that fanatical anglers spent some strange hours in pursuit of their quarry. Some did fish all night and all day, and so, somehow, Pemberton had to find out exactly what the fellow had been doing during those vital hours.

At this delicate stage, direct personal questioning was not an option, he felt. Even if Pemberton began to ask oblique questions, Hadley, being such a seasoned and experienced policeman, would quickly realize that there was a reason for the interest in his movements. It was possible he would refuse to respond. If he felt he was being quizzed or under suspicion, he could simply refuse to answer any questions. Not only would the enquiry grind to a halt, but Hadley's progress towards full health might also be jeopardized, a harsh penalty if he was innocent. Indeed, the stress it generated might even cause a regression.

Finding a way to deal with this problem would not be easy. One alternative was to appoint an officer to shadow Hadley during his off-duty moments, but he or she would soon be noticed. A trained observer such as any police officer, and especially the officer in charge of the firearms unit, was always alert. Pemberton also considered the use of a detective from another force, someone unknown to Hadley; that was a serious option. It was comparatively simple to conceal a watching detective in a busy street – it was not very easy to repeatedly use one on the loneliness of a river bank. As the Chief had suggested, subterfuge seemed to be one option. Pemberton knew there were some very skilled surveillance teams in the neighbouring police forces and felt he could draw upon their expertise if necessary.

Sipping his fresh, hot cup of coffee, Pemberton gazed out of the window while trying to determine the most efficient and effective manner of surreptitiously investigating Hadley. It was easy for the Chief to recommend subterfuge, but how could that be achieved? Hadley was a loner, that had already been made apparent, and he would not respond to pseudo offers of friendship. To find a detective capable of offering genuine friendship to Hadley would be virtually impossible. But worth a try? Maybe the fellow craved a friend? A man friend? A woman friend? Would a sexual relationship reveal the true man, he wondered? Hadley was married, Pemberton knew, but his wife rarely took any part in social events which were linked to the police service. She wasn't a member of the Police Wives' Club, she didn't come to police dances, social events, parties and so forth, and neither did Hadley.

Mrs Hadley's entire life revolved around her husband so a temptress was not a good idea.

Somehow, Pemberton realized, he would have to deploy stealth in his quest. He saw his task as being in two clear sections: first, to establish whether there were any positive grounds for suspecting Hadley of being a serial killer and second, if there were such grounds, to gather the evidence necessary for presentation to the Crown Prosecution Service to determine whether or not he should be charged. The first task would be the more difficult but once that had been completed, Hadley would be suspended from duty as a formal investigation, by the teams of murder case detectives, got under way. The second stage had many more positive elements.

Stealth, then, seemed to be the immediate requirement.

It was while he pondered the alternatives that Lorraine tapped on his door. 'Come in,' he called, not realizing who had knocked. She came in smiling and he rejoiced in the mood of happiness she engendered.

'Hi.' He wanted to kiss her, but refrained, remembering that he was a police superindent on duty and she was a detective constable. 'Just back from Langbarugh?'

'Yes, sir.' She remembered to give him his formal title. 'I'm reporting in.'

'Anything to tell us?' he asked, indicating a chair before his desk.

She explained that the Langbarugh end of the murder enquiries was following its natural course, with their officers trying to establish other links between the victims. While it was likely that they had been murdered because of their criminal activities, some deeper reason might emerge. To date, those enquiries had drawn a blank. No personal links between the victims had been discovered, but three teams were now expressly examining that possibility, one team per victim. Another initiative by the joint investigative unit was to arrange a dawn raid, provisionally and secretly timed to occur tomorrow at 7 a.m., on all criminals in the region who were known to possess or make use of sawn-off shotguns. Every gun found would be subjected to ballistics examination to determine whether or not it had fired the fatal shots. In addition, every holder of a shotgun certificate would also be visited and his or her weapons examined. If any could not account for all the weapons they owned, further enquiries would be made.

Lorraine also reported that the response from the early radio news bulletins and regional morning TV programmes had been beneficial. In both the Langbarugh killings, several new witnesses had come forward, but none had adduced any fresh evidence: their versions of events merely confirmed what was already known and reinforced the sightings of the beautiful black motor cycle and its black-clad rider at the scenes of two murders, each witnessed by several onlookers. In spite of more witnesses to the Langbarugh killings, the moorland Green Tent murder had no such witnesses, other than the Baxtons, but in all cases, the files were growing and information was flowing steadily into the two incident rooms.

After delivering her impressions, Lorraine made as if to leave the office, then said, 'Sir, you look tired.'

'It's been a bit hectic,' he admitted. 'But that's the way with murder enquiries. You work while the work's there.'

'I was thinking of going for a walk this evening,' she said quietly. 'Before dinner, before it grows dark. Just along the riverside at Lainby.'

He pondered for a moment. In the past, detectives rarely took time off when involved in such demanding work, but in the 1990s the mood was more relaxed. Too much intensive work could be counter-productive and besides, he had senior officers to whom he could, and should, delegate some of the responsibility.

'All right,' he said. 'I'll knock off early. I promise. See you at six?'

'Six will be fine.' She swept from his office with a cheerful smile. She was good for him, he knew, she made him relax, take time off, be more human . . . and a walk beside the river on a mild evening would be a wonderful tonic – even if he did have to carry a mobile telephone.

An early finish during a murder enquiry, a shower after work and the change into something casual were a rare treat for Mark Pemberton. He found himself humming in the bathroom as he prepared for an evening out. Lorraine was right, this was a good idea. How nice it would be to be retired from the force and to be able to undertake such outings whenever the mood and opportunity arose. He hummed and sang a tuneless version of music from *West Side Story* and finally emerged ready for their walk.

'There's a nice riverside pub about a mile out of Lainby,' she said. 'How about a bar snack instead of cooking at home?'

'Great idea. I just hope I don't get a call-out! I've left Paul Larkin in charge.' He grimaced. 'Right, sweaters on, boots laced up and some cash in my pocket – I'm ready!'

And so they sallied forth into the North Yorkshire countryside, driving through dales and across the moors until they dropped into Lainby. Parking near the old pack-horse bridge which had spanned the River Keal since the fifteenth century, they left their car and began their walk. Lorraine reckoned it would take half an hour to reach the Trout Inn and they set off, arm in arm, without a care in the world.

Quite deliberately, they did not discuss the murders. Each recognized that some break from work was essential and they found themselves observing nature about them – identifying birds from their songs before sighting them in the woods beside the river, such as willow warblers, chaffinches and blackbirds, noticing the spraints of an otter, the leap of a salmon, the nest of a green woodpecker and the brilliance of the dragonflies which flew like helicopters over the still waters of deep pools which the river had excavated into the banks at bends and corners.

'It's a little bit of heaven, isn't it?' She clung to his arm, revelling in the freedom and the freshness of the evening.

'I wonder why I never did this before?' He shrugged. 'June wasn't one for exploring the countryside, she favoured towns and shops and theatres . . .'

'It's everyone to their own desires,' she sighed. 'But this is my way of relaxing. But I see we have company!' She nodded to indicate someone ahead of them. A man was sitting beside the river, fishing rod high above the surface as he concentrated on the task in hand.

'It's Vic Hadley,' he said quietly. 'So this is where he gets to, eh?'

'We shouldn't disturb him,' she suggested.

'We'll bid him good evening, though,' Mark said. 'We can't just walk past and ignore him . . . although he's so engrossed in what he's doing that he'll never notice us!'

As they walked towards the silent fisherman, Mark made a determined effort to speak to Hadley.

'Hello, Vic.' He halted on the path over where Hadley was sitting. 'So this is where you get to, eh?'

'Hello, sir.' There was a warmth in Hadley's voice now, unlike his unemotional conduct at work. 'Aye, I love it here. So calm, you can sit for hours and hours and watch the world go by – well, the world of wildlife, that is. Otters, water voles, even foxes will come close by if you sit very still. I'm not too fussed about catching trout, to be honest, it's just the peace and quiet that appeals to me.'

'I know the feeling,' Pemberton sympathized. 'That's why Lorraine and I get out for walks like this. My new hobby – a break from police work.'

'There's a good pub along the river bank.' Hadley pointed. 'They do good bar snacks, and the beer's great!'

'That's where we're heading, Vic. Can I buy you a pint? A snack even?' Quite suddenly, Mark Pemberton was a detective again; he knew he had discovered his means of entry into the secret world of Vic Hadley. The countryside, country life, walks by the river, drinks in country pubs. . . . If he could befriend this lonely, somewhat aloof man, then he might discover more about him. If he and Lorraine could meet him on walks, by the river, on the moors, in social circumstances, then he might elicit something of this man's life and movements.

'No thanks, sir. I appreciate the offer, but my supper will be ready when I get in – I promised I'd be back in a wee while.'

'OK, well, another time perhaps. Is this your regular place?'

'This river, aye. It's got trout and salmon – I go for the trout, lovely fish.'

The float bobbed in the water and Vic said, 'Looks like a bite,' and began to gently reel in his line. But the bobbing stopped. 'Just a wee tickle,' he grinned. 'Crafty blighters, trout.'

And so Pemberton and Lorraine walked away, leaving the untidy, sweatered figure hunched over his rod as he cast yet again into the place where he felt the trout lurked. Leaving him, Lorraine and Mark chattered about nothing in particular, but already Pemberton's mind was working on his next strategy. This had been a chance meeting, a pleasant one, and for just a moment Hadley had softened. Pemberton began to see that some kind of relationship might develop between himself and Hadley.

It could be a relationship born of a joint interest in rural matters, and if a false friendship was the cost of finding the truth about those killings, then Pemberton was prepared to befriend this man, or pretend to befriend him. He wondered if he was being a Judas in thinking along these lines; he wondered if a true friend would betray another, even for the sake of law and order. But police work was police work . . .

'You're very quiet,' Lorraine observed as they strolled arm in arm beside the gently flowing water.

'Just enjoying the peace and tranquillity,' he lied, not very convincingly.

'You weren't going over the murders in that head of yours, were you?' she demanded. 'If I know you, you'd be going over the evidence again and again, trying to slot one piece of the jigsaw into place . . .'

'Or trying to work out ways of trapping the suspect!'

'Trapping the suspect?' she asked quickly. 'You mean you've got a suspect, Mark? You know who the biker is?'

She was quick, he realized, too damned quick. He tried to direct the conversation towards the black-suited biker, but she was astute enough to see that he had made a slight error.

'Mark, you said *trapping* the suspect. That sounds as if you know who you want to trap . . .'

'A slip of the tongue,' he muttered.

'You're hiding something from me.' She was not going to let this drop now. 'We said we would never have secrets . . .'

His mind was working rapidly. In seeking someone to share the responsibility of investigating Hadley, he began to realize that Lorraine might be just the right person. She was alert, intuitive, dedicated to him and dedicated to her work, and, after all, the decision about his choice was his and his alone. She knew how he thought and how he responded; she knew what angered him and what delighted him.

A hundred yards along the river there was a bench, placed here in memory of an old lady whose favourite place this was He pointed to the seat and said, 'Can I talk shop for a while?'

'Why do you think I brought you out of the office?' She kissed him on the cheek. 'Mark Pemberton, I can read you like a book. I knew something was bothering you . . . Come along, sit down and tell Aunty Lorraine all about it!'

There was no one else within sight or sound of them, Hadley now being a good half-mile upstream, and so he settled on the bench as she sat by his side.

'Lorraine, what do you make of Hadley?' he asked.

'I don't know,' she admitted. 'Does he worry you?'

He explained the terrible suspicion that had crossed his mind that afternoon and provided her with his reasons. She listened intently, nodding from time to time and asking Mark how or why he had cause to suspect Inspector Hadley.

'I've expressed my concern to the Chief,' he said. 'He wants me to investigate Hadley without Hadley realizing, just to see if there are any grounds for my suspicions. If there are, then the murder teams would take over the work.'

'Oh Mark, what an awful job!'

'Just now, seeing him on the river bank, I realized I might have to befriend him in order to find out what I want. I can't say I relish that.'

'But he'll be suspicious of you, Mark, the minute you start asking questions or following him around. He won't be fooled by casual encounters, not if they happen with increasing regularity and especially if they've not happened before. He'd smell the proverbial rat a mile off! You'd alienate him, Mark, he'd never become your friend. It wouldn't work.'

'I think I knew that all along!' he admitted. 'Anyway, the Chief wants me to appoint someone to work with me on this. I had no idea who to select – until now. So how about it? Will you help me? Officially, I mean. It'll mean snooping on a colleague who's already gone through hell, if we are to believe the official version of events at Millgate supermarket.'

'I wouldn't begin by assuming he's guilty,' she said. 'I'd want to prove he's innocent, if indeed he is innocent . . .'

'So you have doubts, too?'

'Mark, if you have doubts, then I have doubts. I trust your judgement sufficiently well to know you would never lightly entertain such dark thoughts. If you have reason to suspect Hadley of being a killer, then clearly I want to help you determine the issue, one way or the other.'

'All right. You've got the job,' he said. 'Starting right now. So having established that, let's get to that pub and have something to eat. I'm famished.'

11

The following morning's dawn raids, carried out simultaneously by two police forces upon the homes of all criminals known or suspected to use shotguns, had very satisfying results. Even if the raids did not greatly benefit the murder investigations, they did result in the detection of other crimes. A multiplicity of search warrants had allowed the seizure of any goods believed to be stolen, any unlawful drugs, any illegally held firearms of any description or anything which might be the proceeds of crime. The element of surprise did produce several illegally held revolvers and rifles, the proceeds of several major cases of burglary in country houses and two hauls of dangerous drugs. The outcome was that several people were taken into custody and the year's crime detection figures would be considerably enhanced.

So far as sawn-off shotguns were concerned, only two were found. There were several full-length shotguns among the seizures, most of them held without the necessary documentation; of the sawn-off versions, one was in a town terrace house and the other in a coastal village. Each owner was arrested and taken into custody for possession of these illegally altered weapons. They would then have to explain their whereabouts at the time of each murder and submit their guns to ballistic examination. However, neither owned a motor cycle. The gut feeling was that neither man was the killer.

One of Pemberton's wishes had been fulfilled because two of the men knocked out of bed at that early hour were convicts from the Millgate supermarket robbery – Roger Pollard and Robert James Sykes – but neither was found in possession of stolen goods or firearms of any kind. The third Millgate supermarket raider, Shaun Gill, driver of the getaway car, had not been in possession of a sawn-off shotgun during that abortive attempt and so he was excused this morning's visit. Those raids had been carried out before Pemberton arrived at the office – Detective Inspector Larkin had supervised them – and Pemberton's first task that morning was to check the force's own list of shotgun certificate holders to see if Hadley was listed. He was. Although Hadley did not require a shotgun certificate or a firearms certificate in order to use guns during the course of his duty, he did need these documents if he used or possessed such firearms in his off-duty moments. He was listed as holding both types of certificate. Any rifles, pistols and revolvers held could be identified by their make, calibre and serial numbers, but these were of no current interest to Pemberton; shotguns, however, were not identified on their certificates and these were of interest. The holder of a shotgun certificate could possess or buy as many shotguns as he or she wished, and none was identified on the certificate. Thus a man with, say, ten shotguns legitimately held might shorten the barrel of one of them, an offence in itself, and no one in authority might know.

All the shotguns that had been found would now be subjected to close ballistic examination to see if they were linked in any way to the murders.

It was while Pemberton was dealing with the business of that morning, plus coping with the task of preparing the items for discussion at the daily CID conference, that Lorraine had decided to visit the force welfare officer. This was in Lorraine's capacity as Pemberton's special aide in the Hadley enquiry – she wanted to delve into the inspector's private world but knew she must ease herself into the trust of Mrs Marsden. Mrs Susan Marsden was the force welfare officer; she was a forty-five-year-old former policewoman with experience in social work, nursing and all aspects of the caring professions. The visit was Lorraine's idea. She had discussed it with Pemberton last night and they had decided a chat with Mrs Marsden might be fruitful.

'Thanks for seeing me.' Lorraine settled on a chair in the dark office. At the northern side of the building, the gloomy room lacked sunlight, hardly the most suitable place for an office where light and cheeriness were required in abundance. 'It is confidential, you will understand.'

'Like most of my work,' commented Mrs Marsden, a plump blonde whose greying roots were exposed.

'Inspector Hadley, Vic . . .' Lorraine provided her with the reason for the visit. 'As you know, he has returned to work, light work, as a therapeutic exercise, and he is working in our department.'

'Yes, I am aware of that – Admin. did notify me through the usual channels and Vic also keeps me informed.' Her answer was delivered in a curt, sharp tone.

This cold reception, and the lack of an offer of a cup of tea or coffee, made Lorraine suspect that Mrs Marsden was on her guard. Perhaps the appearance of a detective asking about a man who had been under a heavy cloud of suspicion, albeit two years ago, was likely to give rise to some concern? But Lorraine could cope, she believed.

'I have been asked to look to the welfare of all those on the murder enquiry,' Lorraine said, thinking this was a good line of introductory chat. 'It is Mr Pemberton's idea. I try to identify areas of stress among the teams; some will work themselves literally into the ground if we're not careful.'

'It happens. And not just in the CID and not just during murder investigations,' added Mrs Marsden, her cold eyes upon Lorraine. 'Many other officers do suffer from stress.'

'I know that well enough,' Lorraine said. 'But in our case, if I see someone is unhappy or unable to cope, I give advice – which generally entails coming to see you or reducing their work load.'

'Go on, Miss Cashmore.'

'Well, I wanted you to know that we are caring for Inspector Hadley now that he's with us. We do know of his past problems, that is no secret, and I am not breaching any rules of confidentiality when I mention them.'

'I appreciate that.'

'So, Mrs Marsden, my reason for coming to see you is to let you know that I shall be keeping an extra eye on Mr Hadley during the present murder investigation. As you know, we are involved in the hunt for a serial killer, along with Langbarugh CID, and although Mr Hadley's initial task was much lighter, he is now helping us to program current and incoming data into HOLMES. It's a demanding job – all murder enquiries are, but this one especially. The work is very detailed and it has to be completed swiftly and accurately. We've advised him not to work a full day and so far he has agreed to this; he will continue to work the hours we suggested at the outset. He works the hours he wants; it is something he decides.'

'He did tell me that he enjoys the work,' and there was just a hint of a smile from Mrs Marsden. 'I am very pleased with his progress, much of it due to his own determination. I see him every week, you know.'

'I do know the force has been very kind to him,' Lorraine said. 'And in return, he's never let the force down. He's given one hundred per cent commitment, no days off sick before the Millgate affair, a record of health that shows no days of illness.'

'I agree, Miss Cashmore. He's not one for taking time off duty through sickness. He was a very sound and reliable officer with a one hundred per cent attendance record until those newspapers began to smear him. But he tells me that work with your department is all very relaxed and friendly, and I can see he is making good progress. He is a very determined and strong man, emotionally strong, I mean. Physically as well, I should imagine.'

'I don't think anyone would argue with that appraisal,' Lorraine smiled. 'And I do know that none of the senior officers of the CID has any complaints about him or his work. He appears to know how to relax – we saw him fishing last night, clearly enjoying the solitude it offers.'

'He spends a lot of time fishing, by the river, not the sea,' said Mrs Marsden. 'He's not one for the crowded seaside places. He much prefers the solitude of the river bank. The various therapists and counsellors are delighted he is doing this.'

'One reason for my visit', continued Lorraine, 'is to inform you that our current enquiries might trigger off reminders of Millgate. For example, early this morning there was a co-ordinated raid on villains known to use sawn-off shotguns, and two of those visited by our teams were Pollard and Sykes – Vic will associate them with Newton. I cannot guess what effect that might have on Vic Hadley. When their names eventually come through our filing system for entry into HOLMES, Vic might be the one who has to process them. We're not quite sure how he will react, Mrs Marsden. I wanted you to be aware of these factors, perhaps so that you can notify Mr Hadley's therapists and counsellors. We want to resist removing him from that task because he's doing a good job and besides, removal from the work might imply a lack of faith. In his present condition, we do not want him to think we cannot rely on him to cope. Detective Superintendent Pemberton has asked me to say that we are very happy for him to continue working with us, but we don't want the work he's doing to create any kind of reversal of his progress. His health, both mental and physical, plus his welfare, must take priority.'

'Is there likely to be any other link between the current murder enquiry and Millgate?' asked Mrs Marsden. 'I mean, I'm not very *au fait* with the sort of things that emerge during an intense murder investigation.'

'The snag is that a murder enquiry can take all kinds of directions and it can resurrect all kinds of matters which might sometimes be best left alone. But I'll be honest with you, Mrs Marsden, I don't know what else will emerge. No one does. If Pollard and Sykes can't account for their movements at the material times, then they will be subjected to some intense scrutiny and questioning about the current murders – and the Millgate killing is bound to crop up, with Vic's part in it. It's likely that Newton's troublesome brother will raise the issue again, probably through the gutter press. He won't miss that opportunity! Quite honestly, I have no idea how the enquiry will develop – we take each day as it comes, Mrs Marsden – but teams of detectives will be unearthing all manner of new evidence. The fact that Sykes and Pollard have used sawn-off shotguns in the past, and that the present spate of killings all involve sawn-off shotguns, means that the names of those men will continue to appear until they have been eliminated. I know that Mr Pemberton will tell Mr Hadley what is likely to happen, but we felt you should know too.'

'I appreciate your visit, Miss Cashmore. I wish other departments would be so considerate. I will make sure those who should know do know.'

'Thanks,' Lorraine said. 'You've been a great help. You do know that Mr Pemberton is submitting weekly reports on Vic's progress? Any help we can receive about his state of mind and general health, particularly with reference to his continued employment in the CID, would be appreciated. But I must stress I am not asking for any breach of your code of conduct about confidentiality.'

'Call again, Miss Cashmore. If I can help, I will. My first priority is to the welfare and health of Inspector Hadley.'

'So is mine.' Lorraine realized she could not pursue any further questions at this juncture. 'But I must leave now, we have a lot of work ahead of us.'

She left the humourless Mrs Marsden and returned to the incident room knowing that she had not abstracted any worthwhile information from the welfare officer, but she had established contact and that was important. Lorraine departed with a distinct feeling that she had not antagonized the woman. She would find a reason to visit her again, perhaps in a more relaxed atmosphere.

Perhaps a well-organized 'casual' visit to the Hadley household by Lorraine, coupled with a meeting of Mrs Marsden at the same time, might well produce some useful background information? She might even discover his mental state at the time of Millgate.

Lorraine returned to the incident room in time for the morning CID conference and noted that Hadley was in attendance. Like all members of the investigation, Hadley was expected to listen to the discussions which inevitably produced new, mainly minor, lines of enquiry, and answers to nagging questions. As the officer in charge of the statement readers, he would see every piece of evidence and be aware of every twist and turn in the hunt for the motor-cycling killer.

One important piece of information which emerged at the morning conference was that the PNC, the Police National Computer, had been asked to provide a print-out of the names of everyone in the north-east of England who owned a modern black motor cycle. This would take several hours – the computer had to search every recorded machine colour by colour, and then print out details of those black ones whose owners' addresses, identified via their post codes, were within the area in question. There could be thousands of them – and then would follow the mammoth task of interviewing every single owner to establish their whereabouts at the times of all three murders.

So far as the tyre actions were concerned, DCs Pearson and Addyman had traced all outlets for Italian motor-cycle tyres in this region. They were now examining records for recent purchases, although it was discovered that some machines did come already fitted with that make. But it was progress.

There had been no useful outcome of the house-to-house enquiries following the Scott death, although further enquiries around Cressford emphasized his long-concealed paedophilic tendencies. Because he was dead, the villagers were prepared to talk to the police. Further instances of his assaults upon children were revealed but no one could explain why he had chosen to sleep out-of-doors that Saturday night. His route to the camping site remained unknown and no one reported seeing him riding upon any of the local bus services. It was likely he had walked the cross-country route between Cressford and Kesterdale, a trek of perhaps two and a half hours.

While endeavours were being made to catalogue Scott's past life, Hardisty was coming under close scrutiny by Langbarugh police. Their enquiries showed beyond doubt that he was an active dealer in narcotics, mainly in hard drugs such as heroin and cocaine, but he was always willing to supply a spot of cannabis or other soft drugs if requested – and for a price. Several convictions for drugs-related offences had not deterred Hardisty from his enterprise and he had earned a good living from his dealing; he had a modest semi-detached house although one rumour indicated that he owned a villa in Spain. The CID could not substantiate that one.

Pearle's business dealings were also being scrupulously analysed; detectives with fraud squad experience and accountancy skills were examining his business records while others were visiting his friends and business contacts, one question being whether or not Pearle had any known enemies who might resort to such drastic action. To date, none had been found. Enquiries were continuing.

Perhaps the most important outcome of recent investigations, so far as Pemberton was personally concerned, was the re-emergence of the names of Pollard and Sykes. They, along with Gill, had been quizzed at length about their whereabouts at the time of each murder and none could be regarded as a front runner in the suspect stakes. Each had an alibi for all three murders – but those alibis would be meticulously checked. Now released from prison thanks to remission for good conduct, both Sykes and Pollard were back in Fawneswick and Pemberton announced his intention to talk to them. He felt they were more important than Gill, their getaway driver.

Meanwhile, he continued to address his audience, mindful of the fact that Hadley was among them, but the early-morning raids had enabled him to bring the Pollard–Sykes link into the open. Thus this morning's raids had paid dividends.

'I'll do their interviews myself,' he told them without any reference to Hadley's past involvement with the convicts. 'Later today. I want to meet these villains. I want to ask them about the market for sawn-off shotguns, where they obtained theirs, who's likely to be doctoring these weapons now.'

What he did not reveal was that his real purpose was to discover what they could remember about the shooting of Joss Newton. If their past reaction was any guide, they would be willing to expound their views on that.

When the CID conference was over, the next task for Pemberton was to host the daily news conference at 10 a.m.; this morning's news would concentrate on the search for the motor-cycle rider, for anyone who had seen Scott between his home and the scene of his murder and for any discarded sawn-off shotgun which might have been thrown into a river or pond, or been dumped in some unusual place. Places as varied as dustbins, rubbish tips, lakes, ponds, rivers and hedges had to be considered and he asked the reports to highlight their search for the weapon. He produced photographs of similar weapons which were distributed to the waiting news reporters and these were supported by a request that if any member of the public found such a weapon, they should not handle it but should immediately notify their local police station.

When the main conferences of the day were safely over, Lorraine came into his office, closed the door and told Pemberton of her visit to the force welfare officer, referring to its singular lack of success. She did feel, however, that she had established some kind of rapport with Mrs Marsden which might prove useful.

Then she announced she was heading for the Langbarugh incident room for the daily liaison visit.

'And I'm going to interview Pollard and Sykes,' Pemberton told her. 'I'll take a sergeant with me. I want an excuse to ask them about Hadley's behaviour at Millgate.'

'Tread carefully. We mustn't let Hadley know we're investigating him again, not yet. And make sure Newton's big brother doesn't find out. If I can help, I should be back before lunch.' She smiled, and left him to his work.

Half an hour later, with Detective Sergeant Dave Watson as his driver, Mark Pemberton set off to visit Fawneswick to interview

Pollard and Sykes. He had selected Watson because he had been a detective constable at the time of the Millgate raid – he'd been with Swanson in the disguised van.

'Do you think they'll talk to us?' Pemberton asked Watson as they moved out of Rainesbury in the official CID car.

'They might, but I can't see them grassing on whoever shortens shotguns, sir. It's not just anybody who can safely shorten a barrel – it needs a good deal of skill.'

'If I can get them to talk about Inspector Hadley, that might loosen their tongues, eh?'

'Oh, they'll talk about that, sir, they would love to revive that episode. My sergeant at the time, Phil Swanson, wasn't happy about Hadley's actions, not with the outcome.'

'Tell me why,' invited Pemberton.

'He smelt a cover-up, sir, because of Hadley's rank.'

'His rank?'

'Well, he was an inspector and he shot a man. I must say I wasn't too happy either. I'm still not convinced that Newton was armed, you know. There never was a satisfactory explanation about the guns and the number of cartridges recovered. It smacked of a cover-up, sir, rank looking after rank and all that. No one has ever said what really happened.'

Having listened to the comments of his colleagues who had been present at the time, and having known that Pollard had watched Swanson's approach that morning, Watson then outlined his version of the Millgate supermarket incident. His views, not surprisingly, corresponded with those of his superior, Detective Sergeant, now Detective Inspector, Swanson. Watson did believe that Newton was unarmed when he was shot by Hadley even though he admitted he had not seem Newton's arrival on the forecourt. He believed that Pollard had discarded and thrown aside the shotgun which was later attributed to Newton. He did imply, however, that it was Swanson who, from an unknown source, had received the tip-off about the raid and that Swanson wanted to gain credit for the arrests . . . but the shooting of Newton had overshadowed everything else. What was intended to be a carefully planned police operation with a successful outcome had developed into a *cause célèbre*.

'I wasn't on the case, Dave, as you know, and I do have a very open mind, but I'd like to hear what these two rogues have to tell us,' Pemberton explained.

'You're opening the Millgate job then?' Watson asked with obvious interest.

'No, it's over.' Pemberton had to disappoint him. 'But I want to see what these characters know about sawn-off shotguns and whether they can help me in any way with solving the series of murders.'

By twelve noon, Pemberton and Swanson had learned that their two targets were at the Harbour Inn playing pool. Quizzing them separately might not be so simple, not without arresting them, and there were no grounds for that.

'Let's see what transpires,' said Pemberton as he entered the seaside pub. It was busy with tourists and regulars, and he could see a thirty-year-old thick-set individual with tattoos along both arms, about to take a shot. Watson identified him as Pollard, Sykes being a thinner character with a gold ear-ring in his left ear and dark, greasy hair worn long over his collar.

'Drinks first, Dave. I'm having a pint – what's yours?'

'I'm driving, sir, so an apple juice.'

Pemberton paid, ordered a round of ham sandwiches each, and then settled down at a table adjoining the pool-playing area. He pretended not to notice the two players, allowing them to finish their game before standing up to say, 'Roger Pollard, isn't it?'

'Who's asking?'

'Pemberton. Detective Superintendent, and this is DS Watson.'

'You looking for me then? I had your lot round this morning, crack of dawn, looking for bloody guns . . . They'll never be off our backs now, will they, not since we got done for that supermarket job.'

'Drink?' invited Pemberton. 'Both of you?'

'Got nothing to lose – right. Two pints.'

And as Watson went off to obtain the drinks, the two surly men joined Pemberton at the table.

'This morning's raids . . .' Pemberton began. 'It was part of a murder enquiry – everybody who's been convicted of offences involving shotguns, throughout the whole north-east, got a call.

We weren't targeting you two. It was a much wider operation, bigger than you realize. We raided hundreds of houses. It was for elimination purposes – and you two were eliminated from the murder. That's good news, isn't it?'

'If they'd come and talked to us, they'd have learned that,' said Pollard.

'If they'd come and talked, they'd have learned that,' echoed Sykes.

'It wouldn't have worked in every case – there's some right hard cases to contend with. Anyway, I just wanted to ask your help, being a murder enquiry.'

'Help? From us?' grinned Pollard. 'God, Bob, the filth must be hard up, asking us for help!'

'They must be hard up, asking us for help,' grinned Sykes.

'Shotguns,' said Pemberton. 'Three men have been shot with sawn-off shotguns in recent days. What we want to know is who is shortening the barrels, where the guns are coming from.'

'Search me, I don't know,' said Pollard. 'I've never touched a sodding shotgun since Millgate. Didn't have much opportunity, did I? Being banged up like I was. Like we was, me and Bob.'

'We never touched no guns, we was banged up,' said Sykes.

'So where did you get your guns from?' persisted Pemberton. 'The ones you used at Millgate?'

'Bought 'em in a pub, off of this chap, two hundred each. No questions asked. No idea who he was. I told this to your lot at the time.'

'Bought 'em off a chap in the pub,' said Sykes.

'How many did you buy?'

'How many? Two. You know that.'

'So where did Newton get his gun from?'

'Newton? Him that was shot by your lot? He wasn't with us, I keep saying that. There was me, Bob and Shaun. Three of us, all got sent down. I never knew that Newton, Mr Pemberton, he was never with us, not part of our gang.'

'He wasn't with us, Mr Pemberton,' echoed Sykes.

Pollard went on. 'He never had a gun, I kept telling 'em that an' all. Shot in cold blood, he was. Like a bloody rat, Mr Pemberton. Innocent as the day he was born, just walked on to the forecourt to get his bairns something for breakfast and bang, his life went, snuffed out like a candle, he was. As quick as that. Bob fired some shots, yeah, he admitted that, but not at anybody, up in the air, frighteners they were. Newton didn't fire no shots, he had no gun, Mr Pemberton. God's honest truth. That gun they said was his, well, it was mine, the one I chucked away.'

'Frighteners we fired, he was snuffed out like a candle, gone, just like that,' said Sykes.

'Did you see him enter the forecourt, Roger?'

'No, I heard a bang, a shot, and there he was, lying flat out. Dead.'

'He was lying flat out, dead,' came the echo.

'And his gun? Did you see him carry a gun?' pressed Pemberton.

'Never saw him with a shooter, Mr Pemberton,' beamed Pollard. 'God's honest truth.'

'He never had no shooter, Mr Pemberton, God'll swear to the truth,' smiled Sykes.

'You were out of his sight!' snapped Pemberton. 'You, Bob, you were behind the security van, you couldn't see Newton from there!'

'Was I?' asked Sykes. 'Well, I'll be buggered!'

'How many were on that raid, Roger?' Pemberton asked the more intelligent of the pair.

'Me, Bob and young Shaun, he was the getaway driver. Like I said. Didn't getaway very far, did he?' and he chuckled.

'Nobody else?'

'No, nobody.'

'No, nobody,' repeated Sykes.

'So who tipped the police off, then? Our lads knew you were going to do the job, when and where, and the right time. They were waiting.'

'Don't we know . . . no idea, Mr Pemberton. No idea at all . . . nobody could have known, we never said nowt to nobody, did we, Bob?'

'Never said nowt to nobody,' echoed Bob.

'Newton was a thief, gentlemen,' said Pemberton. 'We never caught him, but we knew he was thieving, cash, always cash.'

'Not that day he wasn't, he was nowt to do with us, Mr Pemberton. Your gun-happy Inspector what's-his-name shot him because he was there, no other reason. All that crap about Newton going to shoot a detective, well, it was all crap. I said so in court and I'll say it again, and I don't care what the enquiries said. It was a cover-up, you mark my words. That gun was mine, Mr Pemberton, and I don't care who knows. A bloody cover-up for murder, Mr Pemberton.'

'A bloody cover-up, it was,' added Sykes.

'Who organized the raid, Roger?'

'Organized it? Me and Bob. There was no organizing to do, was there? You just watch the time when the money van comes every week, we knew their changes, different drops an' that, and we worked out when they were due at Millgate.'

'We worked out when they was due,' smiled Sykes.

'Then we set out to nobble it. Got Shaun to be the getaway. We nearly got away – except you lot was waiting with guns.'

'You was waiting with guns,' scowled Sykes.

'Me and Bob would never grass,' said Pollard. 'And Shaun was reliable, he never knew what he was volunteering to do until last minute. He'd never grass anyway. No, we'd never be grasses. Not never, not us.'

'We'd never grass,' said Sykes.

'That confirms my belief that there was another person – not your getaway driver – at the raid.' Pemberton put forward Lorraine's theory. 'Somebody else. Somebody who had set up the scam, somebody who was waiting in the background somewhere, somebody who knew Newton and who brought him along . . . but Newton and him arrived too late. By the time they got there, you two were well under way, waving guns about, so when our detective came on the scene, Newton arrived as well – with a shotgun. And he got killed. The man who set the scam up got clean away, that's what I think – and I think he might have been the man who tipped off the police, Roger. How about that for a theory?'

'Balls!' said Pollard. 'Utter balls . . . there was just me and Bob . . .'

'Balls,' said Sykes.

'Over the weeks before the Millgate raid, there had been other robberies like yours, not done by you, but done by local "volunteers", set up by somebody who knew the timing and value of the loads coming in . . . for a cut of the proceeds.'

'Fairy-tale stuff, Mr Pemberton. Me, Bob and Shaun was alone in this one. Mebbe we should have had help, we might have got a few thousand quid for our trouble instead of porridge. Anyway, you came about them murders and I can't help about the guns. Ours was bought from a bloke in a pub years ago. No idea who he was or where he was from. He just got the guns for us, two guns, Mr Pemberton, one for me and one for Bob.'

'Bought ours from a bloke in the pub,' said Sykes.

'All right, thanks. I appreciate your help. Now, before I leave, there's something else I'd like to clear up, while I'm here. Did either of you actually see Newton arrive at Millgate?'

'No,' said Pollard.

'No,' said Sykes.

'Did you, Roger, notice Detective Sergeant Swanson walking across the forecourt of the supermarket when the raid was under way? Heading for you?'

'No, can't say I did, Mr Pemberton. I was too busy looking for coppers with guns. There'd been shooting, you see, I heard the bangs.'

'He heard the bangs,' said Bob.

'I must admit I didn't see a lot,' said Pollard. 'I was concentrating on what I was doing. Watching them guards close, I was, from behind the truck. Then I saw the old bill coming and thought our number was up. I know what they do to armed robbers, so I broke my gun and tossed it aside. Then I heard a shot and saw the bloke lying there, not far away. He was close to my gun then . . . then I got nicked.'

'He got nicked,' echoed Sykes.

'Was anybody with Newton?' asked Pemberton.

'Never saw nobody,' responded Pollard.

'Never saw nobody,' echoed Sykes.

'Roger, where were you standing when all this happened?' asked Pemberton.

'Behind the security van. Bob was at the side, the passenger side, holding up the guards. I was at the back, watching in case the driver got out . . . he didn't, then all this happened. I told all this to those blokes who were trying to catch Hadley.'

'We told all this to those other coppers,' said Sykes.

'So neither the police nor the guards would see you with a gun?'

'Mebbe not, I dunno,' admitted Pollard. 'I was out of their sight for a few minutes, round the back of the van.'

'He was round the back,' beamed Sykes.

'And you, Bob, you fired your gun?'

'Over their heads, to empty it. We said we'd not kill in the raid, mister, use the guns for frighteners, not to kill. And we stuck to that, eh, Rog?'

'We did – and we got nicked!'

'We got nicked,' said Sykes, grinning as if it had all been a bit of fun.

'Did you see who shot Newton?' asked Pemberton.

'No, just heard a bang, then I got nicked. I saw him lying there . . . there was old bill everywhere . . .'

'Old bill everywhere,' said Sykes.

Pemberton felt he had now gained a clear picture of events that day, and it did not look good for Hadley. But he had no wish to prolong this interview, nor did he wish to make it appear as if he was pursuing that line of enquiry.

'OK, thanks for talking. Another pint each?'

'Never say no to a copper buying a pint apiece, eh, Bob?'

'Never say no to a copper buying a pint apiece,' echoed Bob.

'What do you reckon to those two?' asked Pemberton on the way back to Rainesbury.

'I think they were telling the truth, sir,' said Watson. 'Their side of things matches what we thought. I think they were amateurs setting about a raid which was bound to go wrong. And it did.'

'So you believe Newton was innocent, that he was not part of the raid?'

'I do, sir, yes. It matches what some of us have thought all along.'

'So who tipped off the police, Sergeant? Somebody else must have known . . .'

'I have no idea, sir, you'll have to ask Inspector Swanson about that. He's never told me, not face to face, but from what he's let slip, I thought he was the one who got the anonymous call. And that's why we were all waiting that morning.'

'Sergeant, I want you to keep today's events to yourself. I have no wish to be seen to be reopening the Millgate files nor doubting the outcome of the official enquiries.'

'Understood, sir. But I'm pleased you spoke to Pollard and Sykes. So can I ask, do you think Inspector Hadley shot Newton in cold blood?'

'I wish I knew, Sergeant. But right now we have three murders to solve, haven't we?'

12

As Watson went to park the car at Rainesbury police station, Pemberton walked across the spacious yard at the rear of the building, heading for the rear door with its security coded lock. In those final yards, his eye caught sight of the bike sheds – and there, parked beneath the motor-cycle shelter, was Hadley's black and silver machine. There was no one about and so, not one to miss an opportunity, Pemberton went across to examine it. A Suzuki by make, it was a clean, well-kept motor cycle with gracefully shaped fairings marked with a silver design, dart-shaped. A powerful machine, probably 1100cc, it had chrome wheels glistening in the afternoon sunshine and the familiar Italian tyres . . . Pemberton stooped to examine the tyre tread.

To date, none of his teams would have conducted a detailed examination of these tyres. That would follow in due course, but he did not wish to miss the opportunity for a quick peek himself. Without having the print-outs of the pattern markings found near the green tent, he could not be sure these were identical or even similar, but they certainly appeared to be a good match. The machine had spacious, rigid panniers at either side of the rear wheel and Pemberton made a mental note of its registration number, modern machines having only a rear number plate. He noticed that the plastic plate was held in position by two screws

– it would be the work of a minute or less to remove that number plate and replace it with a false one. So had Hadley done that before embarking on some murderous outings?

Walking away from the machine, Pemberton realized he would have to contrive to make a detailed comparison of those tyre treads – and there was no time like the present. Another thought struck him: Hadley had been at the conference this morning and he was still here, working on the self-same murder enquiry. This was unusual – he usually worked only half-days – and Mark began to wonder whether the fellow was improving in health and therefore working longer hours, or whether his police sense of commitment was compelling him to work a full day alongside his colleagues. Then a more ominous thought crossed Mark's mind: was Hadley working longer hours so that he could monitor the attempts to find the triple killer or even monitor the development of the enquiry which could lead to himself? In that way, he could keep himself safe from capture . . .

Thinking along those lines, Mark realized there was no better place to conceal a suspect motor cycle than the bike sheds of a police station! He found himself wondering whether Hadley was a victim of circumstance or whether he was a clever and dangerous crook, making full use of his police background and acceptability to carry out his crimes. Could that be the real Hadley? If so, he was a very dangerous man.

Letting himself into the building by pressing the buttons in his coded sequence, Pemberton took the lift but called into the incident room before returning to his own office. He found the place a hive of activity, positively humming with vigour, and he noticed Vic Hadley hunched over a pile of statements near the HOLMES terminal.

It would be interesting to discover why Hadley had stayed at work. First, though, Mark located Detective Inspector Larkin.

'I'm back, Paul,' he said. 'It looks busy in here, has something happened?'

'We got an anonymous call about the murder, sir, about an hour ago. A man, ringing from a kiosk. We tried to trace the call but we were too late – he'd gone by the time we got there.'

'What was he ringing about?'

'The black motor bikes, sir. He said he was in Kesterdale last Saturday night, late, with a woman. They were in a car, sir, and she was not his wife which is why he refused to give his name. He said he saw a black motor cycle pull up on the side of the road near the telephone kiosk. It was about half-past one in the morning, Sunday to be precise. In the light from the kiosk, the couple saw the man change the number plate on the bike. The witness said he had no idea what the original one was, except that the figures 1 and 6 were in the sequence. The biker put the original plate in the pannier near the rear wheel and drove off minutes later with a different plate on show. Our witness noted it down, sir . . .'

'And?' asked Pemberton.

'It was the same number as those jobs in Langbarugh, sir.'

'Why didn't he ring us before?' Pemberton asked.

'He was watching the newspapers for something which might be connected with that bike but he's been away on business so he missed the local coverage of the murder stories – the nationals only dealt with them in brief. He'd only just read about the murders and our hunt for the motor bikes. That's when he thought his sighting might be important.'

'I'll say it is!' breathed Pemberton. 'So you couldn't persuade him to come in and make a statement?'

'Not a bit of it, sir. He'd told his wife he was in Scotland on business – she thought he was on his way home after a late meeting, not parked in a Yorkshire dale with his bit of fresh,' Larkin said. 'He rang from a kiosk, we traced it to that one in Lawrence Street, here in Rainesbury. But he'd gone by the time we arrived. We can't identify him – his voice was calm and bore a local accent, that's all we can say.'

'The trouble with anonymous calls is that you never know if they're genuine,' Pemberton observed. 'If only the fellow had come in and talked to us – we could have kept his secret from his wife . . . the secrets we have stored in our files! So what's the frantic activity here?'

'They're going through the PNC print-outs looking for black motor cycles with the figures 1 and 6 as part of their registration number, sir.'

Pemberton realized that those figures did feature upon the registration plate of Hadley's machine – its numerical sequence was

316 – but that was not sufficient evidence, on its own, to justify dramatic action like arresting him or having him charged. But if the tyre marks matched, then his movements at the time of the murders would have to be checked and verified. A thankless task for some detective if the fellow was innocent, but the clues were now beginning to add up into something very sinister even if none of the other detectives appeared to suspect Hadley.

For Mark Pemberton, however, the passage of time and the growing number of unwelcome coincidences were combining to force him into accepting that Vic Hadley could be the avenging motor cyclist. Still reluctant to take action without some positive evidence, Pemberton knew he must soon make a decision about interviewing him. To do that, he ought to be in possession of some hard evidence, something upon which to base the foundation of an oral examination. At this stage, such evidence was lacking.

The obvious move was to make a close check of those tyres against the imprints of the marks found near the green tent. The files in the incident room contained surplus copies of the prints of the Green Tent tyre marks; these were for publicity and for distribution around the tyre dealers and so it was not unusual for a detective to help himself to one – which Mark did. Folding it into three and stuffing it into his inner jacket pocket, he walked downstairs via the flight of steps rather than the lift, and emerged in the spacious car-park. Seconds later, he was once again examining Hadley's motor cycle; crouched beside the machine, unobserved, he held the print-out against the rear tyre. And the tread pattern was identical. This meant the motor cycle which had visited that green tent had borne the same make of tyres as the motor cycle owned by Vic Hadley. But Pemberton knew that millions of these tyres were manufactured and a visual match would not hold sway over a cynical court which was frightened to convict. He would need positive proof, and that meant taking casts of these tyres, every inch of them, and scientifically matching the result with the marks found near the green tent.

Things like wear and tear, cuts in the rubber, the pressure of the tyres and a host of other factors would have to be compared before it could be stated without doubt that Hadley's machine had made that trip. Nonetheless, Mark felt the time had come to inform Hadley of some of his findings. His need to use subterfuge might have been overtaken by events, although he realized that if he wanted an excuse to question Hadley, then he could use the familiar old ruse – 'it's for elimination purposes'. But when Mark returned to the incident room he was somewhat surprised to find Hadley waiting for him.

'Sir,' he said, 'a word, in your office, if I may.'

'Sure, come in.' He led the large, untidy fellow into his private sanctum, indicated a chair and closed the door before taking his own seat. 'Now, Vic, what can I do for you? I see you've decided to work extra hours today?'

'This murder, sir, the one in our area, and those in Langbarugh, I wanted to work as hard as I could to catch the killer. There's a lot of work to do, but I'll not overdo it, I know my limits.'

'OK, whatever suits you suits me.' Pemberton tried to sound relaxed. 'Is that what you wanted to see me about?'

'No, it's worse than that. These print-outs from the PNC, I'm logging them into HOLMES, checking names and so on. Mr Larkin's arranging actions for local interviews of bike owners . . .'

'Yes,' Mark acknowledged. 'We need to get among them all pretty quickly, Vic, to get them eliminated. There's quite a lot.'

'Well, sir, that's why I'm here. You see, my own name has come up, as the owner of a black bike . . . I got that part of the print-out with my name on. I thought I'd better come to see you, to get myself eliminated from the enquiry . . .'

'Yes, well, that makes sense. It would have meant a team coming to visit you and quiz you in depth, as you are well aware. So, Vic, you've saved them a job, eh? Now this means I must ask you to explain your whereabouts on the nights of the murders, Vic. And you need to produce witnesses, independent witnesses. You know the score.'

'That's the trouble, sir, I can't. Can't produce witnesses, I mean I was fishing – even when old Scott was killed in his green tent, I was fishing. I go where you saw me last night, not always in exactly the same place, but somewhere along that stretch of the river. It's common water there, for about two miles up and downstream. I mean, sir, people have seen me there, walkers, strollers, people interested in the countryside . . . but I can't name them and they probably don't know me.'

'Your wife, she would say you were fishing if we asked her?'

'Yes, even late at night, but that's no alibi, is it? Besides, she's not exactly independent, is she? What she'd say is that I was out, and that looks suspicious, because she can't prove where I was. I love night fishing, sir, it's marvellous. I go on the bike as far as I can, then park it and walk. I don't go just for the angling aspect, but for the wildlife . . . badgers, owls, otters swimming inches from your feet . . . I always tell her if I'm going to be very late, especially when I fish all night. I do that now and again, fish all night.'

'I can appreciate your need for solitude, Vic.'

'Yes, it's really great, you know, coming home at dawn with a bag full of fresh mushrooms for breakfast.'

Pemberton studied the man opposite and was unsure whether to regard him as a very honest and frightened man who was desperately keen to be absolved from any suspicion, or a devious killer who had recognized the fact that he might be under surveillance or suspicion even at this stage and who was now looking for a means of escape from the ever-closing net. Pemberton's gut reaction was to go along with the man's requests to see whether or not he ever slipped up in his stories – Pemberton was a great believer in the old maxim that if you give a rogue enough rope, he will eventually hang himself.

'I'll put a suggestion to you, Vic,' he said after a few moments' deliberation. 'How about writing out a statement for me, using your own words, and accounting for your whereabouts at all the material times. You know the rules as well as me, you know what we look for, how important named witnesses are and so on, along with precise times, dates and places. Then, once you've completed it, we – me, probably – would have to question you at length, put you through the third degree to positively eliminate you. I want you eliminated, Vic, and you've shown great presence of mind in volunteering as you have. We would have got around to you in due course, as you know, thanks to the black bike print-out.'

Hadley smiled through his beard. 'Right, sir, yes. It'll do me good, to write it all down.'

'Include details of your bike, Vic, where you got it, how long you've had it and so on. I don't have to tell you that we and

Langbarugh police are both seeking a black-clad biker on a black machine, just like yours.'

'I bought it from Fell's in Scarborough, sir, two months ago. A Suzuki. Brand-new. They had umpteen similar ones in stock, a very popular model, they told me.'

'Good, include all that sort of detail. And the tyres? You haven't changed the tyres, have you?'

'No, they were on when I got it, they were brand-new. Why?'

'Suppose they match the tyre marks we found near the green tent, Vic?' Pemberton looked at Hadley directly into his eyes.

'Bloody hell,' he said. 'And that anonymous call, with two of my numbers being mentioned by that caller . . . I mean, sir, bloody hell, I'm no killer! It looks as if I'm being set up for this lot. Look, sir, you've got to get me out of this, really . . .'

'I will, Vic, you know that, but first I'll need to quiz you and quiz you again and again until you're heartily sick of it . . . like a suspect. You know the routine, you know how hard we can be, how hard we have to be on murder suspects.'

'Sir, I've been ill, I've been accused of shooting Newton in cold blood. I don't want to be accused, or even suspected, of killing those other people – it's not me, sir, not my style. I'm no murderer, it's just not the sort of thing I'd do.'

'You write that statement, Vic, and fetch it direct to me when it's finished – do it here if you want, or at home, or wherever you feel happiest. Don't stress yourself, I don't want you becoming ill again through all this – believe me, I want to help you.'

'Just believe me, sir, just trust me. That's all I ask. A bit of trust. It's so hard getting people to believe what I say. It's always been like this, ever since I was a kid. Always such a bloody battle to get people to believe what I say . . . I never tell lies, sir, never . . .' and Pemberton noticed tears in Hadley's eyes.

He spoke softly. 'Vic, we will have to examine your bike. Tyre treads and so on, to eliminate it, to see whether it was at the Green Tent murder scene.'

'I know that, sir. Go ahead, it's out there now, in the sheds. I'd welcome that if it gets me off the hook. God knows I would.'

And Inspector Vic Hadley, now high in Pemberton's frame of suspects, turned and walked out, rubbing his eyes. Pemberton watched him go, unsure whether he was watching the departure of a very clever killer. His actions were similar to the killer who pretends to have discovered the body, hoping that will convince the police of his innocence. Hadley had done exactly that – had he seen the growing wealth of evidence and decided to take the initiative? That action alone was of enormous benefit to Pemberton and it removed the need for stealth and deception. Pemberton and his teams could now interrogate Vic Hadley just as they would another suspect. And just like another suspect, Pemberton did not know whether he was innocent or guilty. But he had to find out, one way or the other, witnesses or no witnesses.

His first duty was to ring Detective Sergeant Thornton of Scenes of Crime.

'Derek,' he said, 'Inspector Hadley's motor cycle is in the bike sheds behind the building. I want it examined, now. I want you to tell me if it has been at the scene of the Green Tent murder. Check the tyres, look for signs of earth upon it which might have come from that area. Inspector Hadley knows it is being checked – it's being done for elimination purposes, I might add. His bike number is one of hundreds the PNC has thrown up.'

'Very good, sir,' said Thornton, not entirely convinced by Pemberton's reasons for the examination.

Alone with his thoughts, Pemberton decided that he could not treat Hadley like a 'bent' police officer, one who had infringed the discipline code or who was known to have become involved in some criminal escapade. In such cases, the officer was suspended from duty. Hadley could not be suspended merely because his motor cycle was like one which had been used by a killer. Hadley would therefore be allowed to continue in his present role. In that way, and with Hadley in the office, Pemberton and his officers would be able to keep an eye on him. If the suspicions strengthened, then it might be possible to set a trap.

As Mark pondered his next move, he realized that, with all the detailed timings and other information relative to the murders, Hadley, if he was guilty, would be able to compile his statement so that his movements could be explained in relation to the known facts.

But one factor would be inescapable – the tyre marks at the scene of the Green Tent killing would be vital and if they did match Hadley's tyres, then it would be almost irrefutable evidence of his culpability.

Having dealt with Hadley, Mark examined the correspondence in his in-tray, knowing he would have to determine what information should be released to the newspapers this evening, in readiness for tomorrow morning's editions. Apart from Hadley's unpredictable move, there had been little development with the Green Tent murder, and no positive inflow of information from Langbarugh. In other words, the enquiries were all pottering along with no dramatic developments, other than the anonymous caller. His action had revived the enquiry, albeit only briefly, but his information would not be released to the media, neither would Hadley's dilemma.

When he went out of his office, he could see Vic Hadley, head down, working on his statement. He seemed so anxious to get it all down on paper, so keen to prove his innocence. He was writing in longhand on scraps of paper and would transfer his work on to a typewriter or word processor in due course.

Pemberton approached him.

'Vic,' he said, 'I'm having your motor cycle examined by SOCO immediately, tyres mainly. I thought you ought to know.'

'Thanks, sir, at least that'll prove I wasn't at that Green Tent scene.'

Pemberton moved on and found Detective Inspector Larkin in the photocopy room. 'Paul,' he said, 'has Fell's in Scarborough been visited about sales of black motor bikes?'

'No, it's out of our patch, sir. With the Langbarugh link, we've been concentrating on the northern end of the area.'

'Vic Hadley got his bike from them, a black Suzuki which the PNC has thrown up. I think we ought to visit them, finding out how many black Suzukis they've sold recently and to whom – and what sort of tyres they all had.'

'Yes, right, sir.'

'Now?'

'Why not?' smiled Larkin. 'I could do with an outing.'

And so Pemberton asked the press officer, Inspector Dodd, to say that the enquiry team was still concentrating on finding the black motor cycle and some positive leads were being followed. No arrest was imminent, however.

Twenty minutes later, with DI Larkin at the wheel, Pemberton was heading for Fell's, Scarborough's leading motor-cycle retailers. It would be interesting to learn how many black Suzukis had been sold in this area. He found himself hoping there was more than one.

13

Alan Fell, owner of the motor-cycle shop in Scarborough, was very helpful, even more so when he learned that this was part of the Green Tent murder enquiry in the northern part of the county. He kept neat and up-to-date records and was quickly able to show that he had sold a Suzuki 1100cc machine to a Mr Victor Hadley of Rainesbury a couple of months ago. Computer records held by the shop meant that the information was readily available upon request – as long as there was a very sound reason for that request. Fell was able to say that the machine was brand-new, he could provide the registration number, and he confirmed that it was fitted with the Italian Masseria tyres.

He could also provide a list of identical machines sold during the past year; his computer records printed out a list of machines which were not shown on the PNC records, simply because the Scarborough and district postcodes of YO11, 12, 14, 15 and 16 (York areas) had not been included in the request to the computer. Now, Pemberton had a list of thirty other motor cycles which were identical to that owned by Hadley – and fifteen of them had been fitted with Masseria tyres when sold. Fell went on to say that a purchaser could swap the tyres for another brand before taking delivery of the machine if he wished, but few did so.

Mr Fell added that he had received his allocation from the production line and had had sufficient machines to exchange several of his stock with dealers from the north-east, including Newcastle, Sunderland, Durham and Middlesbrough. Those who had wanted this particular model had thus been supplied with their dream bike.

It seemed that those who bought these particular machines were quite content to use the Italian country-style tyres with which they were fitted as standard. Fell showed Pemberton and Larkin examples of the tyres, easily distinguished by their deep tread which was designed for rural motor cycling rather than city or town work; Pemberton saw that they did match those upon Hadley's machine. Fell's computer then showed which of the recently bought machines had been fitted with such tyres after purchase. There were only two – one had gone to a buyer in Lincoln and the other to a holiday-maker from Luton who had had his purchase delivered by carrier.

Neither, felt Pemberton, would be responsible for murders in the north-east of England, but even so they would be interrogated along with all the owners of black Suzukis with Masseria tyres already fitted. They would be asked to provide details of their whereabouts at the time of the killings – and surprises were always likely to happen on a murder enquiry.

Alan Fell was happy to supply catalogues of the machines and publicity photographs of the tyres; he said the British agents in Coventry would no doubt assist further with any more details of the tyres, if they were required. The detectives thanked him and left.

On the return journey to Rainesbury, Pemberton took the opportunity to ask Larkin for his views on Hadley. Larkin, like the other members of the murder team, now knew that Hadley had volunteered to be questioned with a view to being eliminated from the list of black motor-cycling suspects.

Pemberton realized it was putting Larkin on the spot but Larkin was sufficiently mature to understand that this was not a flippant question.

'He's a good solid workhorse.' Larkin spoke honestly. 'He just sits and works on the data, he hardly stops. He's forgotten he's a uniform inspector, he's behaving more like a detective constable. Very dedicated, an asset to the incident room, I'd say. A bit lacking in humour and not very talkative, but knowing what he's been through, I'm not surprised.'

'Had you ever considered him a suspect for the Green Tent murder, Paul? Or either of the Langbarugh killings?'

'Him? Vic Hadley? Good God, no, sir!' There was shock on Paul's face.

'You know he has a black motor bike?'

'I know he comes to work on a motor bike, sir, he leaves his waterproofs and helmet in the locker room. But I have never regarded that as significant – damn it all, lots of people go to work on motor bikes. I must admit I haven't paid much attention to his machine. There was no reason to even consider it.'

'There is now. It's a black one, Paul, with silver markings. We're interested in black bikes, especially those with silver markings and two numerical digits which are the same as on a bike reported seen in Kesterdale shortly before Scott's death. Hadley's bike matches that description, even to having two matching digits on its registration plate. Remember we're talking about a man who was suspected of shooting an innocent shopper during a stake-out, a victim later found to be an unconvicted villain, like the three victims we're investigating . . . they're people apparently killed by some kind of lone vigilante, a vigilante who kills people the courts can never reach, a killer who knows of their unpublicized records and a killer who rides a black motor bike. Our colleague, Vic Hadley, is a man whose hobby is fishing alone, so he says . . .'

'You make him sound like a prime suspect, sir.'

'I'll make no bones about it, Paul. I was on the point of launching a secret investigation into his background and checking his movements when he volunteered for elimination. He said the black bike list which the PNC spewed out had persuaded him to do this – his machine's on the list, as you know. Because of that, he would have been earmarked for interview as a matter of course. It could be argued that we should have known about his bike – he parked the bloody thing right under our noses – but his possession of advanced knowledge has made him jump the queue. That knowledge also removes the need for me to go softly-softly in my interrogation of him. We don't have to hide our activities, Paul, his wish is to be clear of suspicion. Mine is to establish the truth.'

'Won't his mental condition be at risk if we start quizzing him and his wife as we would any other prime suspect? It could make him blow a fuse, or whatever happens in these cases.'

'That's a risk I'll have to take. DC Cashmore is in touch with the force welfare officer, who's a bit of a dragon by all accounts, enough to frighten police officers back to work if you ask me, and we shall maintain that liaison so long as Hadley's with our department.'

'Is he mentally ill, sir?'

'I don't know, that's something Lorraine hopes to learn from the welfare officer, once she's established a stronger rapport. I hope the interrogations will not make him ill again, we don't want to be responsible for setting his recovery back, especially if he is innocent.'

'You sound doubtful, sir?'

'Before this series of murders started, Paul, I did a tiny bit of research into the Millgate supermarket shooting. The outcome of that was that I emerged more baffled than when I started. Reading those reports, and hearing Hadley's reaction to the death of old Scott, I would not be at all surprised if he bumped off Newton, probably seeing it as a service to society. If he is mentally sick now, he might have been mentally sick then. I'm not saying he is mentally sick, though. He's suffering from stress, or has been suffering from stress, which is not quite the same thing, but the point I'm making is that he might have been mentally ill at the time of Millgate. We can't ignore that possibility. That's something no one seems to have established, added to which he might feel he has some God-given right to eliminate wrongdoers. I might be wrong about the Millgate killing but when these current murders started, with more villains being assassinated, I saw there were links, Paul, strong links. For example, who, outside the police service, could know of the criminal backgrounds of all those victims? In two adjoining force areas? Someone with access to police records, confidential records of suspects rather than convicts? There's a lot of unanswered and imponderable questions among it all, Paul.'

'So what you're saying is that we should put a team on to Inspector Hadley?'

'Yes, and it has to be the best we've got. I'd like you to take that on board, Paul. Now that Hadley has opened things up, we can go ahead without any need for subterfuge. So can you select someone to work with you on this, on Hadley, covering all aspects of his life and career, sickness record and so on? I think you should read the Millgate file too, which I have got in my safe. But

I do not want Hadley to be regarded as guilty until we have looked at every conceivable angle. And I need not say that these suspicions must be kept from the press and from all other officers – and especially from the Newton family and those bloody tabloids who crucified him over Millgate. They made him appear guilty of murder when he believes he was only doing his job, so God knows what they'd do with this development.'

'It's a tall order, sir, investigating one of our own like this.'

'I'm aware of that, Paul. I know we're not the rubber heel squad, but it should be made easier because Hadley welcomes the operation. He wants to be exonerated. Let him talk and talk and talk, but never let his chatter and his confirmation of his own innocence cloud your vision. You need to be objective, you need witnesses – or he needs witnesses, to be precise.'

'They'll be hard to find, I imagine?'

'Very. He desperately needs proof that he was where he said he was at the time he said he was there. You know the score, Paul. If you need help, contact me. I've already asked SOCO to look at his bike tyres to see if they can be matched to the tracks at the green tent. Take over from me, Paul.'

'It'll be awful if he is the killer, sir . . .'

'Try not to think of it like that. Be open- minded . . . Hadley has given us the go-ahead and he'll expect you to be frank and open with him, and with the other incident room members. And remember he claims never to tell a lie!'

'Sir,' said Larkin with studied emphasis, 'if he is the killer, then he might kill again – if we don't stop him, that is. Will that mean tailing him day and night?'

'I think that will have to be done, Paul. I would approve the necessary application with expenses and overtime payments – but I think we would have to deploy detectives from another area, someone Vic doesn't know.'

'He's likely to find out, though, surely? He'll know if he's being followed or if his house is being watched.'

'It's a risk we'll have to take,' said Pemberton. 'There are some pretty good shadows around.'

'I'll do what I can.'

And so Detective Inspector Paul Larkin found himself with a very distasteful job. But, in the interests of Hadley and the force as a whole, the truth had to be established. As the two senior detectives drove back to their office, they lapsed into silence, each with his own thoughts. By the time of their return to the Rainesbury incident room, the evening news conference was over and there had been no fresh developments since Hadley's request for enquiries – his personal intervention had galvanized the staff of the incident room.

Because of his open request for elimination, some who knew of his past now thought he was a suspect. Others who had worked with him in recent days were firmly of the belief that it was necessary to eliminate him as swiftly as possible – they believed him innocent. Yet more did not express an opinion either way – they would await the results with interest. DC Duncan Young, the HOLMES expert, was now exhorting his team members to search for any reference which might relate to Hadley, perhaps by description, perhaps by implication, perhaps by omission, while those busy with the black motor-cycle printouts were scanning the registration details of all the machines to see if any did match, or could match, the facts already known. For example, were there any registration numbers among them which could conceivably have been misrecorded? Were there any remotely resembling any of the false numbers already known to the police? It was a mammoth task, checking every figure of every number, but it would be done, and it would be done with immense care.

At this stage of the day, around 5.30 p.m., the teams of detectives were making their way back to the incident room from the towns and villages in which they had been making their enquiries. Armed with files full of handwritten statements, they had made notes of any highlights, any potential breakthroughs, any doubtful facts, and these would be aired at tomorrow's morning conference. A lot of the gathered information would be of no value, but all would be stored in the files and programmed into HOLMES. Like so many murder investigations, there was an inordinate amount of information which appeared to be of no practical value. Every snippet was filed, however, in the knowledge that the tiniest of clues could hold the key to the solution.

Most of the staff of the incident room drifted home after six o'clock, those who needed to work overtime being allowed to do so if it was critical to the enquiry, and at six the night shift appeared. This was a skeleton staff who answered the telephones and who undertook whatever non-urgent chores they were given. Before leaving, Pemberton went over to Hadley who was closing his files and asked, 'Vic, any success? Got your statement done?'

'Yes, sir, I think everything's there. It's in the system now, ready for HOLMES and everything else. It's as truthful and complete as I can make it. I just hope our lads can clear me.'

'We'll give it a damned good try,' smiled Pemberton. 'Are you knocking off now?'

'Yes, been pretty shattering really. I'm ready for home!'

'Me too. It's not been a normal day's work by any standards,' sympathized Pemberton. 'But a useful one. You won't be fishing tonight?'

'No. Jean's expecting me in for our evening meal at six; I'll have a wee dram of the best, then put my slippers on and crash out in front of the telly.'

'You do realize', Pemberton decided to remind him, 'that after our chat this afternoon, you'll be getting visits from some of our teams, and so will Jean. It'll be very traumatic – we'll be seeking witnesses, demanding proof of your whereabouts and so on. You know that it won't be easy, so I think she ought to know what's in store.'

'Sure, sir. Aye, I was going to tell her.'

'Fine, well, have a good evening's rest, and we'll see you tomorrow?' It was a question more than a statement.

'Aye, usual time. Eight thirty. I'll be there.'

As Hadley walked out, Pemberton strolled around the busy room seeking Lorraine. But she was not there.

'Anyone seen DC Cashmore?' he asked of anyone who might deign to reply.

'She went over to Langbarugh, sir, with a copy of those black motor-cycle print-outs. They said it was quicker to get a copy of ours than wait for their computer to make its searches, there's half a day's printing there. Too long to fax as well, pages and pages there were. She said to tell you she'd be back by about six thirty.'

'Right, thanks. Well, I'm off. Thanks for today's efforts, everyone.'

And he left for home.

*

Being first into their shared home, Mark set about cooking the evening meal for himself and Lorraine. He decided on a luscious steak grilled to juicy perfection with tomatoes and mushrooms. A simple dish, but exquisite when done properly. It would be followed by Caribbean bananas and cheese and biscuits. He whistled as he worked in the kitchen, enjoying the chore of cooking for someone else, and decided on a pleasing Bordeaux to accompany the meal. He opened the bottle now, a 1986 Camensac St Laurent, allowing it to breathe before consumption.

The smell of the cooking dish began to permeate the kitchen and then, with Lorraine not being back, he settled down with a malt whisky and *The Times* crossword as the meal simmered in the oven.

Then the telephone rang.

'Mark,' boomed the familiar Irish tones of Barry Brennon from Langbarugh. 'Not disturbing you at dinner, I hope?'

'Not yet, Barry, I'm in the middle of a beautiful malt from Scotland . . .'

'You should try the morning dew from the Emerald Isle,' laughed Brennon. 'I'd back it any day against the Scots drams. But I won't keep you long. I rang your office, but they said you'd gone home. That lass of yours, Lorraine, she brought over the motor-bike list, saved us hours of work on the PNC and yards of paper too, I'll be bound.'

'Nice to be of service, Barry,' said Pemberton.

'I'm sorry to ring like this, but it's that Hadley fellow of yours. Your lady detective . . .'

'Lorraine.'

'Yes, Lorraine, well, she said that he's an inspector in your force, in your office in fact, and that he's come forward, asking to be eliminated.'

'Yes, that's true,' and Pemberton provided his friend and colleague with a brief outline of Hadley's recent history and the reason for his presence in the incident room.

'We've been trying to keep an eye on that fellow,' said Brennon. 'I've been quizzing that girl of yours . . .'

'Lorraine.'

'Yes, that's the one. Lorraine. Well, she told me how he'd come forward when he saw his bike number come up on the PNC print-out, but, you see, we've already been trying to keep tabs on him —'

'Without keeping me informed?' snapped Pemberton. 'Why do that?'

'Well, we knew he was a police officer and we knew he was working with you, so we couldn't tell you, could we? Somebody in your department might have warned him – you know what it's like, Mark, investigating police officers. Secrecy and all that. Or the lack of it. I had no choice, I had to keep mum about it.'

'Thanks for trusting me so well, Barry!' Pemberton was not pleased about this. 'But why have you been tailing Hadley?'

'His bike was seen in Turnerville the day Hardisty was shot,' said Brennon ominously. 'It was bearing its correct number plate. The description of the rider fits Hadley – and also fits the description of the man who shot Hardisty outside the King's Head, by which time the bike had false plates. So how could we tell you that without him getting to know? We've had tails on him for a few days. We knew about the Millgate supermarket shooting too, you know. Hadley is our No. 1 suspect, Mark, which is why I'm ringing you now, at home, on a secure line. I would have told you in due course, when we'd got a bit more information into our system, but with Hadley pushing the whole thing forward, I thought you ought to know.'

'We need to have a meeting, Barry, along with my Detective Inspector Paul Larkin whom I've just appointed to the Hadley action.'

'Tonight, then?' suggested Brennon.

'Tonight? Why not,' said Pemberton, eyeing the opened bottle of wine. 'How about coming to my place? I've got some sirloin and a few bottles of good wine, there's enough for us all. I know you can be here within the hour . . .'

'And that girl of yours will be home by seven,' he said. 'I'll arrive about half-past, to give you time to prepare. Lorraine asked me to tell you, she'll be a little bit late, through talking to me, it was. She's a lovely woman, Mark my old friend, you lucky sod . . .'

'See you then,' said Pemberton with a sinking heart. After the day's activities, he wanted, above all else, to be alone with Lorraine.

'I'll be there,' said Brennon. 'And I'll bring some photographs we've taken of your Inspector Hadley.'

'Photographs?' cried Mark Pemberton.

But the line was already dead. Listlessly, Mark went to ring Paul Larkin, and then set about rearranging his routine to cope with the impromptu supper conference.

14

Lorraine returned before Pemberton's guests arrived and apologized for prompting the sudden meeting.

Smiling, Pemberton kissed her and said, 'You were perfectly right in what you did, Lorraine. There'll be other times when we can be alone . . . I've done most of the work, the table's laid, the vegetables are done . . .'

'Give me time for a wash and a change, and I'll finish off,' she smiled.

Detective Inspector Larkin was next; he had walked and bore a bottle of Mantonico di Bianco, a dessert wine. He and Pemberton were sampling a beautiful Glecoyne malt when Detective Superintendent Barry Brennon knocked on the door. He looked rather too small to be a policeman, but his stature was deceptive. Standing at five feet ten inches, he looked around four inches smaller, but no one quite knew why. As a young man, people said he was not tall enough to join the police – and even now many said he did not have that commanding presence that one expects, or used to expect, from British policemen. Well-built, he had a round cheerful pink face with rimless spectacles and a thin thatch of light brown hair, noticeably absent on top. With a ready smile for everyone, his Irish humour was infectious but in spite of his happy-go-lucky image, he was a skilled and tough detective. Some villains who had thought he was a soft touch had learned the contrary to their cost. He produced a bottle of claret and a bunch of flowers for Lorraine, apologizing profusely for arriving in this way for a business chat on what should have been a social occasion.

He carried a black briefcase too, an indication that work lay ahead.

'I would not have come, but it is urgent, it is important and it is highly confidential, much too delicate to discuss in an office. I needn't tell you that walls have ears,' he said.

Mark assured him he was welcome – which was true; Barry was such good company. His first action was to plant a kiss on Lorraine's lips, saying, 'Now I could never get away with that at the office, could I?'

'Would I complain, sir?' she smiled.

'No sirs here – this is your house, here I am Barry, please.'

He refused a whisky aperitif because he had to drive home afterwards, but did accept a tomato juice. Before eating, they all chatted and joked, the two superintendents reminiscing about their lawless days at the police training centre and recalling jokes they had played upon their sergeant-instructors, such as flying policewomen's knickers from the flagpole on passing-out day and somehow managing to get a car on to the middle of the parade ground in spite of the trees and flights of steps which surrounded the square. Larkin and Lorraine listened to their banter, finding it difficult to believe that these two senior police officers had been such mischievous trainees.

The meal, casually presented but beautifully cooked thanks to Lorraine's intervention, was eaten without any chatter about murders and police work, and then, as they reached the cheese, biscuits and coffee stage, Lorraine said, 'You take your coffees into the lounge. I'll do the washing up.'

'I thought you might want to be part of this discussion?' Pemberton said. 'We have no secrets from you.'

'Mark, if this conference is too confidential for the office, it's far too confidential for a detective constable to hear. No, it's better I do the clearing up, then I can't reveal anything that I shouldn't know about.'

'You have a very wise young lady here, Mark,' smiled Brennon as Lorraine went about her work. Taking their coffees into the lounge, Mark offered his colleagues a brandy, which each accepted. Brennon asked for a very small one and finally they settled in the comfort of the lounge as Brennon opened his brief-case. He lifted out an album of black-and-white half-plate size photographs, the front of which bore a red sticker marked 'Secret', and passed them to Mark.

'Before I begin, Mark, take a look at these. Taken by our surveillance team, over the last few days. The dates are on the reverse.'

Several depicted a motor cycle, some with a rider sitting astride while the machine was parked, and some showing the motor cycle parked with no rider in sight. On most of the photographs, the background was, in Pemberton's view, insignificant, generally being street scenes or car-parks, but two were different. One showed the motor cycle parked outside Canter's Café without a rider near it, and another showed it parked outside the King's Head at Turnerville, this time with a figure astride it. The rider was stocky, male if the appearance could be relied upon, and clad in black leathers. The figure sported a crash helmet, also black, with the visor lowered.

Pemberton noted that the registration number on the rear of the motor cycle was the same as Hadley's. He turned over the print to read the date – it was the day that Hardisty was murdered, but the time was much earlier. Hardisty had been shot at 8 p.m. while apparently awaiting a drugs customer, but this photograph had been taken at 5 p.m.

'That's the crucial photograph, Mark.' Brennon sipped at his tiny brandy. 'It puts Hadley at the murder scene, even if it was several hours before the crime was committed. Now, those other photographs – they were taken in Turnerville the same day, but later. The times are all on the reverse.'

'What are you suggesting, Barry?' Mark asked.

'I'm not suggesting anything, Mark. What I am saying is that a man answering Hadley's description was in Turnerville on the day of the murder, that he was seen by police and photographed by them outside the inn in question, and afterwards, he was spotted in other parts of the town, just passing time. The accompanying statement by the police photographer says that the man went into that café just after seven and emerged just after seven thirty. He appeared to be passing time there, Mark. We couldn't get a picture of the fellow inside the café without his helmet on because he was sitting out of our photographer's sight.'

'Are you saying this is Hadley?' Mark put the direct question.
'Who else could it be?' countered Brennon.
'Someone using his bike?'
'It's possible,' Brennon agreed in his rich brogue. 'But, Mark, we know it was him. How did you think we were able to get those pictures?'
'That was my next question, Barry. A tip-off?'
'Of sorts.'
'But', cried Mark, 'who would want to tip off Langbarugh police about a sick police inspector motor cycling in their patch?'
'A good question, Mark. Yes, we got a tip-off, but not about him visiting that area. After the first murder, Pearle that is, one of our patrol constables noted the bike stooging about the town, doing nothing in particular. He wasn't able to stop the bike and quiz the rider but he did note the number. Remember we were looking for a black motor bike in connection with the Pearle shooting – and he had found one. He passed the details to the murder room, simply because the bike had been seen hanging around town, apparently not going anywhere in particular. We checked the number and turned up Hadley's name – not realizing at that time, I might add, that he was a police officer, let alone that he was working with you. We put a team on to him, with orders not to quiz him or let him know he was being tailed. We wanted to find out who this guy was, what he was doing on our patch and whether he could be linked to the murder – and imagine our surprise when we discovered he was riding that machine into your police station yard. Then, of course, we discovered he was an inspector – and later, we found out he had a dubious record of shooting a civilian in questionable circumstances, and so we concentrated a lot of energy on him. On the day of the Hardisty murder, Hadley did ride his motor bike from his home into Turnerville – we were waiting, we managed to get these pictures. Since identifying him, we have kept this news secret – secret from you because we had to consider that if Hadley was guilty of murder, then he might have an accomplice working with him, in your department. We needed to be sure of our facts before questioning him about the murders – both of them. He has not been questioned yet, by the way.'

'Barry, if he was being tailed and photographed like this, why didn't you get a picture of him right outside the pub at the material time? You might even have prevented a murder.'

'He lost us, Mark. I'm not sure whether it was deliberate or not. After half-seven, he accelerated through the suburbs – he seemed to know his way around the back streets, short cuts and how to avoid cul-de-sacs. The result was that he lost the tail we'd put on him.'

'Could he have known he was being tailed?' asked Larkin.

'It's always possible, Paul, but our men felt not. They were pretty confident he hadn't spotted them.'

'So are you saying he returned to the King's Head and shot Hardisty?' Mark pressed his friend.

'I'm saying that a thick-set man riding a black motor cycle with similarities to the one owned by Hadley arrived outside the King's Head and shot Hardisty,' Brennon said. 'You must admit it all looks very sinister, very sinister indeed.'

'If what you are saying is true, Barry, your men slipped up. If this fellow was hanging around waiting to despatch Hardisty, the gun would have been in one of his panniers, surely? You could have caught the bastard red-handed, we'd have had the necessary evidence, he could have been arrested.'

'That's one of the problems, Mark. We couldn't search his leathers without revealing ourselves and our purpose, but there was no gun in the panniers. Our men managed to search them while the bike was left in one of the car-parks – making sure Hadley was far enough away not to see them do it. If he was the killer, he might have hidden the gun somewhere, going to retrieve it at the very last minute. He had time to do that in the half-hour after leaving the café.'

'Taking care not to have the gun in his possession in case he was stopped?' suggested Larkin.

'That's all very feasible,' agreed Brennon. 'Now, if Hadley is the killer, he will know every trick in the book – which is why we have not yet interviewed him. With his experience, we'll have to have every scrap of evidence to hand before we can nail him. We can't risk him getting away with it on a technicality or through lack of evidence.'

'If he is our killer, Barry, he could kill again,' Pemberton reminded them.

'We have him under surveillance, Mark. I want you to know that – which is another reason for this visit. Not twenty-four hours a day, but if he goes out to kill somebody, we'll be there to stop him.'

'In that case, you'll know we haven't been tailing him, we've never had any reason. The only thing I know about his off-duty moments is that he goes fishing,' Mark Pemberton confessed.

'He tells people he goes fishing, Mark, he tells you he goes fishing. Who can prove that? He can't. Certainly, he does go fishing sometimes, but at other times he takes off on that bike of his. We've tailed him to umpteen places over the past few weeks – since Pearle's murder in fact – always on the bike, always dressed in black and always alone.'

'But none of this proves he is the man we're seeking,' Mark said. 'There is absolutely no proof that he is the murderer, Barry. There's suspicion, I grant you that, but proof? Not a scrap! We can't prove he had anything to do with either of your deaths, Barry. What about our Green Tent murder? Were your men tailing him then?'

'No, we had knocked off for the night. He was seen to go fishing, he was observed walking beside the river with his tackle, that would be around eight in the evening, after which our men left. That would be at nine o'clock that evening. Your murder was four hours later, I believe? In the early hours?'

'True – and he was fishing at the time, he told me so. So you were conducting a surveillance in our area without our knowledge? Our Chief'll blow his top if he finds out.'

'Our Chief did tell him.'

'He never told me.' Mark felt slightly hurt at this lack of trust.

'How could he, Mark? It had to be kept secret, known only to those at the top, the very top. So, now we've provided you with this information – and you may keep those photographs, plus a chronological list of our sightings and observations.' He pulled another grey folder from his briefcase which he passed to Mark. 'What do we do next? What's our next step, Mark? Arrest and interrogation? More observations? Do we risk another murder?'

'He did volunteer to be questioned for elimination,' Mark reminded his friend.

'I know, Mark, but I ask myself why? What prompted him to step forward and offer himself for sacrifice?'

'His bike was listed on the PNC print-out,' smiled Larkin.

'Maybe there is more to his decision,' suggested Brennon.

'A belief in his own innocence?' returned Pemberton. 'So, Barry, we need to clear this up very soon. Hadley will have to be questioned about that trip to Turnerville. I don't think we should let him know he was followed or that we have evidence of his presence in the town; if he denies he was there, then we know he is lying and if he does lie, then we go for his throat, as they say. We'll need to make him account for every minute of every day since Pearle was shot, and if necessary we'll have to search his house and belongings. Remember, he does own shotguns and section one firearms. He's got all the necessary paperwork for them but he's not daft enough to leave the murder weapon where it can be found.'

'But we don't know if he's got a sawn-off shotgun, do we?' Brennon said. 'And our swift search of his bike didn't find one.'

'The murder weapon hasn't been found in your patch, then?' Mark asked.

'No, that's one big stumbling block for us all. But if the killer is Hadley, then he'll know how important it is never to let the police get their hands on the murder weapon. And the same gun was used for all the killings, remember.'

They talked through the crimes, each highlighting similarities and differences, and then Mark said, 'You said you were familiar with the Millgate supermarket raid, Barry?'

'Only what I read in some of those bloody awful tabloid papers, and what inter-force gossip has spread around. I know Hadley was at the centre of that one, I had that in mind when all this bother developed. I know they said he shot an innocent bystander and that the fellow's family have never let the case die down.'

'I went to the scene, Barry, before these murders began, as it happens. I did so because the Chief transferred Hadley to my department. I wanted to see where he had killed his innocent bystander,' and Mark went on to outline his views on that sorry episode. From memory, he recounted most of the matters which had been raised in the press and at the various enquiries, while Larkin and Brennon listened with deep interest. Mark gave due emphasis to Hadley's mental condition and when he had finished, Brennon said:

'So another unconvicted man was executed, eh?' He spoke slowly. 'That makes Newton, Pearle, Scott and Hardisty – with reservations because Hardisty is a convicted drugs dealer.'

'There is a theme running through these killings, Barry. It all suggests a vigilante-type campaign to execute those who consider themselves above the law. The other link is that the victims are all male,' Mark added.

'You're not suggesting a female vigilante, are you? On a motor bike? With a shotgun?' laughed Larkin.

'It's not impossible,' said Pemberton. 'There's some fierce feminists around. Big woman, big bike, big ideas . . . I know some women who could perform that kind of murder without any trouble.'

'Mark, my son, we are going around in circles now, we're getting nowhere at all, but if we look at things closely, your man Hadley is in the middle of all the circles. I think we should have him in for interrogation.'

'Your place or mine?'

'We three together, Mark. If Hadley has volunteered to be quizzed, then it would appear normal if two senior officers from his own force conducted the interview with one from the other participating force. I think the time has come for us to find out just what this man's been doing.'

15

Pemberton and Brennon decided that Hadley should be interviewed the following day. Larkin was sworn to secrecy; the job would be done discreetly so that none of the other detectives would be aware of Brennon's interest in the officer formerly in charge of the firearms unit. With Hadley making it known among his colleagues that he wished to be eliminated from the enquiry, Pemberton's part would not be regarded as unusual. On the other hand, if senior detectives from two separate forces investigating a series of killings were involved in what had all the appearances of a formal interview, then any detective with an atom of common sense would know that something more serious was afoot. And if the entire staff of the murder room became aware that Hadley was in the frame as a suspect, then that news might filter into the realms of the newspapers and other media – and thus to Brian Newton and his family. Nowhere is totally secure. The resultant speculation, fuelled by a resurrection of Hadley's part in the Millgate supermarket death, would produce a furore and there'd be well-publicized speculation that the police service was murdering suspects or introducing its own death penalty for offenders. There was no doubt that the Newton family would make huge capital out of that. The outcome for the police service as a whole would be horrendous and damage to the course of the current investigations might be equally disastrous. It was therefore vital that this interview was treated with the utmost secrecy.

Once the decision had been made, Brennon and Larkin left for home while Pemberton settled down with the papers and copies of the photographs he had been left for perusal. He helped himself to a sizeable brandy and poured a calvados for Lorraine, who came to join him on the settee.

'It looks serious for poor old Hadley,' he said as she settled at his side and curled her long legs beneath her.

'I don't want to know, Mark. What transpired between you two and Mr Brennon is confidential – I mustn't be told. In fact, I'd rather not be told.'

He lapsed into a silence, deep in thought; he was extremely worried about the consequences if Hadley was shown to be the killer, but he knew he must do his job without fear or favour. To accuse Hadley would be wrong, but to ignore the fact that he might be guilty was equally wrong. To interview him would be infinitely more difficult than questioning a civilian suspect. Hadley knew too much about the system – if he was the killer, it would be a very difficult task, probably an impossible one, to persuade him to admit the crimes. Tomorrow, God willing, the truth might be revealed.

'Thanks for clearing up.' He kissed Lorraine as he turned to more mundane matters. 'The meal was lovely.'

'It was nice to share it.' She snuggled closer to him and rested her head on his shoulder. 'We should hold some dinner parties, invite people in.'

'Not police officers though?' He grinned. 'We shouldn't have to talk shop while we're relaxing.'

'Right, how about some of your new rambling friends?'

'Great idea. Once we get this murder enquiry over, we'll do that!'

'Then let's make sure we do,' she said.

She began to chatter about the sort of meal she would like to produce, listing some of the dishes she favoured – Italian, French, Greek – but his mind was wandering. He could not avoid thinking about Vic Hadley. Lorraine realized what he was doing and poked him in the ribs with her elbow.

'You're not listening!' she cried. 'You're thinking about Vic Hadley, I'll bet. Come along, Mark Pemberton. Bedtime. I'm sure I can do something that'll take your mind off murders and mayhem!'

Next morning, news from the forensic lab was not encouraging. A telephone call was received by Sergeant Thornton in Scenes of Crime to the effect that the laboratory experts had examined the casts of the tyre marks found at the murder scene, and had compared them in considerable detail with the tyres of Hadley's machine. Sadly, the marks left in the soft earth were not sufficiently well defined for the scientists to state categorically that they had been made by Hadley's motor cycle. They did say, however, that the treads of his tyres *could* have made the marks because they were of the same design and pattern as the marks in the ground, but the necessary distinguishing elements were absent. Small cuts in the rubber, indentations in the threads, general wear and tear – all these individual identifying characteristics were lacking in definition in the heavy earth and the plaster casts had not perpetuated them. In other words, the evidence from the tyre-mark casts was inconclusive.

Likewise, the tyres of Hadley's machine had been closely examined and no soil of the type which formed the base of the site near the green tent was found in the tread. Other deposits were located upon the tyres but none matched the control sample taken from the scene of the Green Tent death. On these two counts, therefore, the tests were inconclusive. The forensic experts would not and could not state categorically that Hadley's machine had made those marks – but likewise, they could not say it had not made them. Pemberton knew that their evidence could be presented to a court merely as circumstantial and not as real evidence and that any good defence counsel would easily convince a jury of its uselessness. Quite simply, there must be hundreds of motor bikes bearing identical tyres, any one of which could have made those tyre tracks. They provided not a shred of evidence against Hadley, neither did they prove his innocence. For the Scenes of Crime Department, the outcome was something of a disappointment.

Mark, having visited Fell's motor-cycle shop in Scarborough, had a list of some purchasers of motor cycles which had been fitted with identical tyres and they were currently being interviewed one by one, but the inconclusive nature of the detail in the tread marks found in the soil would be unable to link them with any particular machine. Nonetheless, all owners of bikes with Masseria Italian tyres would be interviewed. Another factor was that there were no tyre marks at the scenes of either Pearle's or Hardisty's death. The lab said that a full written report would be sent in confirmation.

Armed with this news, Detective Sergeant Thornton went to see Pemberton and arrived prior to the morning conference of detectives. Pemberton listened and thanked Thornton, saying he would announce these findings at the conference – but without linking them to Hadley. He would simply say that the tread marks found at the scene lacked the necessary identifying characteristics for them to be linked to any particular motor cycle. He would ensure that no details of the tyres, such as size and the name of the maker, would be released to the press because if the killer read the piece, he would simply refit tyres of a different kind or cut or mark his tyres in some way that would have shown on the casts. It might yet be possible that a bike with such tyres was found to have soil deposits within the deeper treads. One could always live in hope.

For Mark Pemberton, therefore, this was another piece of circumstantial evidence which, when added to the others, continued to maintain Hadley as a prime suspect. One difficulty, from Hadley's own point of view, would be the problem of establishing an alibi to counter even this slenderest of evidence. If the police could not prove he had committed one or more of the murders, could he prove that he hadn't? He needed alibi witnesses and seemed to have none.

The morning conference of detectives produced little new material. Owners of all black motor cycles were being traced and interviewed, particularly those fitted with Masseria tyres. At least three of the machines had been stolen and not recovered – they could be anywhere. Garages were being visited to see if anyone had recently been in to acquire a new number plate for a motor cycle of any kind, and motor-cycle outfitters were being visited in an attempt to identify the maker of the black suit and crash helmet.

A telephone call from Langbarugh police indicated that their enquiries were proceeding along similar, unfruitful lines and that no links, criminal or otherwise, had been established between the three victims.

Unable to produce any further news for the press conference which followed, Pemberton had to state that no significant progress had been made, that enquiries were continuing in an attempt to trace the owner of the black motor cycle seen at the scene of each murder, and that the sawn-off shotgun or shotguns used had not been found. No arrests had been made; no one was in custody helping the police with their enquiries. This final sentence enabled the press to continue to speculate upon the crimes – once a person was charged, or about to be charged, then reporting of the case became restricted. Pemberton was happy that proper speculation and publicity was given: this was always likely to persuade reluctant witnesses to come forward.

For Pemberton, though, the next and most distasteful duty was to interview Inspector Hadley.

With Hadley's consent, it was decided that the most appropriate venue was Hadley's home. Other locations had been considered but Pemberton said that, as the officer in charge of Hadley and as the man who had to submit regular reports upon his progress, it was perfectly logical that he should visit Hadley at home. Nothing sinister could be read into that meeting, should it be witnessed by others. And Pemberton was anxious that Hadley's name be kept from the press. Hadley knew the reason for that. The interview would be this afternoon.

During the morning, Pemberton invited Hadley into his office, closed the door and mentioned that Detective Superintendent Brannon from Langbarugh also wanted to talk to him. At that news, he saw the look of concern in Hadley's dark eyes.

'Langbarugh, sir? What do they want?'

Some time beforehand, Pemberton had formulated an answer to that inevitable question.

'You know as well as me, Vic, that there've been two murders in Langbarugh in addition to ours. The two incident rooms are liaising over these killings and Langbarugh are as anxious as we are to trace the black motor bike. We want to eliminate you from all the enquiries.'

Hadley said nothing; he merely gazed at Mark with his dark brown eyes as he continued. 'We want to conduct the interviews discreetly, hence our visit to your home after work. Mr Brennon has asked if he can talk to you too, to avoid the need for another visit. He might have information that I do not have.'

'You mean I'm a bloody suspect, sir? I know the language, remember. I know you let suspects believe you are interviewing them for elimination purposes, just to get them talking.'

'You're no more a suspect than anyone else, Vic. It was you who wanted to be eliminated, remember? That was your request.'

'I'll tell you now that I haven't done those murders, sir. Whatever happens, whatever evidence you have, it wasn't me. I want you to know that. I want you to believe that. You have to believe me, sir. I am telling the truth, so God help me!'

'Vic, I am a senior detective, and I must be guided by the evidence which presents itself. I'll be honest with you, I have no evidence which would convince me that you are the killer. On the other hand, you are in the firing line because of your bike, your choice of riding gear, the tyres on the bike and your recent movements.'

'I'm also a suspect because I shot Newton, aren't I? You still believe I shot him in cold blood, you and the rest of them. I've still got his bloody family on my back, sending me reminders, making life a bloody misery . . .'

'That has no bearing on these murders, Vic – it's over and done with.'

'It bloody well isn't. I'm like a convicted man, aren't I? Just as old cons are always being interviewed as suspect, you'll think of me every time a murder occurs!'

'Vic, that's not true. The Millgate incident is finished, over.'

'Suppose I say nothing? That'll fox you lot – but it'll make you dig deeper, won't it? I know how the CID operate, remember.'

'Saying nothing is your entitlement, Vic.'

'All right, I'll talk, but it's because I'm innocent, sir, because I want to clear myself . . . I just hope I can do that . . . God, this is awful, isn't it? I was just getting over that bloody carry-on with Millgate and now this. Why can't people believe what I say? They never have . . . never . . . and I always tell the truth, sir, always. Ever since I was a kid. I think somebody's got it in for me, you know.'

'What do you mean, Vic? Got it in for you?'

'I don't know what I mean, do I? God, I wish I did! Whoever it is, somebody's gunning for me . . . following me . . . I've been followed lately . . . Did you know that? It'll be those bloody Newtons . . . trying to unsettle me! What a bloody life, having to live like this, under suspicion all the time, watching my back, worrying about my wife and home, having to explain myself when other killings occur . . . me, an innocent man, a policeman. This is wrong, sir. Look, I just want to get on with my life and my job, without any hassle . . .'

'Three o'clock, Vic? Would that be all right?'

'I was going fishing, but I'll give it a miss.'

'I'll see you then, Vic. And thanks.'

Pemberton and Larkin arrived outside Hadley's smart semi-detached home a few minutes before three o'clock and decided to await Brennon. The Irishman arrived a couple of minutes later and emerged from his car with a briefcase. Pemberton left his car to greet his old friend.

'He's expecting us, is he?' Brennon asked.

'He is,' said Pemberton. 'But he's not very happy about your involvement.'

'At least we gave him fair warning,' said Brennon. 'Usually when I interview suspects, I turn up without warning. Catch 'em by surprise, that's my motto. It works, most of the time.'

They were ushered into the lounge by Mrs Hadley, an unsmiling woman with greying hair, but with a round, healthy-looking face.

'I'll call Vic,' she said. 'He's down the garden, in his shed, repairing some fishing tackle. You go in and find a seat, he won't be long. Then I'll bring some tea for you.'

When she had gone, Brennon said, 'I think we should have gone to have a look at that fishing tackle shed.' He grinned.

'Later, perhaps? There's hardly any point now. If he was going to remove anything that might have interested us, he's had ample opportunity,' suggested Pemberton but then Vic Hadley arrived, still dressed in his untidy brown sweater, brown corduroys and heavy brown shoes.

Pemberton rose to his feet. 'Vic, thanks for letting us come and talk. This is Detective Superintendent Brennon from Langbarugh.'

Hadley nodded but made no effort to shake hands, then sat down in an easy chair, facing his inquisitors. He had a green-backed book in his hands, a diary, and also his official police notebook.

'Right,' he said. 'I'm ready.'

16

Pemberton began, with DI Larkin taking notes.

'Vic, this is an interview for elimination purposes, a witness interview. There is no tape recording, it is not being done under PACE regulations. Now, you've been working with us on the current murder enquiry, and that means you've also got a good knowledge of the Langbarugh cases. You know the dates, times and places the murders occurred, and you know both police forces are looking for a black motor bike which is similar to yours in colour, design and registration details. We are seeking a man who dresses in motor-cycling gear, black gear. You know that tyre marks found at the Green Tent murder scene were from the same make and type as yours, with the same tread pattern. You also know, and I must tell you, that you are not obliged to say anything unless you wish to do so, but I know that you wish to be eliminated from our enquiries, Vic, and that means you'll need to explain your whereabouts at the material times.'

'I was fishing,' he said. 'I'm a keen fisherman, always have been.'

'On every occasion there was a murder, then, you were fishing? At the material times? Alone?'

'Yes, quite alone, even when Scott was killed. No witnesses, Mr Pemberton. Well, apart from ramblers and dog walkers and such, sometimes pottering past me along the river bank. I've no idea who they were and whether they noticed me. You know I always tell the truth. I have no witnesses I can call, gentlemen. None at all.'

'Did you perhaps go somewhere else?' asked Pemberton. 'In addition to fishing? Before or after? On your motor bike?'

'Since I went down with stress, I've hardly been anywhere. I used to go with Jean to the supermarket, shopping in town, out for a meal maybe and so on. Not any more, not even since moving to Rainesbury. My wife does the shopping, alone – I don't go with her, not since my face got splashed all over the tabloids. I try to keep away from crowded places where folks'll recognize me. If any of the Newton clan see me, they always take the opportunity for unpleasantness, name-calling, spitting in my face, that sort of thing. Brian never misses a chance to humiliate me if he sees me in a public place – he says he'll get me one day. Too many other folks know me from those pictures in the papers and some were pretty bloody nasty in the things they said and did. They all said Newton was innocent when I knew he was raiding that bloody van and about to shoot Swanson. It's no good arguing, sir, not with folks like that. They've got closed minds. So I keep my head down now, out of circulation I am.'

'The motor bike enables you to be anonymous though?' said Pemberton. 'With your visor down, no one can recognize you. You ride it a lot?'

'Right, I do get about. I prefer the bike to the car. Even in a car, folks can recognize me, but I don't go riding around just for the hell of it. I go to work on the bike, I use it for leisure trips and I use it to get to the river bank when I go fishing. I park it under the railway bridge and walk the rest of the way, half a mile or so.'

'So you've never ridden it to Middlesbrough or to Turnerville?' put in Brennon. 'Or to Pearle's place?'

'Yes, I have been to Turnerville, Middlesbrough and elsewhere. There's no secret in that. I like touring. But look, gentlemen, I know the suspect bike's like mine and I know the tyre marks at the green tent were similar to mine. But it wasn't me. That's the truth. Can you believe me? What else can I say?'

By this stage, Brennon was opening his briefcase and removing his album of photographs. He passed the entire album to Hadley, saying, 'These photographs were taken by our surveillance unit, Inspector. Turnerville is the location. You said you've been there. It's a black motor bike in the photos, just like yours, Inspector – even the number plate is the same as yours. I'd say it was your bike.'

As Larkin scribbled his notes, the burly inspector studied each one carefully, turning them over to note the date, time and place they had been taken, and said, 'You bastards were trailing me. I thought it was the Newtons . . . but that's right, that is my bike. That's me. I won't deny that. Why should I? I've no reason to deny it.'

'You know where these were taken, Inspector?' continued Brennon in his soft Irish brogue.

'Turnerville, like you said,' said Hadley. 'I recognize some of the locations. I did have a ride over there recently – it was the day that Hardisty was killed.'

'Can I ask why you were there?' Brennon was studying Hadley's body language, watching his eyes and his hands.

Hadley lifted a book from the floor; it was his diary.

'I keep a daily diary, gentlemen, as well as my official police notebook. The diary records my off-duty movements,' and he turned over the pages until he arrived at the date in question. Then he passed the diary to Brennon for him to examine. 'If you want proof, this might help. Contemporaneous records and all that. I went to Turnerville to buy some fishing tackle,' he said slowly. 'I wanted a new reel and some lines; there's a very good tackle shop in Church Road. I was uncertain which day to go, kept putting it off because I didn't fancy the trip, and then I got a call from a chap calling himself Lowe. A phone call. He said he had some information about the Millgate supermarket raid which would interest me, if I cared to meet him. God knows how he found me, I'm ex-directory. I told him I was finished with Millgate, I didn't want to talk about it, it was all over so far as I was concerned. But he said it was important and that he lived in Middlesbrough and that he could tell me about Newton. I know Newton was a villain, you see, and I thought this chap might furnish me with some proof of his involvement, just to settle things in my mind – he said he'd read all about me in the papers at the time and believed my side of things. He said he would tell me about Newton's past, something that would be useful, and so I said I was going to Turnerville that day. He suggested meeting there. He mentioned a café. Canter's Café. I was happy to go along with that because it was a public place – you never know whether that sort of call is a set-up of some kind. Anyway, Lowe said he'd be there at seven o'clock and would recognize me. That afternoon, I went on my motor bike but when I got there, I found I'd forgotten to take my wallet. Since I became stressed, I do things like that. Forget things. I forget where I put the car keys or my shoes or my pens and pencils . . . So when I got to Turnerville, I had no cheque book, credit cards or money, other than a wee bit of loose cash in my pockets, and that meant I couldn't buy my reel. I didn't fancy spending time in the shop when I had no money to spend. I only had enough cash for a coffee and a bun, and so, rather than ride all the way home and go back again later to meet Lowe, I hung around the town until my time to meet him. Those pictures are of me doing that, gentlemen, hanging around, waiting with nowhere to go. I went to the café as arranged, but Lowe never turned up. I've not heard from him since and I don't know the chap. His name means sod-all to me.'

'A set-up, Inspector?' asked Brennon.

'I get the feeling I am being set up for something, sir – people following me, those bloody Newtons never off my back, being watched. At least, I thought it was them. It might have been your shadows, but the Newtons have been at it for ages. Your lot might have frightened them off, eh? That'd be a laugh! But they'll be back. They want to pay me back for killing Joss . . . they're like that, evil, vindictive bastards, especially Big Brother Brian. He hates my guts and never misses a chance to say so.'

'So then what did you do, Inspector?' Brennon continued in his formal voice, not responding to Hadley's comments.

'I had a coffee and a bun and came home.'

'And at home, what did you do?'

'Came in, had something to eat, then went out. Fishing.'

'And your wife, Jean, she will verify that?'

'No, she'd gone to the supermarket, late night shopping. She'd left a note, my tea was in the fridge, ready to put in the microwave. I got back about eleven, I think – she was home by then. We had a drink of cocoa, talked a bit about our days and went to bed.'

'And you can produce no witnesses to any of your excursions from home, Inspector?'

'None of my own, sir. Your lot were witnesses surely, Mr Brennon, if they were taking photographs of me?'

'Yes, we were keeping tabs on you. I'll admit that – it was without Mr Pemberton's knowledge, I ought to add. It was because of the bike. After the Pearle murder, we logged the number of every black motor bike we saw, and an alert uniform constable noticed your bike in Middlesbrough one day. He couldn't stop you to quiz you, but took your number . . . We traced it to you, not realizing you were a police officer at the time, and decided to put you under surveillance. Then we found out who you were and where you were working, hence my liaison with Mr Pemberton. And hence this chat.'

'There were people shadowing me before the Pearle job, sir. But your men'll know I was not at the scenes of any of those crimes at the material times!'

'No, I'm sorry to say that isn't the case. You were not under twenty-four hour surveillance, Mr Hadley. The killings happened when our teams were not with you. Can I ask if you were aware that we, the police, had you under our surveillance?'

There was a long pause as the implication of this was studied by Hadley, who then said, 'The short answer to that is no. Not you, not the police. Every time I thought I was being followed, I reckoned it was Newton's mob, out for revenge, waiting to do something to me. That's part of the reason for my motor-bike outings, to lead them away from home, to puzzle them. I tried to lose them on occasions, thinking it was the Newtons. Look, both of you. I shot Joss Newton, I admitted that, and I did it to save a life. I have shot and killed a man but I am not a murderer. I did not kill any of those three men. I want to clear my name, get myself off the bloody hook yet again, but how can I do that without witnesses?'

His voice was weak now, without any of its former and usual force, and Pemberton wondered if this was symptomatic of his condition.

'Can I keep your diary, Inspector? And your official pocket-book?' asked Brennon. 'We can use them to check your movements against our records. And can I come back to you if there are any queries?'

'Sure, yes, I hope it'll convince you that I'm telling the truth. That's why I've always kept notes, to back up my words in case I was being set up for something. But if somebody *is* setting me up, I want to be in a position to fight back.'

Pemberton had to continue, even though this visit might be pushing Hadley too close to his limit of current blighted mental patience or endurance.

'Your firearms, Vic. We need to inspect them.'

'I knew you would have to do that. They're all secure and kept locked as the certificates specify. Come along, they're in the spare bedroom.'

It was a pointless exercise really – if Hadley was the killer, he would never keep the sawn-off shotgun in his house – but the search had to be done. In the bedroom, whose windows and doors were reinforced, they found Hadley's collection of weapons. There were three shotguns, two of which were twelve-bores. One was a side-by-side, the other an over-and-under. The third was a single-barrel .410 and all were locked in one cabinet. As expected, none had a shortened barrel. Shortening the barrels of shotguns was illegal anyway; a sawn-off shotgun was hardly the sort of thing a police officer would keep in the house. His other weapons included two .22 BSA rifles, a .303 military rifle, a lightweight 9mm Steyr carbine rifle, two service Special

.38 revolvers and a Star .45 automatic pistol. His shotgun certificate and his firearms certificate were lying on a cabinet in the bedroom. The two superintendents checked the documents to see that he was in legal custody of these weapons. There was also an array of cups and shields on shelves which adorned the walls.

'Quite an armoury, Vic,' commented Pemberton.

'Shooting was my hobby, sir. Lawneswick Rifle Club, the County Clay Pigeon Shooting Association, the force rifle team, pistol championships . . . I was the force small arms champion for five successive years and I am allowed to hold these weapons because of my membership of various clubs.'

'You're very accustomed to handling guns, then?' said Brennon. 'Quite a good shot too, eh?'

'The best, sir, when I was younger. Winner of all sorts of trophies. They were all legitimate targets, though, not people,' he added wryly.

'You've not been competition shooting lately, then?' Pemberton put to him. 'You didn't mention this as part of your present activities?'

'No, not since Millgate, sir. I've not touched a gun of any kind since then. To be honest, I'm not sure I want to handle a firearm again.'

'But you've kept all this arsenal?' pointed out Brennon.

'I'm keeping them until my certificates are due for renewal, then I'll make a decision whether or not to part with them. If I decide to give up competition and game shooting all together, I'll either sell the weapons or surrender them. I might change my mind when I'm fully fit again. If I do give up guns, then it'll mean giving up my post with the firearms unit.'

'It's easy enough to obtain a gun on the streets, isn't it?' Brennon changed the subject. 'I mean, Inspector, if a villain wants to get himself tooled up, he can buy himself a gun, a revolver, pistol, sawn-off shotgun or anything he wants, for a few quid paid to the right person.'

'No problem, sir. There's a good trade in firearms, especially revolvers and pistols. Shotguns too.'

'Sawn-off shotguns?'

'Always in demand by villains, bank raiders and the like. There's people who'll shorten the barrels and reduce the stock to a handgun grip, sure, sir. But I don't know who they are, that's a matter for CID.'

Pemberton knew that his teams were attempting to interview all those who dealt in this illegal aspect of shotgun work.

They remained in the room for a while as Hadley unlocked the cabinets and allowed the detectives to handle the weapons. Each made a cursory check, matching their numbers against the certificates and examining them visually for signs of recent use. Pemberton was satisfied none had been used for the murders – but the shotguns, even though their barrels had not been shortened, would have to be examined by the ballistics specialists to clear them. Hadley understood and readily agreed – proof that his guns had not been used was a point in his defence. He handed over both twelve-bores against a receipt from Pemberton and they returned to the lounge.

Brennon picked up the diary and said, 'I think that's all for the time being, Inspector. Thank you for being so co-operative.'

'It's in my own interest,' said Hadley.

'You really must get some witnesses to your movements, Vic,' said Pemberton. 'You know how important that is.'

'Sure, but how can I find them if there weren't any? Now, sir,' he addressed Pemberton, 'what about my work? You won't want me in the office now, surely? A murder suspect?'

'You are not a suspect, Vic! I want to emphasize that. You're a witness, one of many who've been interviewed. I have no intention of banning you from the office, nor do I intend to suspend you from work for further investigation, certainly not on the evidence we have so far. There is nothing to implicate you other than some pieces of circumstantial evidence. I have to be very careful how I interpret that evidence. So come to work as usual in the morning. No one in the office apart from ourselves knows of our visit today, and we do need your help in finding the killer of Pearle, Scott and Hardisty.'

'I will not be arranging any more surveillance of you and your movements, Inspector,' said Brennon. 'I'm not saying I entirely accept your reason for being in Turnerville that day, but at least you were honest enough to admit you were there.'

'A good job I did admit it,' and Hadley permitted himself a gentle chuckle. 'That's the value of not telling lies, not even wee ones. Now if I'd denied it, you'd have been down on me like the proverbial ton of bricks.'

'So what are you going to do with yourself this afternoon?' asked Pemberton in a friendly tone.

'I'm going fishing,' said Hadley.

And so Pemberton, Brennon and Larkin left Hadley's house carrying two shotguns and his personal diary, all of which would be subjected to some very close scrutiny. Pemberton and Larkin drove away in one car with Brennon in another, but both vehicles eased to a halt about half a mile away.

'So,' said Brennon, after he had climbed into Pemberton's rear seat. 'What did you make of that, gentlemen?'

'He's either very clever or very honest,' said Larkin. 'I think he knew that we had proof of his visit to Turnerville that day, but I thought his story sounded a bit thin. That tale about the fishing tackle shop and a call from a man called Lowe sounded like fiction to me. There is a fishing tackle shop in Church Lane, I know it, but the tale about Lowe sounded a bit contrived, a bit too convenient. You'll note there's no way we can check whether or not Lowe exists.'

'I must admit I wasn't convinced,' Pemberton had to admit. 'What did have a ring of truth was the fact that he admitted being in Turnerville on the day of the murder. But his movements after leaving the café are not known – your men lost him, eh? Do you think he lost them deliberately?'

'I'm sure he did, but he did provide us with a reason,' said Brennon. 'Harassment by the Newton clan. Is he paranoid about them, I wonder? But whatever his motives, he lost his tail quite deliberately. And once he had lost the tail, he was in a position to carry out his intended purpose – the death of young Hardisty.'

'If that's true, it was a risky thing to do,' said Larkin. 'It smacks either of rank stupidity or total faith in his ability to avoid being seen. I can't imagine someone going out to commit a murder after losing a tail like he did.'

'It's a scenario we can't ignore, especially if he did not suspect it was a police tail,' admitted Brennon. 'But I must admit I don't have any gut feeling about Hadley. You know, Mark, when you meet some killers, you know straight away whether or not they're guilty, even though they persist in their innocence and produce watertight alibis. But I didn't get any feeling about Hadley, one way or the other. I would never place a bet on his guilt or innocence, and it's that that makes me think he is a mighty clever man, Mark. Too clever perhaps for the likes of us?'

'No crook is too clever for us, Barry. If Hadley is guilty, we'll nail him.'

'Do you think I was right to drop the surveillance teams?'

'Only because he knew he was being followed, whoever he thought it was. If he is guilty, he's likely to go out and kill another person, especially if he's not being followed.'

'I find that a very worrying thought,' admitted Brennon. 'But I don't think any surveillance unit could get close to him now.'

'I could always recruit from another force, Barry, bring some strangers in to monitor his movements?'

'I think that would be wise. Imagine the situation if another murder occurred while we suspected Hadley and didn't have him targeted!'

'One other point arises, Barry,' said Pemberton. 'In checking the intelligence records of your victims, Pearle and Hardisty, did you find that Hadley was involved in any way with them? You know, as arresting officer in our patch, court officer if they were at any of our courts, that sort of thing.'

'No, I checked that. Apart from Hadley's arrest of Pearle years ago, there are no common factors, Mark, other than that they were villains, male villains, who were apparently operating heedless of the law.'

'We still need to find out who would know that, don't we? Who would know they were criminals who had not been caught? I get the gut feeling there's some kind of police input into all this. I don't think the deaths are pure chance,' Pemberton stated.

'I agree. Some serial killers do kill indiscriminately, but this smacks of some inside knowledge, Mark. Somebody settling scores, protecting the public from villains, acting as judge and jury. We can't escape the fact that we might be looking for a police officer who's gone wrong. Or an ex-police officer.'

'We're going round in circles again, Barry,' said Pemberton. 'Well, I must return to my incident room to continue our fruitless search. But I've another job for you now, Paul.'

'Sir?' asked Larkin.

'Delve into Hadley's background, will you? We haven't finished with him yet. Start with his file in Personnel – find out what he did before joining the force, jobs, hobbies, general background.'

'Yes, sir,' acknowledged Paul Larkin.

'Great idea,' said Brennon, leaving Mark's car. 'Keep in touch.'

'And you,' said Pemberton, starting his engine.

17

Gaining access to the personal records of police officers is almost as difficult as stealing the Crown Jewels. The individual files of all personnel are kept under lock and key in the Personnel Department and viewing of them is restricted, almost without exception, to the staff of that department. Their job is to protect them and to keep them up to date. From time to time, however, personal files have to be scrutinized by the heads of other departments, perhaps when an officer is being considered for promotion or transfer to another department, or when a disciplinary matter is pending. Even then, it is seldom that the entire file is released for examination.

What is generally offered is the Personal Record Card. This is an A4-sized card printed with boxed sections and it details the officer's career in a concise form. It bears his or her photograph, and it provides personal details such as date of birth, marital status, number of children, address, previous occupations, date of joining the force, examinations passed and qualifications gained, places at which the officer has been stationed, specialist departments in which he or she has served, any commendations won or medals awarded, any special training or skills acquired, courses attended, disciplinary proceedings (if any) and penalties imposed, driving qualifications with due note of additional skills such as PSV or HGV qualifications, firearms training, underwater section experience, first-aid qualifications – and more.

What is rarely seen, even by heads of departments, is the actual file which accompanies that record card.

This contains the history of the officer – it will even contain original documents like birth certificates, a copy of the officer's fingerprints and his or her application to join the force along with early written references. Those references are checked for authenticity, and there is a record of those checks. The file also contains written reports of the officer's progress – assessments from courses attended, confidential reports upon work and progress, assessments for promotion by supervisory officers, details of commendations and sometimes newspaper cuttings if an officer has been in the news for any reason. Requests from the officer for a transfer to another department, or for specialized training, or indeed for any career consideration, are kept in those bulky files. They are very personal indeed and are considered most confidential. Even when an officer makes a written request to examine his or her own personal file, it is the record card which is given to them, not the file itself.

When Detective Inspector Paul Larkin decided to examine Inspector Hadley's personal file, he realized he would be opposed by the bureaucracy of the civilian staff by whose care it was maintained. He had no criticism of that attitude – it was most important that confidentiality was assured – but when a police officer was under suspicion of committing a crime, particularly as a murder suspect, then it was vital that the file, in its entirety, be released for examination. Detective Inspector Larkin therefore sought an interview with Chief Superintendent Richard Redfearn, head of the force Administration Department. He did not explain his reason over the telephone but the interview was approved.

Paul Larkin therefore found himself waiting outside Redfearn's office at Great Halverton police headquarters at 3 p.m. one afternoon. Eventually he was ushered inside the smart, clean office with its deep blue carpets and smart furnishings – a far cry from the CID offices whose desks were battered and whose floor covering was not a carpet, but well-worn linoleum. Redfearn, a heavily built man with a cheerfully pink complexion and thinning hair, rose from his chair with some difficulty and extended a hand in greeting. In his late forties, Richard Redfearn had suffered serious leg and back injuries in a car crash while in pursuit of a stolen vehicle, and was now lame. He walked with the aid of a stick, but always remained cheerful. He now worked in Admin. because operational police work would have been most difficult for him. A friendly man with a wealth of practical experience, he made Paul feel welcome by offering him a seat, a cup of tea and a plate of chocolate biscuits.

'So what brings the CID to see the paper-chasers?' he smiled.

Enjoying the tea and biscuits, Larkin explained the scope of the current murder enquiries and provided Redfearn with details of Hadley's role and his request for elimination. 'What we need,' said Larkin, 'is a sight of his personal file. We need to know something of his personal history, sir, his previous occupation, sicknesses while serving in the force, any disciplinary hearings, problems he might have encountered during his service, that sort of thing.'

As Larkin explained his requirements, Redfearn listened intently.

'He always was a bit of a loner, was Hadley,' said Redfearn. 'I served with him for a while. He was a strange man in many ways, very deep. He didn't have many close friends. He seemed to prefer his own company. He was honest, though, I remember that claim of his, about not telling a lie. Something to do with a strict Scots Presbyterian upbringing, I think. When he was a young constable, he told us he would never lie about anything. Very keen, he was, a very able policeman too, I might add. He had the makings of a good thief taker even then, Paul – he'd never let a villain get away with a crime if he could help it. He really did believe that sin and crime should be punished.'

They chatted about the Millgate supermarket incident and Inspector Larkin revealed Pemberton's recent suspicions about Hadley; a sight of his file, with any personal or medical documents, might provide some useful leads to the investigation. As they talked, Redfearn realized that if the CID really wanted access to this file, and if such permission was not given informally, then Pemberton could make due representations, in writing, to the Chief Constable. But Redfearn had the sense not to stand in the way of necessity.

'I'll request his file,' he said. 'I'll do it now. As head of the department, that is one of my privileges – my request will not be challenged. But you'll have to study it here, in my office.'

'I appreciate that, sir,' said Larkin with some relief.

Five minutes later, Paul Larkin was studying Hadley's personal file on a table in the corner of Redfearn's office.

It began with his application to join the force; after his initial approach by letter, written in a youthful hand, there had been a printed form to complete, references to secure and an entrance examination to take. Larkin read these briefly and was tempted to skip the trivia of those twenty-two-year-old documents, but a question caught his eye.

One section of the application form asked: 'Have you a police record or have you been the subject of any police investigation?' It was a true test of honesty because, whatever the answer given on the application form, a check would be made in police records. Even a juvenile conviction would be revealed – and while someone with a juvenile record of minor crime such as vandalism or petty theft might be accepted as a constable, someone who refused to be honest would never be accepted. And the ultra-honest Hadley, then aged a mere twenty-one, had completed that section. He had written:

'When I was eleven, I had to attend the inquest on a boy who was drowned. He was my friend Stephen Bainley aged ten. He fell into the River Keal at Plockwood and I was the only witness. I was seen by PC Oxford and had to attend the inquest. It was accidental death.'

The entry had been endorsed by the recruiting sergeant of the time as 'Report checked and accurate' but no further details were given. Larkin knew the system: at his interview by the Chief Constable, Hadley would have been invited to give a more detailed account of that incident from his childhood, but what he said to the Chief Constable was not recorded.

He had been accepted as a member of the force, however. There was no date for the incident, but Larkin knew it had to be further investigated if only because Hadley had been involved in yet another death, albeit as a boy of eleven. A report of the inquest would be available or, failing that, a report in the local paper. Larkin was confident that he could locate a full account of the case. He was able to determine an approximate date simply by taking Hadley's birthday and adding eleven years. He made a written note of the entry and continued through the file. But this turned up another drama. As a young constable, Hadley had shown an aptitude for outdoor pursuits such as hiking, abseiling, rock climbing and mountaineering and so he had been seconded, as an instructor, to a Forward Thrust training school in the Lake District. The students on such courses came from a wide variety of backgrounds, such as industry, commerce, local authorities, the emergency services and even from juvenile detention centres or former approved schools and remand homes, now called community homes. The secondment was for twelve months during which time he would live and work at the training school, not as a policeman but as an instructor in Forward Thrust skills and techniques. He had been twenty-seven at the time and it had been felt that such a background would be useful for the training of police officers in their own training schools. Hadley was clearly destined to be a training officer within a police training centre, but this never materialized. The reason might have been the contents of a thick file which Larkin found among Hadley's papers.

He read the report.

During his secondment to the Forward Thrust school, a sixteen-year-old youth had fallen to his death while rock climbing in Borrowdale. The youth, a juvenile with a string of convictions for stealing motor cars and for burglaries in shops, had been under the supervision of Hadley at the time. The youth, called Darren Johnson, was an habitual offender and all other attempts to dissuade him from crime had failed. The authorities felt that a spell of tough physical activity, of the kind found on a Forward Thrust course among the Lake District hills, might persuade him to adopt other interests and outlets for his energy. It had also been felt that mixing with young people from more secure backgrounds might help him. On the day in question, with other young people in the vicinity plus three more instructors from the centre, Darren Johnson had been rock climbing on a crag with Hadley in attendance. He'd been fully roped and secured, and always under close supervision, but for some unexplained reason, he had fallen. According to Hadley's statement, which was in the file, the piton had failed to support the weight of the youth as he fell, and he had crashed more than a hundred feet on to some rocks below. Later in hospital, Johnson had died from multiple injuries.

The inquest had delivered a verdict of accidental death; the rider had been that organizations like Forward Thrust should ensure that their equipment was always in first-class condition, and always checked rigorously before use. Hadley had given evidence at the inquest; he'd said that the equipment was in first-class condition, that he had employed all the safety measures and that Johnson had been under close supervision by him at the time.

He could not explain why the piton had failed. From the notes of the inquest, and of the police enquiry into the tragedy, it was clear that some blame had been levelled against Hadley. The criticism was that he had not done his job properly. There was a newspaper cutting which highlighted Hadley's evidence at the coroner's court, in which he'd said, 'Why doesn't the court believe me when I say that everything possible had been done? I had checked the equipment, I had tested everything myself, I did follow the rules . . .'

But PC Hadley, as he had been at that time, was sent home to resume normal police duties. No negligence could be proved, and so the death of young Darren Johnson had been written off as accidental.

As Larkin read this account, he shuddered. Even in this brief summary of Hadley's life, he had discovered that the fellow had been associated with two deaths, one at the age of eleven and another at the age of twenty-seven, one as a child, the other as a serving police officer. And two years ago, this time as a police inspector in charge of the firearms unit, he had been associated with yet a third – the shooting of Joss Newton during a supermarket raid. He continued to study every piece of paper in the file, including Hadley's sickness record. Apart from the occasional dose of flu, he'd never been ill, either physically or mentally. Paul found that a full account of the incident at Millgate supermarket was included, along with the outcome of the disciplinary hearing, but it threw no new evidence upon his current investigations. He found no other references which might have a bearing on his present enquiries.

'I need to photocopy some documents, sir,' he asked Redfearn when he had finished his study. 'Highly confidentially.'

'My secretary will do that for you,' he said. 'She is totally reliable.'

As Mr Redfearn's secretary took away the documents for copying, Larkin explained to the superintendent his findings. Redfearn listened carefully, his clear grey eyes revealing something of his concern as Larkin made his revelations.

'Are you saying he's been bumping off criminals all his life, Paul?'

'I'm saying he's had a remarkable association with people who've died when he's been in the vicinity,' said Paul Larkin. 'I do know that Mr Pemberton is very concerned, and those deaths I've uncovered today will add to his worries. I'll pop into the *Gazette*'s offices on the way home to see if I can dig out anything on that drowning when he was eleven.'

'A ten-year-old kid can hardly be a criminal, can he?' asked Redfearn.

'You're wondering if the young Hadley pushed him in, are you?' asked Larkin.

'It's a possibility we can't ignore. I'd better warn the Chief,' said Redfearn.

'Yes, sir, I'm sure that would be wise. But Mr Moore does know that Langbarugh police have been keeping Hadley under surveillance.'

'It's got that far, has it? You're not suggesting that Hadley should be suspended from duty, are you, Paul? As a prime murder suspect?'

'No, sir, not yet. That's the last thing we want. At the moment, there is no real evidence to link him with the murders, it's all circumstantial. Mr Pemberton will want something more substantial before we take that kind of action.'

'He's under supervision, is he? Hadley, I mean? In case he goes out to kill someone else?'

'Langbarugh have called off their watches, sir, but Mr Pemberton is considering similar action. It won't be easy, Hadley knows he's under suspicion. Perhaps a word from you, sir, might help? Mr Pemberton would welcome ideas, or further background about Hadley.'

'Right, I'll ring Mark Pemberton before you get back,' promised Redfearn 'I can assure him money will be found for that! Ah, here's Juliet with your photocopies.'

The visit to Personnel had been most successful and from there, Larkin went to the offices of the *Gazette* where, after showing his warrant card to the librarian, he was shown into the cuttings library of the newspaper. Many of the papers were now on microfiche and, having determined the year in question, he settled down before the viewer to make his search. The death of a young boy in a tragic drowning incident was a major story for such a paper and had been featured on the front page; Larkin had no difficulty tracing it.

'Drowning tragedy at Plockwood' was the headline, and it was accompanied by a photograph of a stretch of the River Keal. The report went on, 'Ten-year-old Stephen Bainley of Plockwood was drowned in the River Keal yesterday while bird-nesting. He had been playing with his eleven-year-old friend, Victor Hadley, and had ventured on to the top of Plockwood Dam, intending to inspect the nest of a moorhen among some shrubs on the dam, when he lost his footing. He was swept down the fast-flowing sluice of the ten-foot-high dam, helpless against the powerful current, and was drowned in a deep pool below. His friend, Victor, said, 'I tried to reach him with a branch, but the water was too deep for me to paddle over. He couldn't get hold of the branch.'

A week later, the same paper reported the inquest. Victor Hadley, being the only witness, had to tell his story before the public and as the coroner had gently questioned the lad, he had appeared to stumble in his account of the accident. The discrepancy arose when the coroner had asked whether Victor had also been on the dam at the time his friend slipped into the water. It seemed that there was a clump of shrubs part way across the dam. On the edge of the sluice, they were growing from cracks in the concrete and as the water flowed past, branches of those shrubs caught drifting straw, twigs and grass. A moorhen, otherwise known as a water hen, had nested there, and Stephen had gone across to look at the nest. It was possible to walk along the top of the small dam, the flat area being about eight inches wide, but it was a mere inch or so above the surface of the water and always wet and slippery due to wavelets lapping across it. The constant dampness had encouraged a growth of moss which added to the danger.

As the coroner quizzed Victor, Victor first said he had not been with Stephen when he'd been looking into the nest, but later indicated that he had walked along the surface of the dam, otherwise he would not have known that the nest had contained eight brownish speckled eggs.

The unanswered question was whether Victor had been close to Stephen when he had slipped – had the two lads bumped into each other on the narrow strip of concrete? Had Stephen in fact been pushed into the sluice, accidentally or otherwise? When the coroner raised the latter question, Victor had burst into tears, saying no one believed him, and that he had been told by his parents never to tell a lie. He said he had not been there to steal the birds' eggs, but Stephen was going to take some of the eggs and blow them. Victor was not that sort of child. His parents had always told him never to harm the eggs or any bird and never to destroy a nest. Victor went on to say that Stephen had slipped over the edge of the dam without being pushed or shoved in any way, and that he, Victor, had run back to the river bank to pick up a branch with which to reach his friend as he had struggled in the pool below the dam.

He had failed. The coroner decided that both Stephen and Victor had been on the top of the small dam – that must have been the case if Victor had known the contents of the nest and had to run to the bank to obtain a branch – but he also stated that Stephen's death was due to a tragic accident. There was no evidence that he had been pushed into the water or that the actions of two boys upon a very small and slippery surface area had contributed to his death. He praised the eleven-year-old Victor for his efforts to rescue his friend and recorded a verdict of accidental death.

Larkin scanned the papers which followed in the ensuing weeks, but found no further references to that accident.

He made photocopies of the reports and left for Rainesbury police station, thoughtful and somewhat unhappy. He began to see that Hadley could have pushed young Bainley into the river because he stole birds' eggs; he could have allowed Darren Johnson to use defective equipment and so sent the lad plunging to his death, all because he was a persistent stealer of motor cars. And if he had contributed to those deaths, all those years ago, it was perfectly feasible that he might have taken a God-sent opportunity to dispose of Joss Newton at Millgate supermarket, not to mention Pearle, Scott and Hardisty.

Perhaps Brian Newton had just cause to continue his campaign against Hadley? Larkin hoped Pemberton and his team were capable of finding out the truth. But if Hadley was a murderer, then he would surely kill again? So who was next? They'd have to catch him in the act if they were to prove a case against him – and that would be far from easy.

Detective Inspector Larkin pressed his accelerator.

18

Even before receiving Larkin's news, Detective Superintendent Pemberton knew that he had to immediately begin to monitor Hadley's off-duty movements around the clock. It must be done until it could be proved whether or not he was the motor-cycling serial killer. Pemberton was acutely aware that if another murder occurred without steps being taken to prevent it, his own job, plus the reputation of the police service as a whole, was at risk. And he had suddenly identified a point of major interest.

Pemberton realized that the murders had occurred in an identifiable sequence – the first had been on a Saturday, the second on a Sunday and the third on a Monday, all with a period of seven days between them. If that sequence was continued, the next death would be today – Tuesday.

At Pemberton's urgent request, therefore, and with the full approval of the Chief Constable, Holderness police provided a unit of seven officers who were skilled in surveillance techniques, both with electronic listening and watching devices and by the simple device of human observation. The unit comprised one inspector, two sergeants and four constables who, between them, could operate throughout a twenty-four-hour spell, if only for a limited period of three days. The situation would be reviewed after that time and repeatedly reviewed thereafter, but the team did make use of local officers too, the latter seldom knowing the extent of their involvement. Quite often, local mobiles or foot patrols would be asked, by their Control Rooms, to undertake what appeared to be a routine task whereas in truth it was part of a much larger and more complex operation.

Having listened to the unit's requirements and proposals, Pemberton said it was ideal for starters; it was agreed that the Holderness officers should attend immediately, with the officer in charge of the force Control Room being advised of their presence and the likelihood of some possible requests for assistance, all of which must be given priority. Pemberton agreed to rendezvous with the group that evening at 6 p.m. in a secret location, when he would provide them with photographs of Hadley and details of the task in hand. Meanwhile, a discreet watch would be maintained on Hadley's home by his own officers. Thanks to some buildings conveniently situated nearby, that could be achieved without Hadley being aware of their presence. Following Hadley whenever he left his home would be infinitely more difficult – that would be the task of the Holderness officers.

It was after Pemberton had established this surveillance of Victor Hadley that Paul Larkin returned to the incident room armed with his new information. For Pemberton, the revelations were devastating. It took but a few seconds for him to discern a pattern, and to realise that his request for surveillance was most opportune and timely. He told Larkin about his own theory of the sequence of deaths, but it now seemed, from the accrued information, that Hadley was capable of executing anyone who infringed the good laws of society, whether by stealing birds' eggs or by sexually assaulting children.

Pemberton began to see that Hadley's work in the police force had provided the perfect cover for such activities and had also offered the opportunity to discover the secret lives of such citizens. If a killer wanted to instigate a war on villains, what better place was there to hide and what finer base from which to operate? It was increasingly possible that Hadley's despatch of the hapless Newton had been a calculated killing . . . Who else knew Newton would be involved and who else could have undertaken such an execution in the presence of his colleagues? So how many other victims were there?

Mark felt an awful hollowness in the pit of his stomach as Larkin revealed his news. He was aware that one aspect of serial killers was that they did increase the frequency of their killings – one killing a year could become one killing a month, and then one killing a week, and then at even closer intervals as the killer became addicted to the crime. And these local crimes were being committed at the rate of one every eight days . . .

In spite of everything, there was insufficient evidence to justify an arrest – even now, it was all suspicion and supposition. Hadley had to be caught in the act, it was the only positive means of proving his guilt. Even now, there were unanswered questions, such as how Hadley had known the whereabouts and movements of the victims. Those questions, and more, would have to be answered. To justify the arrest of Hadley, and to warrant a prosecution, there was a lot more work for Pemberton's team to do.

'The only way to stop him, Paul, is to catch him in the act . . .' and Pemberton went on to outline the surveillance operation he was about to establish. 'My gut instinct is that today is crucial. Hadley will be watched for every minute of the day when he leaves our premises. When those watchers get into position, they will maintain contact with me, through radio, which means my office will have to be staffed continuously. I shall be in my office for most of the time but you will be needed to relieve me if the exercise goes on for very long. Clearly, if Hadley is at home or in bed, we can relax a little, although the surveillance team will always be there and we'll always be on call. But if he's out on that confounded motor bike of his, or ostensibly fishing on the river bank, then we shall have to be here, in my office, at the end of a radio link. He will be monitored at every inch of his journey, wherever he goes and whatever he does . . . and he must never know we're tailing him. I've warned the Holderness team that he will be alert to any surveillance attempts, but they're good, very good. And, Paul, this is top secret. Catching him in action is going to be a most difficult task, but no one else must be part of this activity. It has to be executed with the utmost secrecy, but we will require a team of officers, some armed, to be on standby and to move urgently when commanded. There is no need for them to know what they are waiting for, just have them immediately available from six o'clock this evening, until we decide to stand them down. And if we have to shoot Victor Hadley, so be it. We'll call it Operation Moth.'

And so Operation Moth was put into operation.

*

That Tuesday, the subject of Operation Moth, Inspector Victor Hadley, had finished his day's work in the incident room at 1 p.m. and, after some lunch, had gone fishing in his favourite spot on the banks of the River Keal.

At that stage, he had not been under any supervision by detectives. Larkin's revelations and Pemberton's theory had injected a new urgency into the matter, and it was now realized that Hadley had to be supervised day and night – beginning at the first possible moment. As it happened, he had returned to his home at 5.30 p.m. for a meal. By six thirty, the surveillance team was in position, Hadley's home was being electronically monitored and contact had been made with Pemberton's office at the incident room, Larkin taking the first spell of command.

Pemberton had gone home for his own meal, but knew he would be unable to refrain from returning to the office. Things were beginning to happen, the work of the past weeks was gelling and he had a gut feeling about this case. With the instinct of many years of detective work, he knew the climax was very close and he wanted to be on duty when the killer of Scott, Pearle and Hardisty was caught. But who was the next intended victim? If the identity of a future victim was known, plans could be made to intercept the killer, but in this case, no such steps were possible. The identity of the next victim was totally unknown.

A very difficult job lay ahead. When Pemberton returned to his house, Lorraine was out. She had been to Middlesbrough earlier that day as part of her liaison duties with Langbarugh police, but this afternoon, according to Barbara Meadows, she had driven down to the ballistics lab in Nottingham. She'd gone with some samples and had left a message asking that Pemberton be notified. He was out when she had made her decision, but she had not revealed any more of her purpose to anyone.

'Samples?' he asked Barbara. 'What samples? There aren't any more cartridges to go there, are there?'

'She didn't say.'

'Maybe she's discovered something on her trip to Langbarugh. I don't think we asked for our earlier samples back for any reason, did we? She hasn't gone to fetch those, surely?'

'No,' Barbara confirmed. 'Ballistics always retain them in case they've got to give evidence at a trial. They need them as their exhibits. She said she was taking a sample for urgent analysis, and would I inform you. I'm just relaying what she said.'

'Oh, well, she'll know what she's doing.' He shrugged his shoulders. 'Such are the wiles of women, eh, Barbara?'

'I'd call it intuition not wiles,' smiled Barbara. 'Anyway, it's a two and a half hour drive each way, plus her time there, so don't expect her back before seven at the earliest.'

It meant that Pemberton would be engaged upon Operation Moth by the time she returned; it also meant he had to eat alone. He found a shepherd's pie in the freezer, along with some frozen garden peas, and was able to knock up a quick meal in the microwave.

He showered, changed, enjoyed his meal with a glass of red wine and then left a note for Lorraine. 'Gone back to the office, don't bother to follow. Top secret task,' he wrote on a writing pad which he left on the table. 'Back sometime.'

And so he drove out to his office in the incident room to await developments. Larkin was there, in Pemberton's office, with the unintrusive radio network installed.

'All quiet so far, sir,' the inspector smiled. 'He's still at home, we can monitor his conversation in the house.'

'We could be in for a long wait, but I couldn't sit at home all alone.' Pemberton took a chair and sat down. 'Not when all this is happening. Has anything else arisen, Paul?'

'Not a sausage, sir. He's having his tea. That's all.'

'Have you eaten?'

'As a matter of fact, no, sir, I haven't.'

'Right, well, I can take over for a while. You sneak off if you want. I'll cover until you return. We can't operate on empty stomachs, Paul.'

'Thanks, sir, I might make do with fish and chips. I'll pop round the corner to get some. I don't want to miss anything either. I've a gut feeling about tonight . . .'

'Me too,' said Pemberton. 'So on your way. Fish and chips first, surveillance second.'

An hour later, at eight minutes past seven, Victor Hadley left home on his motor cycle, telling his wife that he was going fishing.

His words were picked up by the sensitive listening device deployed by the team, and they heard him say he was going down to the river and that he'd return about eleven o'clock. She said she'd wait up – there was something on television she wanted to watch. They heard him go to his shed for his fishing tackle, heard the motor-bike engine strike up, and then he emerged to ride down to the river bank. At that point, the personal surveillance began but not with the obvious device of putting a car or a motor cycle on his tail. That would have been too simple, too readily noticed. His departure was noted, and at the next junction in the road, a police car in smart livery was waiting. Hadley, it was felt, would never suspect that a brightly coloured police car complete with blue light and flourescent stripes was tailing him. If he was going to be tailed, he'd have expected something like a plumber's battered van or an innocuous old banger of some kind clinging to his rear bumper, and so the operators of this system felt they had engineered a good beginning. And so, for the first leg of Hadley's outing, he was observed by the simple means of using a marked police car.

'Here we go,' said Pemberton to Larkin, now back in the office and replete with a helping of delicious fish and chips. 'Is he going fishing or not?'

They listened to the commentary of the police driver, but Hadley did not turn towards the river. He continued along the main road, heading for Lawneswick as the police car overtook him and settled into a steady speed ahead of the black motor cycle.

'He's not turned towards the river,' said Larkin, now wearing an earpiece. 'But we've a tail on him. There's no mention of him being armed. According to the surveillance team, it seems he collected only fishing tackle before setting off. They managed to search his bike panniers too, while the bike was in the garage. They'd make good burglars, those lads, but there was no shotgun.'

'Maybe he's going to pick up the weapon? Let's hope he doesn't lose us!' grimaced Mark Pemberton.

Having told his wife that he was going fishing, and having placed the strap of his bag around his shoulders with his rod, gaff and nets upon his back, Vic Hadley left home as daylight was turning to dusk. With his long rubber waders upon his feet, where they served as protective motor-cycling gear, his leather jacket and black helmet completed his outfit. The beautiful black Suzuki sprang to life at the touch of the starter button and, with the engine as smooth as a sewing machine, he swung from his drive with all the skill of a very experienced biker.

The well-maintained machine quickly reached the maximum speed limit – 40mph in this part of town – and Vic felt the cool evening air on his face and the wind in his ears. Even with the protection of a helmet, there remained the joy of feeling the wind about his head and face and the touch of fresh air upon his cheeks as he controlled the speed of his machine until he reached the open road. The sight of a police car at the junction with Castle Road reminded him of the obligatory speed limit and he reduced his speed to 30mph, an unconscious reaction.

The police car emerged from the side road and tucked in behind him for a short distance before easing into the outside lane and overtaking him. It settled down in front of him, cruising at 40mph until it reached the town boundary where it accelerated slightly. Vic followed. Ahead lay the open road, with Fawneswick twenty minutes away. He opened the throttle, the bike responding immediately until he was cruising along at 60mph with the wind whistling about him and with an immense sense of freedom within. The police car continued ahead, not speeding away, apparently not going about any particular task, but enjoying a leisurely patrol along the deserted moorland road which linked Rainesbury with Fawneswick. This route was patrolled regularly by mobiles of the Road Traffic Division and thus the presence of that car did not strike Hadley as being out of the ordinary. For those who were watching him, on the other hand, it had been a very good beginning to their task.

After a ride of some fifteen minutes, with cars both behind and ahead of him during the journey, Hadley came to a lonely moorland junction; there was an inn at this point – the Moorcock Inn – and a direction sign pointing towards the coast. That signpost said, 'Bleawick only. 3', and it pointed along a very narrow, winding lane with high hedges which led towards the coast.

Bleawick, a former Roman signalling station, was a cliff-top hamlet comprising little more than a huge hotel and some former coastguards' cottages, now occupied by sturdy dwellers and holiday-makers. A coastal footpath ran through the hamlet and there was a large car-park for visitors who flocked here during the summer season. There was a magnificent viewpoint with climbs down the cliffs to the sandy shore below.

Hadley turned along the narrow lane towards Bleawick. The police car, still within his sights as he had arrived at this point, continued towards Fawneswick. Now alone on this rural lane and requiring headlights due to the rapidly fading daylight, Inspector Vic Hadley accelerated towards Bleawick with a rising sense of excitement. For him, a satisfactory conclusion was near. His own enquiries had proved very fruitful: he knew that Swanson was corrupt and that he was a womanizer, an adulterer. Adultery was bad, but a corrupt police officer was the basest of creatures, the scum of the earth. Hadley now had the evidence he wanted and he hoped he would remain calm enough to conclude tonight's business.

'Moth One. Subject has turned towards Bleawick,' said an anonymous voice from the police car.

'Ten four,' said Control.

Another voice said, 'Moth Two to Control. Am behind subject, distance four hundred yards, his rear lights are in view. Now proceeding to Bleawick.'

'Ten four,' said Control. 'Moth Two, for your information, the road terminates at Bleawick. There is a public car-park, suggest you avoid that. Exercise the utmost caution.'

'Ten four,' said Moth Two.

Moth Two was a blue Ford Escort, some five years old, and inside were a young man and a young woman, both casually dressed in jeans and sweaters. They had all the appearances of a courting couple, but each was in fact equipped with a throat microphone in addition to the car's own radio. When Moth Two arrived at the public car-park on the cliff-top at Bleawick, Hadley's motor cycle was there. On its stand, it gleamed in the light of a street lamp beneath which it had been placed and they were in time to see the bulky black figure of Hadley walking towards the splendid Beacon Hotel. There was no other vehicle in that public car-park but they drove on and parked on a patch of waste ground overlooking the sea, apparently a courting couple seeking solitude.

Within seconds, though, the walking figure of Hadley was lost in the darkness, his black clothing making him invisible. The site had been a beacon in Roman times, and even in later years fires were lit on the cliff-top to warn ships of danger, or to provide signals for smugglers; now the lights of the hotel provided seafarers with any necessary warnings of cliffs and rocky beaches. The hotel was shown on all maritime maps of the locality. The 'courting' couple had now left their car for a cliff-top stroll.

'Moth Two, subject entering grounds of the Beacon Hotel. Over.'

'Received, Moth Two. Keep him under surveillance. Identify other persons present if possible. Over.'

While the young male detective shadowed the sturdy figure of Hadley as he materialized in the glow of the light from the building, his partner walked among the cars already parked in the hotel grounds.

Through her throat microphone, she listed all the registration numbers, these being recorded by Control. Each would be immediately checked on the Police National Computer. Some would surely belong to members of staff; others would be guests, residents and non-residents alike. The place was popular with diners, the restaurant being particularly well known.

'Moth Two to Control,' said the male voice. 'Subject now in hotel grounds. He is sitting on a bench among some shrubs, almost hidden. He is alone. He is not holding any weapon. Am maintaining observation. Over.'

'Ten four,' said Control, knowing that these words were being monitored by Superintendent Pemberton at Raineswick.

'What's he doing there?' Pemberton puzzled in his office. 'For a man who says he never tells a lie, it's a funny place to go fishing!'

'It seems to me that he's waiting for somebody,' said Larkin.

'Exactly. But who?' Pemberton sounded frustrated.

Two minutes later, the telephone rang. It was the inspector in charge of the Control Room. 'Morton here, sir,' he said. 'Those cars at the Beacon. We're putting the numbers through PNC, but one's already of interest. It belongs to Detective Inspector Swanson, sir; it's his private car.'

'Swanson? What's he doing there?' asked Pemberton.

'He'll be with his bit of skirt, sir,' said Morton with a chuckle. 'He has a woman, you know, a bit of spare. He's had her ages – it's that widow of Newton, the chap Hadley shot at Millgate. I don't think his wife knows a thing about it.'

'Newton's widow?' cried Mark Pemberton, who then realized that some people would regard that kind of liaison as both sinful and criminal. Certainly adultery was a worse crime than hunting for birds' eggs. And he remembered Swanson's meeting with him, the meeting where Swanson claimed he'd seen Hadley murder Newton.

'God!' he said suddenly. 'I wonder if Swanson was seeing her at the time of Millgate!'

'Sir?' questioned Morton.

'I'm talking to myself, Inspector. But I'm going to the Beacon Hotel,' he announced. 'Get the firearms unit to meet me in the public car-park, urgent and secret. And tell Moth Two not to let Hadley out of his sight! He might well be intending to shoot Detective Inspector Swanson!'

19

It was nearly nine o'clock when Lorraine returned to the incident room from Nottingham. She was tired and hungry after the long round trip; an accident on the Al(M) had caused her to lose an hour or so on the return leg. The place was deserted apart from the evening's skeleton staff although she did see a light emerging from beneath Pemberton's office door. She tapped and walked in; she was very surprised to find Detective Inspector Larkin sitting alone among a bank of radio receiving equipment. There was no sign of Pemberton and her first request was to ask his whereabouts.

'He's out on a job,' Larkin told her. 'He's rushed out, Lorraine. Top secret. I'm holding the fort at this end. You've not been home?'

'No, I had to rush down to Nottingham without telling him or you – you weren't around, either of you.'

'It's nice when people use their initiative, but I'm afraid he's out of touch just now, and likely to be for some considerable time, certainly for the next few hours.' Larkin was sympathetic. 'It's well past your knocking-off time, so why don't you go home and put your feet up? Have a relaxing night.'

'I think he'll want to know what I've discovered, sir.' There was an insistence in her voice which he could not ignore. 'But what's he got involved with now? Am I allowed to know?'

'No one's allowed to know, Lorraine, except a handful of top brass. But let me put it like this – it wouldn't surprise me if we caught the motor-cycling killer tonight.'

'That's great! I'm really pleased – but it makes my information even more important! So I must speak to Mark . . . er, Superintendent Pemberton, it's about Hadley.'

'Hadley?'

'Well, to be honest, it's about the Millgate supermarket incident.'

'Can it wait?' he asked. 'Your Mr Pemberton's in the middle of a very tricky operation.'

'If Inspector Hadley's involved in whatever's going on out there, then Mr Pemberton must know what I've discovered – it's vital!' and she almost snapped out the words.

He recognized her anxiety, but said, 'If it's all that important, Lorraine, you'd better sit down and tell me all about it, and I might be able to make contact. He's on the road now, there's a while before he's due to arrive, before he's irrevocably committed, so we've a few minutes in hand. Time for a coffee perhaps? For you and me? I'm parched, it must have been the salt on my fish and chips.'

'Fish and chips?' She licked her lips. 'I'd give my right arm for some just now . . .'

'Right, we've enough time for you to dash round the corner for your fish and chips. I'll put the kettle on, then we'll talk.'

Larkin put on the kettle as Lorraine hurried out; less than five minutes later, she returned with her chips wrapped in newspaper. Two steaming mugs of coffee were waiting.

She settled down to her meal, finding it odd that Larkin was using Pemberton's office and occupying his chair.

Larkin allowed her the luxury of enjoying a few mouthfuls before asking. 'So what's this important news you bring from Nottingham, Lorraine?'

'You're familiar with the Millgate supermarket incident, sir?' she asked.

'I am. Mr Pemberton made me read the file when the current series of murders began.'

'Then you'll be familiar with Inspector Hadley's claim, sir? That Newton was carrying a shotgun?'

'Yes, I am aware of that. It was a gun that no one else saw and which has never been seen since,' he added wryly. 'The cause of much speculation.'

'Well, I was in SOCO early this afternoon and they told me they still had the cartridges recovered from the supermarket forecourt. They'd been sent back by Ballistics after the trial. There were four of them, as the report mentioned. Three from twelve-bores, and one from Hadley's own weapon.'

'So?' asked Larkin. 'We all know that. One of the twelve-bore cartridges was unaccounted for, wasn't it? A throwaway, everyone thought.'

'Well, I remembered the story of that time, about one of the gang firing two shots, the other firing nothing at all, and Inspector Hadley firing one shot. Three shots were fired and accounted for, sir, but four cartridge shells were recovered This led to speculation that a fourth shot had been fired.'

'Those discrepancies were considered at the time, Lorraine. The fourth shell was never satisfactorily explained. I think the conclusion was that it had nothing to do with the raid.'

'Exactly, sir. But I now believe that Inspector Hadley was correct in what he saw. That's why I took those cartridge cases to Nottingham this afternoon. I wanted them to examine the fourth one. They'd examined it before, at the time of the supermarket incident, and said it had not come from any of the guns involved in the case. More correctly, they said it had not been fired from any of the shotguns recovered at the scene.'

'So what are you saying, Lorraine?'

'I asked Ballistics to compare that old cartridge with those we've recovered from the scenes of the murders of Pearle, Scott and Hardisty.'

He was now regarding her with interest and respect. He could guess what she was about to tell him. 'Go on, Lorraine.'

'It was fired by the same gun, sir.'

'Bloody hell! Are you sure?' he cried.

'Ballistics will confirm it in writing, but I asked them to do an immediate examination. They've got the shells from the three current murders, and it was the work of a moment to compare that old one from the Millgate incident. The firing pin's punch mark on the ignition cap, and the extractor claw marks are identical, sir.'

'My God, Lorraine. This changes everything!'

'The old cartridge is not the same make or age as those recently used, but the marks produced by the gun's firing mechanism are the same.'

'So all this means that there *was* another shotgun?' breathed Larkin.

'Yes, sir, that's exactly what it does mean. And that same gun is now being used to kill again,' stressed Lorraine. 'And I very much doubt if Inspector Hadley will be using it. And there was another thing, sir.'

'Go on, Lorraine,' he whispered.

'That list of black motor-cycle owners . . . I don't know whether anyone familiar with the Millgate incident ever studied it.'

'No, they wouldn't. It was given to a team to work on – they'll be contacting all owners.'

'But I read it, sir, when I was waiting around Langbarugh headquarters this morning. There's a very significant name on it.'

'You have been busy. Who is it?'

'Brian Newton, sir. He can't drive a car, but he does ride a motor bike. He bought one which is identical to Hadley's, even with the same tyres and colouring . . . He got it from Sunderland, two weeks after Hadley bought his.'

'Are you saying Hadley's being framed for these crimes?'

'It wouldn't be difficult, would it?' she put to him. 'I think he is. And Brian Newton does have good reason for getting his revenge against Hadley.'

Larkin thought hard. Revenge was sweet, he knew, and if Newton had been deliberately setting up Hadley, it was clear that he had worked carefully on his plans.

Larkin closed his eyes as he tried to recreate the scene on the Millgate supermarket forecourt at the time of Newton's death; he realized that it would be impossible for Hadley to have seized and retained that weapon, the weapon that Newton must have been carrying, the one that had disappeared from the scene.

'You have a theory about all this?' he asked Lorraine.

'Yes,' and she told him what she had earlier told Pemberton, that she believed a fifth person had been present at the scene of the Millgate supermarket raid. That person, she believed, had accompanied Newton along Acorn Alley to the point where it entered the forecourt. That person had probably been a few strides behind Newton, who was leading the way armed with a loaded sawn-off shotgun, but when Newton had literally taken two steps into the arena, he'd been shot. He'd fallen to the ground only a few strides from the exit of Acorn Alley. The gun had been blown from his grasp by the force of Hadley's shot and it had fallen to the ground where the impact had harmlessly discharged one of its barrels, that shot being lost among the others being fired at the same time. Hadley had been quizzed about that, but had no recollection of the gun being hurled into the air. His concentration had been on the man as he'd collapsed on the ground. But if the gun had been blasted from Newton's hands it could quite easily have discharged a harmless shot – which could explain the phantom fourth shot.

She went on, 'I think the gun must have fallen close to his body, sir, on the blind side. His body must have concealed it. In the confusion that followed – and there always is confusion in a case like that – the fifth person simply reached out along the ground and dragged the gun into the alley to make off with it, leaving Newton's car to be found by the police. That fact alone would suggest Newton alone had been involved. No one would have seen that gun; Newton's body would have obstructed any view of an arm reaching out.'

'And now you are telling me that that very same sawn-off twelve-bore was used to kill Scott, Pearle and Hardisty?'

'I don't say it, sir. Ballistics say so. They're the experts.'

'So if Inspector Hadley is not the motor-cycling murderer, who is?' asked Detective Inspector Paul Larkin.

'We might know tonight, sir, might we?' She smiled. 'I think Mr Hadley has been slowly drawn into a trap, sir, and I'd lay bets that Brian Newton is involved.'

'And I'll have to stop our armed units from targeting the wrong man,' he muttered. 'I hope we're not too late. This throws a whole new complexion on the matter . . . I'll call Superintendent Pemberton immediately.'

In the grounds of the Beacon Hotel, Moth Two was still observing the silent figure of Inspector Hadley. Hadley had remained on the bench in the grounds for nearly two hours, moving very occasionally and sometimes standing up to stretch his legs or move his arms. In the darkness of that night, and taking advantage of the shadows cast by the lights of the hotel, he was virtually invisible as he maintained his watch.

In the meantime, other cars had arrived at the hotel. Some two dozen people had entered for dinner or as overnight guests; every registration number was recorded by the watching police, and now two officers, a man and a woman, both dressed for the occasion, had entered the hotel ostensibly as diners. Unknown to Inspector Hadley, who had a clear view of the dining-room from his seat, and unknown to Detective Inspector Swanson and his lady love, they asked for and were given a corner table. From there, they could observe the entire dining-room.

Their throat microphones were neatly concealed and thus it was possible to relay information to those waiting outside. But nothing appeared to be happening. Outwardly, this seemed to be a perfectly ordinary evening with diners enjoying a good meal in pleasant surroundings. No one was aware of the watching Hadley in motor-cycling gear as he remained hidden in the shadows of the garden and no one, not even the vigilant police, could know the reason for his presence.

But Pemberton was beginning to understand.

*

Being a fisherman, Inspector Victor Hadley had infinite patience. Just like a patient angler, he was prepared to wait until he had secured a worthy catch. The bait, Hadley knew, was already in position; he hadn't been a policeman and a detective without learning something about secret enquiries.

He would wait for as long as necessary.

Pemberton, along with officers from the armed response unit, his own CID and the observers from Holderness, was also waiting. The influx of police vehicles, none marked but most of them recognizable to a police officer, had been distributed around the small community. Some were parked outside the row of former coastguard cottages; some were in the hotel grounds; several had been moved into quiet lanes and fields; two were parked at the public toilets a few yards along the lane which formed part of the cliff-top footpath.

One of the vehicles which had entered the hotel grounds and parked opposite Swanson's private car was a parcels delivery van. According to its livery, the firm was called Javelin Express Deliveries. It was a dark blue van with a gold flash around a javelin logo along each side of the van portion. It was just one of several vehicles which had arrived and departed during the last hour or so, but this one had remained.

It was out of the sight of the waiting Hadley, but had he watched, he would have seen a man climb out with a parcel, take it to the hotel and return to the van. But the van, which was the size of a bread van, had not left the premises. The driver must have decided to have a rest and was slumped in his seat, apparently asleep. Inside the rear compartment, however, were Detective Superintendent Mark Pemberton, two detectives and two armed police officers in uniform; they were out of sight but equipped with their listening equipment and radio transmitters.

To anyone entering Bleawick, the tiny hamlet looked absolutely normal. For the waiting police, it was anything but normal.

Their target, Hadley, was still being watched by the anonymous Moth Two, but as he waited, Pemberton's mind began to reassess his knowledge of Hadley, of Swanson, of the events at Millgate. If Swanson had been seeing Newton's wife, and if Swanson had wanted her as his own, how easy it would be to persuade him to raid a security vehicle. If Swanson had slipped information to Newton that an extra high amount of cash was there for his picking . . . Newton would take the bait and organize the raid – and be arrested by the waiting Swanson and his officers. Thus Newton would be out of the way while Swanson made merry with his wife . . . but Newton had been shot dead. No one had bargained for that, no one had even considered Hadley's swift response . . . and, Pemberton realized, Newton could have been about to shoot Swanson having discovered his adultery with his wife. If he'd realized what Swanson had been doing – and what lay in store for him if he was arrested – he might well have tried to kill the detective. Maybe Hadley was right? Maybe Newton had tried to kill Swanson . . . but if so, where was his weapon? If the recovered gun had belonged to Pollard, then it ruined that theory . . .

'Still no movement,' said Moth Two as Pemberton's mind was in a turmoil.

'Ten four,' said Control.

'Moth Five. Anything happening in the dining-room?' asked Pemberton.

'Swanson has reached the coffee stage,' said the woman's voice very quietly. 'It's the custom to take it in the lounge.'

'Moth Six is in the lounge,' said Pemberton.

Pemberton then addressed the men in the rear of the van.

'I can't see Hadley attempting to shoot Swanson in the hotel,' he whispered eventually. 'Be alert for another killer; we might have been on the wrong track. Repeat, don't ignore the possibility of another killer. Hadley's bike is in the car-park outside too, which means he has a gallop of, what, two hundred yards in order to make good his escape on the bike. His fishing gear is on board, strapped to the panniers. In the past, the killer has been astride the machine while committing his crimes . . . Don't ignore Hadley, he has time to fetch his bike into the grounds, but do consider another killer . . . Repeat, do consider another killer! If there is another, he will have seen Swanson leave the table and go into the lounge, so he has a few minutes before Swanson leaves the hotel. Over.'

A colleague in the rear of the vehicle whispered, 'I think chummy will take Swanson as he tries to enter his car, that's when he'll be at his most vulnerable. And that's when we need to be ready with a reception committee. Guns loaded for use if necessary. Remember, Hadley's a crack shot and he's a trained police firearms officer, he won't be easy. Even if he's not the killer, the killer's shown himself to be pretty effective at close range with a shotgun.'

'There's more of us than him,' grunted another voice in the rear.

And then Pemberton's radio whispered his call sign. He acknowledged it. It was Larkin.

'I distinctly said no calls here, Paul,' snapped Pemberton in a stage whisper. 'Especially not now, things are beginning to move . . .'

'Sir,' said Larkin, 'it's vital . . . Hadley's not the killer. Lorraine's been to Nottingham – the gun that Newton had during Millgate is now being used by the killer . . . so it can't be Hadley.'

'Then what the bloody hell is Hadley doing here, leading us all into this situation?' cried Pemberton, angry with himself. 'If he's not here to shoot Swanson, then why is he here?'

'I don't know,' said Larkin. 'I'm convinced he's not the man we're looking for.'

'Sir,' said a detective in the van. 'Sir, a motor cycle. A black one, heading this way . . .'

The motor cycle drove into the car-park of the Beacon Hotel, circled the entire parking area twice and then came to a halt between two cars. It was the distance of two cars away from Swanson's. The rider switched off the engine and doused the lights. And in the light of the hotel, Pemberton could see that the machine was a black Suzuki with silver markings on the fairing. The rider climbed off and stretched his legs, coming to inspect Swanson's car. He was a large man, well built, and he wore a black helmet; his motor-cycle suit was black leather. Having seen the car, he returned to his machine and sat astride it, waiting.

Pemberton whispered, 'Moth Two, is Hadley still on the seat?'

'Yes, sir,' he said. 'But he heard a motor bike arrive, he stood up, I heard it too. He's beginning to walk away now, sir, towards the main car-park —'

'Radio silence!' snapped Pemberton. 'Operation Moth is entering its final phase. Everyone to their stations, everyone sharp and ready. Execute Operation Moth as arranged. But, repeat but, Hadley is not our target, repeat Hadley is not our target. Target is astride a black motor cycle outside the main entrance of the hotel, believed to be awaiting Swanson. Man, bulky build, in black leathers and crash helmet. He will surely be armed. Beware, beware, beware. Take him when Swanson appears . . . Moth Three, prepare to block the hotel gate with your vehicle, not too early . . . good timing essential. Dog section? Be alert in case he runs for it over the wall. Everyone to their posts.'

And so the trap was set.

20

The wait seemed eternal. It was as if all noise ceased, all activity halted and every person vanished into the darkness. Inside the brilliantly illuminated hotel there was light and happiness, but none of that noise permeated to Pemberton and his waiting officers. They could near nothing of the chatter or the sound of cutlery or even the soft music which played in the background. The only sound, discernible if one listened carefully, was the constant crash of the waves somewhere in the dark distance, breakers crashing on to the rocky shore deep below the hotel at the foot of the cliffs.

Everyone was waiting for Swanson to appear. From his hiding place in the van, Pemberton could see the main entrance of the hotel, a wide double door standing open to emit light which bathed the steps and paving stones in a pale unobtrusive glow, and inside he could see the antique furnishings, the mirrors on the wall, the paintings, the beautiful mahogany furniture and hall table. And outside, beyond the reach of the light, stood the motor cycle, engine silent and lights extinguished as the silent black figure astride it also waited. He was watching that doorway; the police were watching him. Hadley was watching him too. Hadley, equally invisible, had left the seat now; having heard the arrival of the black motor cycle, he began to move through the shadows towards the machine, silently moving among the trees and across the grass of the grounds with all the skill of a trained stalker. A countryman stalking his prey, a fisherman endeavouring to outwit a fish, a hunter with a will to outwit an animal with the keenest hearing and most alert of senses.

Moth Two, charged with the duty of observing Hadley, could not relay this movement to Control; radio silence had been ordered and Moth Two knew that if he moved, he might reveal himself. And if he did reveal himself, the entire operation could be aborted or ruined. He said a silent prayer that Pemberton and his men close to the scene of the forthcoming action might be aware of Hadley's departure from the seat. Moth Two therefore remained in the shadows, as still and silent as a nightjar, wondering whether or not he was going to witness a death this evening, or whether or not he was going to be instrumental in preventing a death. He could do no more and he began to perspire in spite of the chill of the night.

Pemberton did see Hadley's approach. An officer in the rear of the van noticed him first. In the quietest of whispers, he said, 'Sir, Hadley's moving, he's left the seat. I can see him heading this way, he's bloody difficult to see but the light of the hotel keeps glinting from his helmet . . . he's coming towards the bloke on the bike.'

'We might have to head him off.' Pemberton's voice was calmly reassuring; there was no sign of tension or of panic. 'Is anyone close to the chap on the bike?'

'One armed response member, one detective, both concealed.'

'They'll not let Hadley get shot . . .'

Then Swanson appeared in the doorway of the hotel. The woman on his arm was clad in a fur coat and was clinging to him with all the love and desire that she could display . . . They began to descend the steps.

Pemberton heard her say, 'Oh, damn, Phil, I've left my handbag in the lounge . . . I'll just pop and get it. I'll see you at the car.'

'Right,' said Swanson.

'That's Newton's wife!' someone hissed. 'Joss Newton's, I mean – well, his widow.'

'Has she set Swanson up for this?' whispered another officer. 'Led him into a trap?'

'Quiet, all of you!' snapped Pemberton.

And as the woman turned and melted into the glow of the hotel, Detective Inspector Swanson, off duty and having enjoyed a wonderful meal, continued towards his car. He strode quickly towards it, not using a torch or any form of light to guide his way.

'Prepare for action,' breathed Pemberton into the microphone.

There was no reply from his colleagues but he knew they had heard and understood him. There was not a sound now, except for the breathing of the officers entombed in the van; the tension was threatening to cover the windows with condensation, but they had been left open just a fraction to allow a saving current of air . . . visibility was still good. They watched Swanson move towards the parking area, walking in front of the row of cars as he made for his own vehicle. The biker was waiting; he was watching Swanson. Whether Swanson would see the waiting man could not be guessed – he was tucked between two cars in the darkness, well back and beyond normal vision. One would have to look deep into the space to see him. Swanson passed the gap in which the man was parked; the man never moved.

Swanson gained his own car and, as so many police officers are prone to do, walked around it to inspect it, just to see if anyone had bumped it while it had been parked there: an automatic reaction from a police officer. Satisfied that no one had smashed his headlights or scratched his paintwork, he took the key from his pocket and unlocked the driver's door. The watchers heard the click of the central locking system as all the doors were simultaneously unlocked.

The interior light came on as Swanson settled in the driver's seat and placed the keys in the ignition. He started the engine, probably to get the heating system working while awaiting his lady love.

It was then that the motor cycle moved. Quite suddenly, the engine burst into life and the lights came up as the rider emerged from his parking place two cars distant. He drove out, then into the next space, weaving behind that parked car until he approached Swanson's car from behind. He parked his bike near Swanson's car, lifting it on to the rest with the detective not aware that the bike's movements were in any way odd. Then he got off the bike, strode to Swanson's door and hauled it open with his left hand.

'Go, go, go!' shouted Pemberton into his microphone.

Even as the man was hauling the sawn-off shotgun from his leathers with his right hand, a firearms officer shouted, 'Police! Stay where you are. No one move. You are surrounded. We are armed.'

Hadley was now in the middle of the car-park and running towards Swanson's car, unarmed and shouting, 'You bastard . . . you bastard . . .'

The gunman saw Hadley's approach and in a flash, raised the weapon to his shoulders, aimed it at the oncoming Hadley and pulled the trigger. There was another shot at precisely the same moment. The shotgun was catapulted from his grasp as Hadley, reacting with split-second timing, sank to the ground, uninjured. The shot went wide. A police van moved across the hotel gateway to block it entirely; no vehicle could leave at this stage.

'No one move, stand still everyone. The hotel is surrounded by armed police. We are armed and will respond if any move is made . . .'

'Get that woman,' shouted Pemberton. 'Find Mrs Newton . . . she can't be far.'

The shotgun was lying on the ground in front of the row of parked cars and now, as the tension eased, a policeman went forward to retrieve it. He broke it, ejected the second unused cartridge and said to the man in the biker's suit, 'You are under arrest for attempted murder . . .' and then chanted the long and complicated new caution.

Pemberton was on the scene now and went to Hadley who had risen to his feet and was looking totally baffled.

'Are you all right, Vic?'

'Sir? How did you get here . . . I mean, all of you . . .'

'I think it's a good job we did, Vic, don't you?'

'This bastard was framing me, sir, making as if I was killing those people . . . He even bought a bloody bike like mine, even fitted with the same tyres, and look, he's using my registration number. He never spoke during his crimes, he couldn't fake my accent, but he left enough clues to lead to me. Who'd have believed me if I'd said that was happening?'

'I believe you, Vic.' Swanson stood as still as a rock, shocked into immobility by the sudden turn of events as Pemberton turned to the black-clad rider. 'So who have we got here?'

'I think it will be Newton's brother Brian, sir, trying to get his revenge against me for shooting Joss. Joss was armed, you know, sir, he really was. Nobody would believe me about that either . . . He and Brian went on the raid, the Millgate job. Brian got the gun away. It was the Newtons we were waiting for, not those other bloody idiots.'

'We know, Vic, and that's the same gun he's been using to kill Scott, Pearle and Hardisty. So what now, Vic?'

'You arrest Newton, sir. I want to arrest Swanson.'

'Swanson?' Pemberton looked at the detective inspector, now sitting in his car, drained and silent.

'Yes, sir, for corruption. Who do you think fed the villains with details of the raids, for cash? That's why he was going to be shot tonight, to look as if I'd done it. They'd have said I'd shot a policeman who was committing crimes and getting away with it.'

'He set the Millgate job up, then?'

'Yes, he drew Newton into the proverbial net. And he told Brian Newton about Scott and the others, passed on information he'd gained from his detective work, all to implicate me . . .'

'But you saved his life, Vic, at Millgate.'

'I did, but he didn't see it like that. Swanson wanted Joss put inside, a short sentence, that's all, so he could firm things up with his wife, but when Joss got shot, you can imagine what the family felt. Swanson's life became hell, sir, they'd got him by the proverbial short and curlies, and he helped the Newtons get their revenge on me. Until he was no further use, and then he was going to be shot as well, with me being blamed for shooting a corrupt officer.'

'You've evidence of all this, Vic?'

'You bet I have, sir! I wasn't as sick as people thought I was, you know.'

'So Newton was part of that raid, Vic? In spite of what Pollard and his mates said? He wasn't an innocent bystander as lots of people believed?'

'It wasn't quite so simple, sir. Swanson had the gen about the amount of money on the Cerberus van, an extra lot on that occasion due to the forthcoming bank holiday weekend. Swanson was having an affair with Newton's wife at the time, so he told Newton and his brother about the raid, the timing and so on, but set a trap because he wanted Joss Newton to be arrested and put away, leaving the coast clear for himself to enjoy having his wife. He hadn't bargained upon Newton being shot – and the family thought it had been done on purpose. They thought the police had drawn Joss to Millgate deliberately to shoot him. So they blackmailed Swanson afterwards. They concocted the story about the innocent man buying cereals for the children – a pack of lies because Newton and his brother were both on the raid. Brian couldn't drive and so he had to leave Joss's car behind, but that fitted the idea of a dad rushing to buy his kids something . . . But the van arrived a few minutes early and caught them by surprise. They were late for the raid, daft as it may sound.'

'You worked all this out, Vic?'

'I did. I had to, to clear my name. I could see no one was going to believe my account, even if the official enquiry did exonerate me.'

'But those other three lunatics, Pollard, Sykes and Gill? They said Newton had nothing to do with the Millgate raid.'

'He had nothing to do with *their* part of the raid, sir. They came by chance – Newton was not with them. There were two raids that day, sir, on the same van! A sheer coincidence, sir. It threw us all out of gear. And Pollard was right – the gun he threw down was his own, it was loaded and never used. Newton's brother managed to sneak Newton's twelve-bore back in those micro-seconds after the shooting, and he's been trying to get me sent down ever since – killing others and blaming me, using Swanson for background knowledge, wiping out people who had offended him in the past and working against me, all the time.'

'It's a complicated way of getting revenge,' said Pemberton.

'He's a complicated man, sir, and clever. It nearly worked,' said Hadley.

Pemberton turned to Swanson who was being restrained by two detectives.

'All right, Vic, do your stuff.'

Hadley clamped a heavy hand upon Swanson's shoulder and told him that he was under arrest on suspicion of corruption; he chanted the formal caution and noted that Swanson made no reply.

'I fear you have a lot of explaining to do, Detective Inspector Swanson,' Pemberton said. 'Take him away, take him to Rainesbury police station, we'll deal with him there. And you . . .' he addressed the biker, now helmetless, and saw the resemblance to Joss Newton. 'Brian Newton, you are under arrest for the murders of Frank Scott, Harold Edwin Pearle and Wayne William Hardisty . . .'

'They deserved it,' he said as he was led away.

'Vic,' said Pemberton as the drama eased, 'you said you were going fishing tonight, I believe?'

'Fishing for men, sir,' smiled Vic Hadley. 'Some people fish for men, others just fish. But I cannot tell a lie, so after I've done the paperwork for Swanson's arrest and before I go home, I will just pop down to the river, only for a short while . . .'

'I'll need a statement from you, Vic, in writing, about all this.'

'It'll be a pleasure, sir. Tomorrow all right?'

'Tomorrow's fine,' laughed Pemberton 'See you back at the office, then?'

'I might just catch Muriel Brown's killer, sir,' smiled Hadley, pulling his helmet over his head. 'I'm enjoying being a detective.'

'Thanks, Vic,' smiled Pemberton as his officers began to flood the scene. They had a lot to do now; the scene had to be sealed off, witnesses had to be interviewed, suspects interrogated and charged. They would seal off the area now and gather all the vital evidence. It could take until daylight.

Then, as Vic Hadley roared away on his motor cycle, Pemberton remembered the little boy who had died in the river and the youth who had fallen down the mountain side. And he remembered Joss Newton who had died on the Millgate supermarket forecourt.

A lot of puzzles remained, and tomorrow it was time for Pemberton's weekly report to the Chief Constable on the subject of Inspector Hadley's progress and his continued suitability as a senior police officer. Mark knew it would not be easy to compile a fair report – but whatever the outcome, he would have to speak to the Scotsman about his general untidiness. If the fellow was going to continue in the force, the least he could do was to dress in some smarter clothes and get a haircut.

Then there was the question of who would continue the work on the Muriel Brown case.